For Anne

e-ISBN 978-0-9573711-2-5
Paperback ISBN 978-0-9573711-7-0

Cover design © Jessica Bell

Visit www.helenahalme.com for more books by the same author
and for news and reviews of Helena's work.

Coffee and Vodka

Helena Halme

To Malin and Rebecca
Lots of love
Mum / Helen
x x

NEWHURST PRESS

Acknowledgements

Again I am in greatest debt to my family, particularly to David, but also to Markus and Monika. If it hadn't been for their patience and encouragement, I'd be no kind of writer at all.

Thanks must also go to Bath Spa University and my excellent tutor, Lucy English for this particular novel, as it was during my crazy year learning about the craft of writing that this story was conceived. Also Gavin Cologne-Brooks and Jonathan Neal for their tireless enthusiasm, and Mimi Thebo for her insightful comments. Without my fellow students including my editors Pauline Masurel (Mazzy) and Robin Pridy, Tania Hershman, Sadie Walters, Charles Berridge and Tom Bass, I would not have had the courage to embark on writing this novel.

My editor Dorothy Stannard and cover designer Jessica Bell are both to be congratulated for not losing heart with the many changes and additions. You are the best team any writer could hope to have.

Last, but by no means least, I want to thank Anne Halme, Jaana von Rettig and Mirja Sundström for their friendship and unfailing belief in my writing ability.

One

Tampere 1974

I WAS sitting on the wide ledge of the corner window. The pane felt cold against my cheek, even though it was a warm and sunny day outside. It was the fourth week of the summer holidays, and I had nothing to do. Our old flat was outside the town centre, next to a large cemetery, where dark-green pine trees and headstones with black crosses lay behind a thick brick wall. Anja and I would sometimes sneak over the other side of the wall and walk solemnly between the graves, pretending to be looking for a relative, copying the adults as they stooped under the weight of the wreaths they were carrying. My favourite gravestone had a boy's head drawn on it, and always had a pot of flowers in front of the inscription: 'Juhani Simberg, 1953 – 1964'. Juhani had been the same age as me when he was 'crudely taken away from his beloved parents'. I wished I'd known Juhani, but he'd have been 21 by then and unlikely to want to know an 11-year-old girl like me.

The smell of sausages made me turn my head away from the window. Mamma was cooking in the kitchenette. She wore an apron over her light blue trousers. The ribbons at the back were tied with a big bow and she had a white sleeveless top underneath. She wore her straw-coloured hair in a bun, and she smiled at me when she turned her head. 'Are you alright, Eeva?'

'Yes, Mamma.'

I turned my eyes towards the cemetery again. Then I saw Pappa park his red Triumph on the side of the road. He waved to me and I jumped off the ledge, 'Mamma, Anja, Pappa's home!'

Anja was sitting doing her Swedish homework at the table and Mamma said, 'Anja, can you move your things now. Quick before Pappa comes in! Dinner is almost ready.'

Pappa came through the door and went to kiss Mamma on the lips. 'It's all arranged, Kirsti.' He didn't seem tired and he didn't once glance at the mess Anja had made on the table.

'What's arranged?' she asked, her blonde head still bent over the exercise book. She'd flunked her Swedish exam at the end of the year and would have to retake it at the beginning of autumn. She hated Swedish, she told me, but I envied the time she spent with her teacher at the school. I'd have given anything to spend my summer holiday learning a new language with Neiti Päivinen. I wished she'd start clearing up so that Mamma could set the table and Pappa didn't have to wait for his dinner. The only thing he usually said when he came home was, 'Where's my dinner?' and then Mamma would have to hurry to get the food on the table.

But instead of looking at Anja, and the mess, Pappa came

over and gave me a hug. He smelled of aftershave and I noticed that I could touch his shoulders without being on tiptoe. Everyone said I looked much older than I was. I was the tallest girl in my class and had caught up with Anja's height. I wished I had her curves, though. I was as straight as an ironing board, with long thin legs. Pappa lifted me back onto the window ledge and one of his soft earlobes brushed my cheek. He looked at Anja and then at Mamma. His face looked very round. It had been that way ever since he'd had his hair cut short.

'Shall we tell them?' he asked Mamma. His eyes were bright and blue and he was smiling. Almost laughing. Mamma took Pappa's arm and said, 'Yes, go on then.'

'We're moving to Stockholm!'

Anja and I stared at each other. Anja put a strand of her wavy blonde hair behind her ear and tuned her eyes towards Pappa, 'When?'

'Soon. Before you go back to school after the summer holidays.'

'Why?' I said.

Pappa laughed and ruffled my hair, 'Eeva, the "Why Girl". It's because I can earn lots more money in Sweden. After just one year we will have enough to buy our own flat!'

'Wow!' Anja said. Then, 'Does this mean that I'll have to leave my friends here?'

Pappa's mouth became a straight line, 'If you mean that junkkari, that drunkard and the other layabouts you call friends, good riddance!'

Anja was thirteen and always knew what she wanted. She got her way because she was very beautiful. Even Pappa

7

sometimes gave into her. She had a way of speaking, saying the right words. I tried to copy her and sometimes got what I wanted, especially from Pappa. But my hair was the same colour as the fur of the squirrels that in winter ran up and down the tree trunks in between the headstones at the cemetery. And it was straight and thin. I sometimes wondered how I could look so different from Mamma and Anja, who were like peas in a pod, although Anja's eyes were a bit darker. Anja was so grown up compared to me, too. One morning when she got dressed just before the end of term, I'd noticed she had breasts. She told me that on Saturday Mamma had taken her shopping for bras. She'd bought two: one white for sports and one with pink and blue flowers for every day. She put on her new underwear quickly, as if she'd been doing it for ages.

'All the girls in my class have a bra, have had for ages,' she told me while I watched her from the top bunk bed.

Anja now crossed her arms over her chest and gave Pappa what he called her cocky look. This, I knew would annoy Pappa even more. I couldn't understand why she wanted to make him mad. Last week Anja had been caught drunk in the centre of Tampere. Mamma and Pappa came out of the cinema and saw her sitting on a park bench with a teenage boy. Anja had a half-empty bottle in her hand and Pappa said she could hardly speak.

'I've never been so embarrassed in my life,' Anja had told me. 'They dragged me away from an innocent walk in the park with my friends. I'll never forgive Pappa,' she said.

'Pappa called the boy you were with a waster,' I'd said.

'I know, it's so unfair,' Anja replied. 'It's only two

months till I'm fourteen and then he can't tell me what to do.'

Mamma now looked from Anja to Pappa and said, 'C'mon let's eat. Anja put your books away. It's sausage soup.'

Mamma was worried about the move to Stockholm. I heard her talking to Grandmother Saara about it when we were standing in her kitchen. Grandmother was painting, and Mamma and I watched her dab tiny amounts of blue, which she'd mixed with yellow, onto the canvas.

'I don't know how we shall manage,' Mamma said.

Saara's kitchen smelt of white spirit and coffee. She'd started painting right after Vaari died. I missed him too, but Pappa said Grandmother Saara couldn't be consoled. First she'd painted the walls of her flat different colours. The hall became orange, the small bathroom at the end of the hall yellow. It reminded me of the chicks Saara bought one Easter and raised into hens in her two-bedroomed flat. Pappa just shook his head when we went to visit, while Anja and I held the soft furry things in the palms of our hands.

Saara painted the bathroom with a small brush, creating swirly patterns on the walls. Pappa said he was glad not many people would see that particular room. Saara used a roller on the other walls in the flat. She chose light green for the lounge, and left the kitchen white. Her small bedroom, which had two single beds side by side, though one was always empty, she painted orange like the tiny hall. Pappa said his mother would soon come to her senses and see this was a silly hobby.

'It's no hobby,' she said to me, letting me mix her colours.

Sometimes when I stayed with her she gave me an old canvas to paint. Now Saara turned her head away from the painting.

'But Kirsti, rakas, Mikko has a job to go to that is well paid, doesn't he?'

'Yes, but…' Mamma replied, then saw me and stopped.

'Eeva, why don't you go and get some cakes from the bakery?' Saara said, turning her head away from the canvas towards me.

I worried the colours would dry and be wasted if Mamma didn't let her carry on painting. The picture was of a very pretty town with stone houses and trees, and a blue sky with white fluffy clouds.

Saara seemed to love Mamma more than Pappa, who was after all her son. They were always talking, Mamma's blonde curls close to Saara's black and grey ones. They laughed and smiled at each other when Mamma and I visited. But then, I guessed, everyone had favourites. I knew Mamma loved Anja more than me. And Pappa was always mad at Anja and nice to me.

I looked at Mamma. She was very pretty. Today she was wearing a pair of light-blue trousers and a pale yellow blouse with white spots. Her glasses were dark brown, which she got from her youngest brother, Uncle Keijo, the optician. When they were orphaned he'd been taken by the rich side of the family and had a good education, Mamma had told me. I decided I, too, would get my glasses from Uncle Keijo when I needed them. I wondered if he could send them to us in Stockholm.

Saara's flat was just a walk through the park from my school. After Anja started at Tampereen Lysio, and left me alone in the junior school, I would walk through the park to Saara's place and watch her paint.

Often, like today, she sent me down for cakes from the bakery on her street. I skipped down the stairs, deciding not to risk the lift. It jolted at each stop and made me think one of the ropes would give way and drop the cage, with me in it, all the way to the cellar.

The lady in the shop knew Saara and gave me the best Mannerheim cakes, with runny raspberry jam in the middle and soft and warm sponge. My favourites, though, were laskiaspullat, large sweet dough buns cut in two and filled with whipped cream. They were only baked in February for the Sleigh Day, when the streets were slippery and I had to keep to the sanded parts to avoid falling. The round-faced woman behind the glass counter smiled at me when she placed the Mannerheim cakes in a clean, white cardboard box.

'Tell Saara we're baking a new batch of rye bread tomorrow morning,' she said as I took hold of the string loop she'd made for me to carry the box.

Saara, Mamma and I had coffee at the round table spread with a rose-printed cloth and watched young mothers push prams on the street below. We saw older children playing in the sandpit outside her house, or on the two swings. When I was little I used to play there too, and sometimes Saara came down and pushed me higher and higher on the swings. Now they made an awful jarring sound and Saara said they should be fixed or replaced. 'The little ones will get all sorts of disease from the rust on those iron chains, or get hurt on the splinters from the seats.'

Watching people come and go, like always she told us who they were. Sometimes she waved at someone. She was disappointed if they didn't see her. She knocked her fifth-floor window so hard, I was afraid she would break the pane.

When we left, Saara squeezed me hard in her large uneven bosom and said, 'You're a good girl, Eeva.' Then she adjusted her artificial breast and went over to the window, ready to wave us goodbye.

Two

THE NEXT day Mamma was sitting on my bunk bed helping to pack my books. She said I should take only the grown-up ones, not the baby books.

'You haven't looked at those for a long time,' she said, nodding at a shelf. 'We'll put them in the storage boxes – you won't lose them, they'll be waiting for us at Saara's. The white boxes are for storage and the brown ones go with us,' she reminded me.

Saara would have to take a load of stuff, I thought, and felt good that at least Charlotte, my doll, would be in a safe home with her. It was a baby thing, and I was nearly a teenager, not a child who played with dolls! Besides, Pappa told us we couldn't take everything.

'We can buy new things in Stockholm,' he'd said.

Anja had no difficulty deciding what to take and what to leave. She'd finished her packing the day before and was sitting listening to the radio in the living room.

'Anja, Mamma needs your help with the cleaning,' Pappa said.

'Why should I?'

'Because it is your room, too!'

'And Eeva's. She's still packing, and the rest has nothing to do with me.' Anja was looking through one of Mamma's old magazines.

'Anja, we are all very busy packing, now please do as I say!'

'Jag är färdig!' Anja replied in Swedish.

Pappa didn't say anything, but sat down on the sofa opposite and picked up the Aamulehti. Anja turned the radio up when a song that she liked came on and Pappa glanced at her over his paper but said nothing. I couldn't wait to learn Swedish too.

'It's a shame you chose English instead of Swedish like Anja.' Pappa had said when he told us about the move to Stockholm. I couldn't remember being asked to choose, but I liked my English classes so I didn't really mind. Or hadn't until now.

'How much are you expecting my mother to store? Some of it must be thrown out, don't forget. Especially the old toys,' Pappa shouted from the lounge. Mamma looked at me and sighed.

'I'm going to put Charlotte on the top. I don't want her in a dark box all by herself,' I said.

Mamma gave me hug and said, 'You do that, Eeva.'

We spent the night before going away in Saara's flat. Anja and I slept on the sofa, top to tail, which Saara called a sister bed. We had to get up very early to catch the first train to

Turku, then a ferry to Stockholm. I was very excited but Anja hated waking up early.

Outside it was still dark when we all sat at the round table eating bread, cheese and salami. I had a cup of milky coffee with three spoonfuls of sugar. It was sweet and felt warm in my tummy. I only managed to eat one piece of rye bread with liver pâté. 'Liver makes you strong,' Saara said, so I had some even though I didn't really like it.

'Anja, aren't you having anything for breakfast?' Saara said pouring more coffee into the cups.

Pappa was glaring at Anja. She was sitting at the table, looking like a lifeless doll. Her hair was a mess.

'Anja, did you hear what your Grandmother asked you?' Pappa said.

'Please have just one piece of bread,' Mamma said, stroking Anja's back.

Anja shook her body so that Mamma's hand dropped away. She looked straight at Pappa and said, 'I'm not hungry.'

'You won't get any food until the ferry,' Pappa said. Anja just shrugged her shoulders.

'Sit down, Saara,' Mamma said, and smiled up at her, 'This is a lovely breakfast.' Saara sat down at her painting chair with a heavy sigh. She looked sad. Then she got up again and said, 'I'll make you a couple of sandwiches just in case someone gets hungry on the train.'

Mamma looked at Pappa and said, 'What a good idea. I'll make them.'

'Don't be silly, Kirsti, you have to get ready. I don't have anything better to do.' Eventually Mamma gave in and we all rushed around the small flat to get our things ready. As I was packing a book into my canvas holdall, I saw the set of colouring pencils and a small drawing pad that Saara had given me for the journey. I looked up and saw her in the kitchen through the narrow hall. She was standing sideways, wiping her eyes with a kitchen cloth. Pappa was still sitting at the table reading a paper. He put yesterday's Aamulehti down and looked at Saara. She sat down facing Pappa and he put his hand on her arm. I couldn't hear what he said. Saara got up again and started clearing the plates while Pappa continued reading the paper.

Anja was sitting on the unmade sister bed.

'What a stupid idea to leave so early in the morning!' She still hadn't brushed her hair, nor packed her bag. 'I read the brochure Pappa has. The night ferry looks really good, they've got a disco and everything!' Anja stood up and said, 'Not that they would have let us go there.' She was finally getting ready. Pappa had finished reading his paper and came over to the lounge.

'Are you ready?'

'Yes Pappa,' I said, and looked over to Anja who was examining her bag.

'Anja?' Pappa said.

'Alright, alright,' she said. Pappa took a deep breath in and went to Saara's bedroom. I went to the kitchen where Saara was standing at the sink. Her head was bent over and I went to stand by her. This is where I often stood to dry the dishes while she washed up. I had no time to do that today. I looked up at her.

'All packed?' Saara asked. Her eyes were red and wet. I pushed myself against her large body and started crying.

'Eeva, don't you start me off again,' she said. I pulled away and looked at her. She was smiling. 'Soon you'll be on that ferry and then Stockholm, and you will have a wonderful time,' she said, holding onto both of my hands.

'Don't forget to open up the box and check up on Charlotte every week,' I said.

'I won't,' Saara said. I hugged her again and thought how warm she was and how soft her cotton apron felt against my cheek.

'The taxi's here!' Pappa said from the door. Everyone started rushing. I went out first with Anja. I ran down the stairs and was at the bottom well before her. I opened the heavy front door and said, 'Hello' to the taxi driver. He wound his window down and rested one arm on it. He was wearing a black leather jacket and smoking. He blew puffs of smoke out, making rings with his lips. I watched them rise and then disappear into the air. He turned around to look at me, tapping the ash off the end of his cigarette onto the pavement. His eyes looked small and watery. 'Hello,' I said again, but he didn't say anything.

I turned to look at the lift. I saw the wires moving inside the cage. The lift was slowly coming down. It creaked and I hoped it wouldn't give way under the heavy luggage Pappa had with him. With a loud thump the lift stopped and Pappa carried the suitcases one by one into the back of the taxi.

'Good morning,' the driver said to Pappa. But he didn't get up to help him with the cases. Then Mamma and Saara came down in the lift. I heard them talking over the luxurious humming of the taxi. I'd only been in a taxi once before.

'Where's Anja?' Mamma asked.

'I'm here,' Anja said. She was still coming down the stairs. She looked very tall and grown-up in her cropped trousers and stripy t-shirt. She'd tied her hair back and the end of the ponytail rested on her shoulder. Uncle Keijo had said she looked like Brigitte Bardot. I wished Mamma had let me have trousers like hers instead of a pair of white cotton ones. Mine were far too big for me and I had to roll the hems so that they wouldn't drag on the floor.

'We are going to Keskusasema,' Pappa said to the man. When the taxi started to drive off I glanced back at the door. Saara stood there, large but lonely, her arms hanging loose by her side.

Three

Stockholm 2004

IT WAS as if the lock was trying to tell me something. I didn't want to panic; this had happened before. Two months ago the key had initially refused to work on my front door. I'd resolved to phone the caretaker, whose offices were an hour outside Stockholm, to make an appointment to have the lock replaced. Of course, I hadn't. I now cursed myself for being saamaton, one of those Finnish words that were impossible to translate. Neither 'inefficient', nor 'incapable' came close. The word meant something immoral, like laughing in the face of life and its commitments. As I was thinking of this word, the lock suddenly clicked open and I sighed with relief.

I picked up the pile of post lying on the threshold. I scanned the useless advertising flyers and other junk mail for a long, thick envelope, with Saara's scrawling handwriting on it, but it wasn't there. How long had it been since I'd had the last letter? Must be over three weeks, I decided, and then started to worry again. This was the longest gap between her letters I'd known. I thought of phoning her, but by the time I was home it was usually too late. The hour's time difference to Finland and her habit of going to bed early meant I might wake her up. I hung up my coat and took off my boots. I wiggled my toes on the wooden floor of the narrow hall. My feet in the high-heeled boots had started aching on the walk from the bus stop to the flat. I should have worn something more sensible. I went into the kitchen, a narrow galley-shaped room with cupboards on either side, and made myself coffee. Out of the window I saw it was still light; at last the nights were getting longer. I sat at a round table, which I'd painted cornflower blue. The chairs had been the hardest. I'd used a small brush and the paint had run down my hands. I had the stains on my fingers for at least a week afterwards. I could sit four people, squeezed up, if I had a dinner party. Usually, though, it was just Janne. He often sat opposite me for breakfast on a Sunday morning if he'd stayed the night. He would lean back in my blue wooden chair, reading Dagens Nyheter, while blindly drinking milky coffee and eating bread with cheese. I'd watch his hand come out from behind the paper, looking for his plate or cup. He ate with ink-stained fingers, and I thought of the poisons entering his body through his dirty hands but said nothing. Occasionally, he'd make a comment about something, folding the paper and looking me straight in the eyes, so it was hard to ignore him.

From the kitchen, through a half-open door, I saw a stack of papers sitting on top of my desk in the bedroom. This was translation work I was due to finish in a week's time and should really work on tonight. The day's lessons at the Stockholm Language Centre had worn me out. It was strange how differently the foreign students learned the language. Jacob, a man from Somalia, had just moved into the advanced class. His progress had been quick, though he still found it hard to verbalise in Swedish. He'd pick that up once he started working, I thought. He was one of the lucky ones. The exams were all written papers, and he'd certainly get a good mark. Unlike Irina, a dark-haired woman who was 42, like me, and came from Russia. She'd been in Sweden for a year and was a mathematician, but she struggled with the language. Today I'd explained the Swedish sentence structure to her at least five times while the class was chatting in low voices around me. I'd felt like a children's schoolteacher, like my first teacher in the school in Rinkeby, trying to keep the class's attention. Irina should not be in my class; how many times had I tried to tell the Head of Learning, Stefan Andersson, that she should be in the beginners' group? But Stefan, a small man with a flabby body, had to think about his performance figures.

'Eeva, Irina will soon come along. If anyone can, you'll teach her the language,' he'd said, with his smarmy smile, touching my arm as if we were close friends. The looks he gave me made me shiver. Besides, he was a married man with two, or was it three, children? I'd rather have sex with a slug than him. He often made me so angry I felt like spiking his coffee in the canteen those times he insisted in joining me for lunch. I'd daydream about putting my eye-drops in his cup while he wasn't looking. My old school friend Harriet, who worked as an air hostess for Scandinavian Airways, had told me that the drops gave you the runs. She'd given them to drunk passengers to stop them drinking more.

'The Finns, you mean,' I'd said.

Harriet smiled wickedly and said, 'Actually, more often than not it's the Swedes these days.'

I'd smiled back at her; she never forgot my roots however much I wanted to.

I thought of Saara again, alone in her flat. Perhaps she was painting a new picture, and had forgotten to write? I opened a drawer and took out her last letter. The envelope felt soft and full in my hands. The lilac-coloured crepe lining rustled faintly as I opened the flap and took out four sheets of writing paper:

Tampere 17th February 2004

My Dearest Eeva,

I hope you are keeping well. You must look after yourself and try not to work too hard. I know all you want to do is help those foreign people, but you can only do so much. I do like the sound of Irina, although I have never known a nice Russian. But I suppose the world is a different place now and we all must try to get on. I'm glad to hear the weather is getting warmer for you in Stockholm.

Here there is still a thick covering of snow on the front lawn but the sun is beginning to warm a little now. In places the ice on the pavements has melted, but then we have a frosty night and are back to winter again. I have been going out to the shops every day, the pavements towards the Konditoria and the bus stop are very well sanded, though Marja next door tells me in town it can be terrible. She says the council have no money and couldn't care less if old people break their necks walking on the street. It would only save them money in hospital costs, she tells me. Well, you know how she is, likes to complain about everything. When I've been to town to get more paints I've had no such problems.

I laughed at the picture Saara had drawn in the margin of a woman with a stick, toppling cartoon-like on ice. The shaky writing in green ink, which at times faded to an almost invisible watery mark, made me smile. I put the sheets down on the table and took another sip of coffee, but it had gone cold. If I made another cup, I wondered, would I be awake all night? My thoughts were interrupted when the phone rang.

'Eeva Litmunen,' I said knowing it was Janne before he spoke. He phoned the same time every day, about half an hour after I'd got home.

'Eeva, how are things?' Janne always asked that, and I wondered what he really meant by it.

'I'm OK.'

'Shall I come over and cook you something soothing?'

'Well...'

'I got a nice bottle of Shiraz from the Systembolaget, and I could do my mushroom risotto. Then later I could rub your feet or massage your shoulders...'

'Janne,' I said, interrupting him.

'Yes, what is it?'

'I haven't heard from Saara.'

'Your Grandmother?'

'She writes every week and it's been three now.'

'Why don't you phone her?'

'No, I can't. She'll just worry and...'

'I'll come over, I'm at work, so it'll take me just twenty minutes to be with you.' Janne was speaking quickly now.

'No, really, I'm very tired.'

'I see.'

'I've got some translation work; it'll take my mind off Saara.'

'If you're sure.'

I heard the disappointment in his voice and thought of how he must have looked. Mouth in a straight line, eyes a darker green than normal, his fair eyebrows knitted together, his wiry body tense. Why couldn't he understand that I had to concentrate on not thinking about Saara and what if?

I looked at my desk. There was dust around the PC, and I went to fetch a cloth from the kitchen to wipe it off. Then I felt the need for some air and went into the lounge where I opened the balcony door. I took in a deep breath. The balcony floor was wet. I thought of the summer evenings when I had sat there having a glass of wine, or beer, listening to the other people around me enjoying their balconies. Soon it would be time to fill the window boxes again. I looked at the empty containers on the floor. Now it was too cold to leave the balcony door even ajar, so I closed it and went back to my desk to start the translating. The outside air had invigorated me. I turned on the PC, took off my skirt and blouse and put on a dressing gown.

Then the phone rang again, and I wished I had one of those machines that tells you who's calling. I sighed and went to answer it.

'Can I speak with Eeva Litmunen?' The voice of an older man asked in Finnish.

'Speaking' I said, thinking, I really must not accept any more translation work before I finish the lot staring at me from the desk.

'Eeva?'

'Yes,' I said and in the briefest of moments I knew who this was. I wanted to double over and hold my stomach, but put my right hand on it instead. Holding onto myself like this, I sat down at the desk, waiting. Then the words came:

'Pappa täällä,' he said. The voice was soft, as it always had been, a little deeper perhaps, but still silky.

'Pappa,' I said, sounding like a little girl.

For a while neither of us spoke. I was thinking, 'Why is he phoning me, after twenty, no, nearly thirty years, what does he want with me?' I wondered if I should just put the phone down, but that would be childish, and cowardly, it would confirm all his beliefs about women.

'Eeva, I'm phoning about Saara.'

'What's happened?'

'She's in hospital and she asked to see you.'

'What's wrong? When did this happen?' I wanted to know everything, I was feeling dizzy and my mouth was dry.

'I'm sorry to have to tell you this over the phone,' he said.

I listened to Pappa recite 'doctor speak'. A stroke, they thought, in the night, two days ago. Saara had improved, but today had worsened, and in a faint whisper had asked for me.

I looked at my watch. If I packed quickly I could make the overnight ferry. 'I'll try to get there by tomorrow morning. Where is she, where shall I come to?'

'You'd better come to my house.'

'Your house?' I couldn't believe his arrogance, why would I go to him?

'I'll take you to the hospital, you won't find it on your own,' Pappa's voice was dry, matter-of-fact, 'It's Lauttakatu 7.'

It was the same street as Saara's. I didn't know they lived close to one another. I couldn't think straight.

'I'll phone and tell Anja,' I said.

Pappa coughed and said, 'If it's what you want.' Then, 'You'd better take my number as well.'

After I'd put the phone down and looked at the note I'd made of Pappa's telephone number, I wondered how he'd known where to find me? Saara must have told him. I had a sick feeling in my throat and ran to the bathroom and retched, but nothing came out. I looked at my face and wondered how I could look so normal. It was the bone structure, the high cheeks, as Mamma used to tell me.

'I remember when you became beautiful,' she once told me, years before, 'you must have been fifteen or sixteen.'

But I knew I wasn't beautiful, not like Mamma and Anja. But I was slim and tall. 'Striking,' Janne said when I asked him why he started talking to me in the Tunnelbana. He told me he'd seen me for weeks on the platform waiting for the underground train, and had taken the same carriage. Eventually he'd summoned up enough courage to approach me.

I washed my mouth with cold water. I went into the bedroom and dialled Anja's number but got her answer machine.

'Anja, it's Eeva. I didn't really want to say this in a

message, but I've just had a phone call from Pappa. The thing is, Saara isn't very well. It's quarter to six now, I'm taking the ferry over tonight. Ring me as soon as you get this message.'

I put the phone down and covered my face with my hands. How was I going to tell Anja about my correspondence with Saara? They were never close, I knew, but still, if she didn't come back from hospital, if the worst happened, would or should I tell Anja I'd been in touch with Saara all these years? I didn't think Anja would want to see either Pappa or Saara now, but she was my sister after all and Saara's first granddaughter. She'd never hidden her disgust for Pappa, not even when she was younger. Now, of course, we never mentioned him. What a weird, dispersed family we were. But it was all Pappa's fault, and now Saara was ill. I looked over to my bed. All I wanted to do was to climb in and hide my face in the pillow, hoping it would all go away. But I needed to hurry, I needed to get to see Saara and not think about it, just get organised.

I dug out an overnight bag and put in my toiletries, underwear and a couple of tops. I took my black trouser suit from the wardrobe. It was by Sand, the best one I owned, and made of a fabric that didn't crease. A travel suit, it had said on the label. As I changed I decided to pack a pair of flat indoor shoes, black courts. I looked at myself in the mirror, which had been fixed to the inside of my wardrobe door by Janne. The suit made me look tall and slim. I'd bought it in the NK designer shop for that reason alone, though at the time I'd told myself it was a practical purchase. When I showed the suit to Janne, he said I should wear the jacket with nothing underneath, he said I would look sexy like that, but I'd never dared. I decided to wear my Clarks short boots with rubber soles and a warm lining. I put on my heavy Ulster. It would be cold and the pavements would be slippery in Tampere.

The lock will have to wait until I come back, I thought as I shut the door behind me and ran down the two flights of stairs. Outside it was raining a fine drizzle and the light was fading. I saw people going about their mundane tasks. On the other side of the road by a cluster of shops, a woman lifted two heavy plastic bags into her car. She slammed the boot shut and then strapped a child into the back seat. A man, hunched up inside his grey coat, was walking a dirty-looking poodle. Putting my bag on the passenger seat of the Volvo, I thought that I should phone the Language Centre. Inside the car I checked for the mobile in my handbag, then for my wallet and credit cards. As I started the engine and turned left onto the Lidingö Bridge that would take me to the Silja Line ferry terminal, I checked my watch again: there were only forty minutes till the ferry was due to leave.

Four

THE RAIN was now falling steadily and there was mist on the horizon. Not many people were travelling midweek from Sweden to Finland by ferry; no other cars were ahead of me as I drove up to a small booth. The girl inside was wearing a blue uniform and her hair was fixed up in a loose bun. When I asked for a single cabin, she didn't look at me, but at the screen on her desk.

'You realise you're paying double for a cabin for one person only?'

She cast an uninterested look at me through her little window. Leaning out of my car I wanted to shout at her that I couldn't share. I nearly said, 'My Grandmother is dying, just let me get on board.' But instead I said, 'Ja, I do,' and gave her the look.

'Here you go then, have a nice trip,' she said handing me the tickets. Then as an afterthought she added, 'Drive up to lane six.'

I parked behind a large Mercedes. The sea was calm. I

remembered there was only an hour or so of open sea and then nine hours sailing through the archipelago.

There was a knock on my car window. A man in a fluorescent jacket, with a hood, was staring impatiently at me. I wound down the window and said, 'Yes?'

'Please drive in, you're holding up the lane,' he gestured behind me and I looked in the rear view mirror. A single car was revving its engine, smoking in the misty air. Rain was dripping from the edge of the man's hood. I said nothing, just started my engine. Ahead of me, another man in a yellow wax jacket waved his arms, guiding me into the dark belly of the ship.

On the passenger decks it was all plush carpet and polished brass. It had taken me a while to get to the right cabin. There were several lifts, but eventually a woman, in a sailor's suit and wearing an insincere smile, guided me to the right one. The tired, smelly ships of my childhood were long gone, I realised, as I stepped into a blue and white designer space. There was a window at the far end of the cabin overlooking a shopping mall in the middle of the ferry. I opened the door to the toilet and found the old smell still resided in some places. I shut the door quickly, the nausea from earlier on was still there. I looked through the window at the shops and restaurants in the mall. People were walking in twos, holding hands, browsing. I wished I'd asked Janne to come with me. I decided to call him as soon I felt a bit more settled. I read the glossy brochure placed on the table next to the sofa. The ship had a swimming pool, a sauna and several eating places.

You could have steak, fish, or oriental food. I was oddly pleased to see they hadn't done away with the smörgåsbord, or the more expensive alternative that Anja and I had always wanted: the à la carte restaurant. I decided to try her again and dialled the number, but got the answer machine. I wished I'd talked to her before leaving. I realised I hadn't told anyone about this trip. Anja might have wanted to travel with me. I brushed this thought aside. She had her family, and would be driven by her husband to Tampere, or even fly. Or she may not be able to go at all. That wouldn't surprise me.

I took a book out of my bag and left the cabin, taking the credit card-style key with me. In the lift there were several people who were obviously travelling alone and a few families with very young children. No drunks. Still, just in case, I kept my eyes lowered to the floor of the lift and, clutching the book, went to find the à la carte.

After my meal I found a seat at the back of a bar in the bow of the ship. I dug my mobile out of my bag and saw that Anja hadn't tried to return my call. I needed to phone Janne but kept putting it off. I knew I should have called him before leaving; I didn't know why I hadn't. I thought about the last time we made love, slowly and pleasurably. Janne was very attentive, never too demanding or rough. It was good with him and I thought of Yri less and less.

I felt the ship move. We must be on the open sea, away from the shelter of the archipelago, I thought. I remembered the first time I'd felt the motion of the sea, on our way to Stockholm thirty years before.

I wondered if Tampere had changed at all. Was our old block of flats still standing? Our tiny flat in Tampere, overlooking the large cemetery with its imposing statues. Where a red brick wall sheltered the dead from the road running between the flats and the tree-lined rows of headstones. We had only two bedrooms and a kitchenette, separated from the living room by a stripy red and yellow curtain. Both rooms had large windows. The flat occupied a corner of the house and had two aspects: one to the road and the cemetery, one to the children's play area between our block and the next. The flats were built after the war – made of solid stone to house the new generations. Three of them stood side by side, with young families, like us, inside.

My sister Anja was two and a half when I emerged quietly and with little pain to my mother. She'd walked two kilometres to the maternity hospital, Naistenklinikka, past the cemetery into the centre of town. Pappa and Anja were still asleep when the phone call came that another little girl had been born prematurely. There was disappointment in Pappa's voice, I was told later, but when Mamma came home with me, and Pappa held me for the first time, he said, 'This little girl I like! We will call her Eeva.' From that moment on Pappa was my hero and I could do no wrong.

Pappa was a big man with blue eyes but delicate feet and hands. Those hands could fix anything: a broken vase, a punctured bicycle tyre, a creaky door. His mouth was curved, and when he smiled his eyes had a kind look, instead of the sad one he usually wore. When times were good, he'd joke and make up stories while I sat on his lap, tugging his fleshy earlobe between my thumb and forefinger. The softness of Pappa's earlobe made me dreamy, the silky feeling of it comforted my whole being as I rested my wispy blonde hair against his strong chest. Now, looking at the rain dripping down the black windows at the bow of the ship, I realised we were both happy then.

Finding it hard to concentrate, I lifted my eyes from the pages of my book, and looked around the bar. At the small round table next to me a man was sitting nursing a large pint of beer. He had one hand around the tall glass while the other held a cigarette between his lips. When he looked back at me, I quickly moved my gaze down. Then loud laughter startled me. It was coming from a blonde woman sitting at the other end of the bar. She had a short black skirt and her legs were crossed. They looked long and slim in her black stockings. A man standing close to her was admiring the curve of her neck. I sighed. At that moment the man turned and my heart stopped.

Yri was wearing a suede jacket over a pair of light beige trousers. His hair was a bit thinner, but, standing sideways a few tables away, he didn't look any older. I touched my hair and remembered I'd not had time to wash it before leaving the flat that afternoon. And my make-up was old and faded by now. My lips were pale and unpainted, unlike the giggling woman's. Then I thought for a moment. Could she be his wife? No, I'd seen a picture of her, and their two children, smiling into the camera. She'd had short, dark hair and slight features. Somehow I'd always imagined she was short too, nothing like the flirty, leggy blonde sitting close to Yri now.

I didn't want Yri to see me unkempt like this. He'd think me old and mousey. But just as I was about to get up and sneak past the couple unnoticed, he turned and looked squarely at me. I saw in his eyes that he'd recognised me. I looked at his piercing eyes first, and then his mouth.

It was his mouth that most haunted me. He had wrinkles either side – laughter lines, he'd said. Two years ago that mouth had told me in Polish: 'Kocham Cie' after a day locked up in bed in my flat, a snowstorm raging, listening to the harsh wind outside. At the end of the night, when it was calm again and the fresh whiteness illuminated the streets below, Yri had stood at the door. Turning around, he'd taken hold of my face in his strong hands and said the words while looking into my eyes, making sure I knew what they meant. Standing there in his overcoat he'd asked me, 'What's "I love you" in Finnish?'

'Minä rakastan sinua,' I'd replied, my body abandoned in the palms of his hands. I took in his scent, of cinnamon and coffee, as I buried my head into his neck, the tips of his blond hair tickling my face.

'Don't go,' I'd said. But he did, over and over, until it was too late and he had to go for good.

Facing him now I knew I had to be strong again. It will be easy, looking like you do, I told myself. He obviously had other interests anyway. So I decided to take the bull by the horns and slowly, in a measured way, got up from the seat and, picking up my glass of wine, walked up to the bar.

'Yri,' I said.

He smiled made a little bow. Still the charmer, I thought.

'Eeva,' Yri held my gaze a little too long and I struggled to breathe. The leggy woman was silently watching us. Then she started to rock her leg, which was perched over the knee of the other, as if in protest. I looked away.

'This is a surprise,' I smiled at the woman. Whenever I

was in a strange place, I thought, I was afraid I'd bump into Yri. Perhaps I wanted to see him, thinking he might have got divorced. His children would be teenagers by now and need him less. But I never thought it would actually happen. Besides, why would a Polish man, a dentist, be travelling midweek to Finland by ferry?

'Isn't it!' Yri said, and I thought I heard breathlessness in his voice too. I turned my face to him again.

'You're on your way to Finland?'

Yri shot a sideways look at his companion and said, 'Yes, a conference. Meet my colleague, Ms Puuhtonen.'

Though Yri's pronunciation was terrible, I could tell the name was Finnish.

'Terve,' I said.

The woman was startled for a moment, and then replied a curt, 'Hello' in Finnish too. Her reaction made me smile; here we were on a ferry, yet two Finns who have settled in Sweden would never acknowledge each other's roots. Being Finnish still carried a stigma of sorts.

We stood there for a while in an awkward silence, only broken by more people entering the bar. Yri nodded to a few of them, as did Ms Puuhtonen. Some of the men were eyeing me and I thought I couldn't look that bad after all. I smiled at a tall, dark-haired guy on the other side of the half-moon shaped bar, when he lifted his glass of beer to me. Yri noticed him and said, 'Eeva, can I get you another drink?'

'I was just about to go.'

But I found myself returning Yri's smile. It had always been like that, just the thought of him made my lips curl upwards. Even when I had been broken-hearted and angry after the break-up, I'd smiled at the memory of his lips.

'Ok then, just one more. White wine, please.'

'I know,' Yri said, and touched my arm. I saw the glint of the simple gold ring on the fourth finger of his hand. 'Still married, then,' I thought and decided I'd drink up quickly and leave. Ms Puuhtonen had turned her back to us and was now laughing with another man.

Yri said nothing while we waited for the barman to take our order. He just smiled at me and, as always, seemed in full control of the situation. I felt oddly safe in his company, although I knew that was the last thing he offered: safety. When eventually he handed me the drink, his fingers brushed against mine. It was as if a spark had been lit inside me. My heart started racing and I knew I wanted him back. I wanted to kiss those full lips, be held by his strong arms, and nuzzle my face into the wispy blond hairs on his neck. Instead, trying to control my breathing, I looked down at my feet and sipped my wine. But I found my hands were shaking so much that I had to put my glass on top of the bar, leaning closer to Yri as I did so. Catching the scent of him, I felt momentarily dizzy. Yri took hold of my arm, 'Are you OK, Eeva?' His eyes were on me. When I lifted my face up to him, he bent down to whisper in my ear, 'I've missed you.'

During the night the ship was never quiet. When the wake-up call came, I felt as if I hadn't had a wink of sleep. There had been the drunks bouncing off the walls of the narrow passage-way and shouting to each other, the slow humming of the engines and some strange clanking noises. As I clambered into the shower and washed myself under a steady, but weak, stream of water, I wondered what the odd noises were. The drunks that I remembered from my first ferry journey frightened me less now. But the intermittent banging had been new and disturbing. It was as if the ship had hit icebergs on the way.

I remembered Yri's face close to mine when we squeezed up together in the narrow bunk in my cabin. He'd made love to me urgently, not even removing his clothes after he'd pushed me hard against the wall of the cabin, sitting me up with his strong arms and pressing his lips over me, his tongue probing inside my mouth, claiming me. I was like a rag doll in his arms, trousers pulled off, legs parted and lifted. Thinking of him now made the whole of my lower body ache, smart with lust and longing. He'd promised to phone me, when I told him about Saara. Afterwards, when he'd gone, I'd lain in the uncomfortable bed trying to sleep, but had felt stronger, more able to deal with Saara's illness and with seeing Pappa again.

While the water was warming my bare shoulders I thought of Saara and how she would look now. I realised that my image of her was thirty years old. The black and grey hair must be white by now. I couldn't wait to see her and I started to hurry, hardly taking time to lather the shampoo into my hair. Then I rubbed myself quickly with the thin, white towel that smelled of old washing. I wished I'd thought of taking my own. I found a socket for the travel drier underneath a small table screwed to the wall of the cabin, and blew the warm air onto my fringe. The rest of my shoulder-length hair would have to dry during the drive to Tampere.

I looked at my watch and smiled as I thought about Yri at his breakfast meeting. He'd be tired and yawning his way through the presentation. He left my cabin in the early hours, well past three o'clock. I let out a small giggle when I thought about the leggy, young Finn wondering what he'd been up to all night. He'd told me it was just a company that produced dental equipment launching a new product. 'Eeva, it no problem! I will sleep with eyes open and no one will notice!'

He'd made me laugh, even while tears were stinging my cheeks.

Walking down to the car deck, I wanted to phone Yri, but he'd told me not to. His conference was scheduled to last through the docking in Turku. He'd stay on board and return to Stockholm that same evening.

'So that nobody jump ship!' Yri had said, his eyes wide and clear, making me laugh.

I noticed people were carrying plastic bags full of tax-free shopping. I'd not thought of that. I looked at my watch and saw I might still have time. I rushed back up the stairs, dodging sleepy people. I followed the signs to the shop and found it was just shutting.

'You've got ten minutes,' a young boy, surely too young to be selling alcohol, told me, pointedly jangling his keys. I rushed into the first aisle and picked up a bottle of Koskenkorva and a pack of Karjala beer. I could always take the booze back home if Pappa had stopped drinking. As I joined the queue of last-minute shoppers at the till, I caught a waft of the chocolate. I saw the huge Fazer chocolate bars and decided to get some. How, as girls, Anja and I had feasted on those bars! I picked up the bars and breathed in the smell of intense, milky sweet chocolate mixed with the sharp aroma of the packaging. I thought of the first time Pappa went to Sweden and brought back a massive bar for each of us. 'You eat them as if they were bread,' he laughed when he saw the empty wrappers.

The beer was heavy. I struggled with my shopping down the four flights of stairs that I'd descended that morning. When I finally sat inside my car I felt as though I'd done a day's hard labour. I then realised I had no map of Finland, and wondered if it would be easy to find the road from Turku to Tampere. Suddenly there was a violent movement backwards, and then a rocking forward. Hearing shouts above the noises of the deck and the engines, I realised some eager drivers had already started up. Then there was sunlight ahead of me. We had docked. The engine fumes became stronger and I wound up my window. I followed the car in front of me and drove over the rickety steel ramp between the ship and land.

The morning was cold and bright. It looked as if it had snowed recently. In March, I thought. The sea was solidly frozen, apart from the wide shipping lane. The sun shone on the slate-blue water and sparkled on the snow and ice around the lane. In the distance the solid line of pine trees along the shore was green and dark. The sun was low to the east and warming, its force barely diminished by the thin layer of dreamy clouds.

Looking at the view I felt as if the past thirty years hadn't existed.

I was at home. I was in Finland again.

Five

Stockholm 1974

THE NEW flat was huge.

'This part of town is called Rinkeby. It's ten stops on the Tunnelbana from the centre of town,' Pappa told us. 'That's what the underground train is called.'

We walked up the stairs to the second floor of a large block. Ours was the fourth door along a covered walkway. I counted the doors so that I would find it again. When we arrived it was dark and there were orange lights along the walkway. Inside the hall was large and square and led into a big kitchen on the left and into a bathroom on the right. By the window in the kitchen there was a round table. It had a plastic tablecloth and four wooden chairs. You could see the walkway and the car park from the window. Along the walls of the kitchen were lots of cupboards. The stove was shiny. Mamma looked inside the oven and said it had never been used. There was a big fridge but it was empty and the door was open. Mamma shut it and turned the fridge on, but nothing happened. Pappa told her to plug it in on the wall. A slow humming started, and Mamma said, 'All we need now is some food.'

'Tomorrow,' Pappa said.

At the opposite end from the table was a door that led to the corridor. Pappa went through and we all followed. He walked back to the hall and opened the bathroom door. It was nearly as big as the hall and had a blue plastic-looking floor. It had two doors just like the kitchen. Anja walked in one and out of the other. I followed her.

'Stop copying me,' she hissed in my ear when we were standing in the hall again. From here, you could see straight into the lounge. There was a big arch-like opening. This was the biggest room in the flat. But there was no furniture apart from an old-looking sofa against the wall. There was a large window at the end with light brown curtains hanging either side. Pappa went to open a door to the balcony. 'Come and look at this!' Even in the dark you could see the large space that ran all the way along the flat.

'There is another door from here into our bedroom,' Pappa said, turning around to look at us standing in the doorway. It was too cold and dark to go onto the balcony. I really wanted to see how high up we were, but Anja and Mamma were standing in my way. Pappa came back in and said, 'The new sofa and chairs should arrive next week.'

'What new sofa?' I whispered to Anja, but she just shrugged her shoulders, 'How am I supposed to know?'

Anja and I had our own bedrooms. Mine had a low bed made out of white wood against one wall. Anja's room was opposite. She'd chosen hers first, but I didn't mind. Pappa looked at me and said, 'You sure, Eeva?'

'Yes Pappa, I like this room,' I said.

'Come on girls, let's make up your beds,' Mamma said. She took tightly rolled sheets from the large suitcase that lay open in their bedroom. She handed me a pale blue set and Anja a pink one. Apart from the colour, they were exactly the same. You could tell which was the top sheet from a narrow strip of embroidery at one end. Mamma helped us make up the beds and told us to go and wash in the large bathroom and then sleep.

'It's past eleven o'clock Swedish time,' she said. 'And that's past midnight in Finland.'

It felt strange going to bed in Stockholm. I didn't feel sleepy, so I lay on my back under the fresh-smelling sheets listening to the strange hum of the new flat. Mamma and Pappa were talking in muffled voices and Anja was moving about in her room. There was a strange echo to everything I heard. And there were no cars outside. At home, I could always hear the traffic on the road by the cemetery. I wondered what Saara was doing now. She was probably asleep on one of the beds in her small bedroom. I wished I could kiss her goodnight.

Though I was lying absolutely still, I felt as if the bed was rocking. It was as if I was still on the ferry. But it wasn't a bad feeling. I liked the thought of sleeping at sea, being able to wake up and walk straight onto the deck and see the white horses, the ship pushing against the waves. I wondered how far our new flat was from the sea. I must ask Pappa tomorrow. I couldn't believe we were actually in Stockholm, in the brand-new flat. My skin felt prickly all over at the thought of tomorrow.

The white walls of my new room glowed even though the room was dark. I could see a street lamp through the curtains. Its light painted a long orange strip along the wall and the door. I'd left my door ajar; it had felt too lonely to shut it completely. I heard Mamma laugh softly. Then she said, 'Shhh, Mikko.' I turned to face the door and thought about what Rinkeby would look like in the daylight. Would there be a children's playground outside the flats here like at Saara's? Would my school be a tall building like Anja's new school in Tampere? What were Swedish girls like? I wished that I'd find a friend like Kaija and that my teacher would be a nice person like Neiti Päivinen. She never got angry with me. I'd heard her shout only once, at a boy who kept pulling the girls' hair. But he was horrible and smelt of cooked cabbage. Oh, I hoped there wouldn't be lots of boys like him in my new school.

In the morning Mamma knocked on my door. 'Breakfast is ready,' she said. Anja was still asleep but Pappa was reading a newspaper in Swedish at the kitchen table. He was still in his pyjamas and I could see his large bare feet under the table. He looked over the paper at me and said, 'Sleep well, Eppu?' That was his nickname for me. He hadn't used it for ages, so I smiled and said, 'Yes Pappa.'

There was a funny smell in the kitchen like fried onions. Mamma said it was the strange furniture and that when she'd cleaned the flat properly, the smell would go.

'Your nose, Eeva, is very sensitive,' Pappa laughed.

Mamma was smiling, unpacking boxes in the kitchen. It was nice to see our old cups and plates. Then Mamma found one plate that had broken during the move. Pappa said it was a very expensive Nuutajärvi glass plate, but that it was lucky nothing else was broken.

'I told you we shouldn't have taken everything,' he said to Mamma.

Mamma just looked at the large chip on the plate and said nothing. I thought how lucky it was that my doll was safe in Saara's cellar.

After we'd had breakfast around the kitchen table, Mamma said, 'Eeva have you unpacked everything in your room?'

She knew I hadn't so I got up to go to my new room. I walked along the corridor past Mamma and Pappa's new bedroom and went in to have a look. At the far end the balcony door was open. The air was blowing the white, thin curtains about. Mamma had put the old yellow bedspread on the large double bed. At the foot of the bed was a row of wardrobes. I opened one narrow door and saw Pappa's winter shoes and his heavy Ulster hanging above it. I closed the door quickly.

The room looked very tidy even though there were two large suitcases and several unopened boxes stacked on the floor. On either side of the bed there was a small table, and a white lamp screwed onto the wall above. I flicked the switch and a bright light came on. I imagined Pappa lying on the bed reading a newspaper, his legs crossed and his socks shiny and loose on his feet. Sometimes, on his old bed in Tampere, he fell asleep like that in the middle of the afternoon with the paper folded neatly next to him, his arms crossed over his chest. I closed the door quietly behind me and went to my room.

My bedroom had a white desk against a large window overlooking a path between the blocks of the estate. I could see a group of boys cycling there. They were shouting to each other and peddling without holding onto the handlebars or pulling the front wheel up off the pavement. They laughed, daring each other to do more tricks. Suddenly one of them looked up. I moved behind the thin cotton curtain.

'Do you want to come to the shop with me?' Mamma was standing at the door. She looked at my unopened boxes.

'Yes please!' I said.

'You'll have to promise me you'll unpack as soon as we come back.' But I could see she wasn't angry, she was smiling. 'Take your coat. It looks warm but there is a wind and it's a bit of a walk, I think,' she said from the corridor. Then Anja stood there, sleepy-looking.

'Are you coming to the shop?' I asked.

'Yes, Mamma wants me to come because I can speak Swedish,' she said and walked out. She wasn't even dressed yet so I knew it would be a while before we left. I sat down on my bed and opened one of the boxes.

On the way to the shop we walked past the boys on their bicycles. I tried not to look at them, but I saw from the corner of my eye that they were still being silly. I wondered if they went to the same school Anja and I would start at on the following Monday. That was the day after tomorrow, I thought.

'Can you believe we're here?' Mamma said, and linked arms with us. Anja said, 'It's so cool, there are so many girls the same age as me. I saw them walking on this path.' Anja was wearing a pair of red jeans and a shirt that she had tie-dyed in the bath in our flat in Tampere. The jeans were very tight.

Mamma pointed at a low building in the distance and said, 'That's your new school.' She knew where everything was because she'd been here with Pappa before. Pappa had shown her the flat and they'd walked around to our new school and met the teachers.

The path went under a road. In the tunnel our voices made an echo and we laughed. 'Wow,' Anja said. 'So cool!'

Then there was a long hill and steps up to the square. At one end was a shop with a glass door. Inside, the shop smelled of sweet fruit. There were large baskets of bananas and apples, mounds of tomatoes and different coloured peppers. Pappa was right, everything was bigger and better in Sweden. Anja and I found the sweet aisle and looked at the different unfamiliar packets. They all looked so delicious, but we had no money.

'Let's see if Mamma will buy us some,' Anja said and took my arm. We ran along the aisles and aisles of foodstuffs, finally finding Mamma at the bread counter.

'Ah, Anja, thank goodness. I want some of those cakes but the lady doesn't understand, and I can't say it,' she said. Mamma looked red in the face and the woman had her eyebrows raised. She wore a white apron and had very blonde, curly hair. She said something but Anja didn't understand her either. Anja pointed through a glass case at a green cake that had four ready-cut slices left. She put up four fingers and said something in Swedish. The woman didn't reply but took a knife and slid the four slices into a cardboard container. Then she closed the lid and wrote a number on it and handed the box to Anja. We all smiled and said, 'Tack', but the woman just crossed her hands over her chest and stared at Mamma and Anja in turn.

Mamma had lots of food in her trolley. 'I'm ready, let's go,' she said. Her face was still a bit red and she looked sad. 'She was very rude, that woman!' she said to Anja.

Anja shrugged her shoulders and said, 'Can we have some sweets?'

Mamma looked at her and said, 'Alright, one each.' 'But not a big one,' she shouted after us. A woman with an equally full trolley was coming the other way and we nearly bumped into her. I said, 'Anteeksi'. She looked at me angrily and I realised I'd said 'sorry' in Finnish.

'Jävla Finnar,' the woman said and pushed her trolley away.

'Come on,' Anja said.

'What did she say?' I asked Anja. She was pulling my arm and we were running. Anja didn't reply, so I thought she didn't know either.

'What's sorry in Swedish?' I asked when we were standing in the fully stacked sweet aisle again.

'Förlåt,' she said and picked up a heavy bar wrapped in a golden-coloured paper.

'I'll have the same,' I said. Then, looking at her I said carefully, 'Vorlat?'

'No, you copycat, it's FÖR - LÅT!'

***

47

On our first Sunday in Stockholm Pappa said we should all take the Tunnelbana the ten stops to the centre of the city and walk the famous streets and see the famous places. Drottningatan, where you could buy anything in expensive glass-fronted shops. Gamla Stan, the old part of the city, where there was a street so narrow even I could touch the sides with my outstretched hands. And Kungsholmen, where the King lived.

There was a bus stop by the next block of flats that took you to Rinkeby underground station. Pappa let us get on first and paid for us. The bus was empty and no one came on board.

'It's Sunday afternoon, everyone's staying at home,' Pappa said. At the Tunnelbana station we went through a gate and Pappa showed our tickets to a man with long hair inside a booth. He waved with his hand and said nothing. Then there was a long escalator moving downwards. I had never been underground.

'It's fine, c'mon girls,' Pappa said to us. I stood next to Mamma and we both held tightly onto the side of the moving staircase. There were escalators at Stockmann's department store in Tampere, but none were as long or steep as this one. I felt dizzy and Mamma said, 'Just look right ahead of you, you won't fall.'

Anja whistled and swayed from side to side in front of me. 'Be careful, Anja,' I said, but she just laughed at me. I felt silly and childish. I pulled my hand away from Mamma's.

'You must stand back behind this blue line,' Pappa said when we walked on the platform. 'And it's always the left hand side train that goes into the centre of Stockholm. Remember that, Kirsti?'

'Yes, Mikko! Girls, remember that.'

There were a couple of other people waiting for the train too. A tall man with long blond hair was reading a newspaper. He looked at me, then away into the tunnel. Pappa told us to sit on a bench.

I heard the train well before it came and stopped in front of us. The sound was a long rumble, getting louder. Then there was a screeching sound when the train stopped.

'C'mon Eeva, we'll miss it,' Pappa said and took my hand. 'Watch for the gap in between,' he said and nearly lifted me in his strong arms into the compartment. It was bright and I nearly fell over when the train moved again.

'Eeva, here!' Mamma said. Anja and Pappa were already sitting on small benches facing each other. The cushions were made out of green plastic, and on the other side of the aisle the seats were ripped. Someone had drawn with black felt-tip pen underneath the window and on the walls all around the carriage. Everything looked dirty. There were handles on the ceiling and they swayed back and forth with the motion of the train. I could just make out the tunnel walls whooshing past through a window.

Pappa put his hand on Mamma's knee and squeezed it.

We came out of the underground at Hötorget. This time the escalators were much shorter and less frightening. Outside was a big market with so much colour, it was like a very bright sunset, but not really because there were shades you never saw in the sky, expect on a good rainbow. It looked more like a huge set of watercolours, or palette, the kind Saara used for her paintings. Mamma laughed at me and said my eyes looked like two round lakes. She asked if I wanted to buy a bunch of feathered twigs, but I couldn't decide which colour and she said we'd come back to the stall and get some when I knew what I wanted. She smiled at the man in a green apron and pulled me away.

It was a sunny day and there were people everywhere. At the other stalls there were dark-haired men standing behind tables full of shiny silver jewellery, leather purses and hand-bags, clothes, little carved wooden dolls and red painted horses and even more fruit than in the shop in Rinkeby.

'We don't want to buy any of those,' Pappa said. 'You don't know where they've come from.'

I wanted to taste the delicious looking peaches. I'd never had fresh peaches, or the furless fruit next to them, which Pappa told us were nectarines, a new fruit just invented. I didn't know you could make new kinds of fruit and asked Pappa how it was done, but he didn't know. Anja wanted to buy a red and yellow leather purse, but Pappa said she'd not need one since she always spent all her money straightaway. Anja walked away then, and Mamma had to run after her. Pappa was angry with her when Mamma brought her back.

'We must stay together – it's very easy to get lost here and then what would you do?' he said to Anja.

'I'd find my way,' Anja said.

'Oh yes, you know Stockholm after one day.'

'I can speak Swedish and I know how the Tunnelbana works.'

Pappa didn't say anything then. But Mamma looked at her and, linking arms with Pappa, said, 'Where are we going to next?'

Pappa smiled at her and took a map out of his pocket.

'Happy families,' Anja whispered to me, and then said to Pappa, looking up at him, 'Please could I have the purse, so I can keep all my pocket money in one place?'

Mamma smiled at Anja and then turned to look nicely at Pappa. He said, 'Alright Anja. We'll all go and get it for you. We don't want you to get the wrong change.' He looked at me and said, 'Eeva, do you want anything from the stall?'

I chose a purse in blue and white, the colours of the Finnish flag.

Six

THE MORNING that school started was sunny. It felt as if it was still summer even though it was the first day of September. Mamma walked Anja and me along the path to the school. I had on my new jeans and Anja was wearing white trousers and a yellow T-shirt. Looking at Anja I wished I was older and had studied Swedish at school in Finland like her. Pappa made her take the extra lessons in the summer.

'You'll thank me once we're living in Stockholm,' he told her.

It was strange finally walking up to the school. We'd seen the building the day before when we went past it on our way to the shop. It was a newly built school. Just like all the blocks of flats around it. It looked like grown-up Lego, all the walls in different colours. Mamma took my hand and told Anja to go to a yellow building in the distance. Her class number was 2C in room D253. Anja said she'd find it and there was no need for Mamma to take her. Mamma and I walked up a set of steps and into a big hall.

'This is the teacher's office,' she said. A small woman with thin straight hair and gold-rimmed glasses walked out of a room and smiled at us. She was wearing a flowery cotton dress. She shook Mamma's hand and nodded to her.

'This is Fröken Andersson,' Mamma said. 'She's your teacher.' I looked at her friendly face. She took my hand.

'Don't forget, Anja will look after you, and you must walk home with her after school,' Mamma said.

I let go of Fröken Andersson, hugged Mamma, and said, 'Yes, I won't forget.'

Then I turned back to my new teacher. She took hold of my hand again and we walked into the large courtyard, now filled with pupils. A bell sounded and the children disappeared into the different coloured buildings. Fröken Andersson led me through a door with a large letter 'A' and a strange word. We went through a corridor and then she opened a door into a classroom.

The class was very noisy. I was surprised when the pupils didn't stop throwing things at each other when the teacher appeared, or turn around to face the front. I stood slightly behind Fröken Andersson when she raised her voice. It sounded shrill but not frightening. When the noise continued, she took a deep breath and walked up to her desk. I followed her. One boy turned around to face the front, said something to the others and pointed to me. Everybody stopped and stared. Fröken Andersson grabbed her chance and spoke with authority into the silence. She turned to me and said: 'Eeva', then spoke to the other pupils. They laughed and jeered.

I looked down at my jeans to check that the zip wasn't

undone. It wasn't, but I pulled my jumper further down over the jeans just in case. I wished Fröken Andersson would let me sit down somewhere out of sight.

My new teacher ignored the laughter and handed me a book and a pencil and a rubber in a plastic box. Then she took me to a seat at the back of the class next to a girl with short ginger hair and a freckled nose. The girl looked like Pippi Longstocking. She had friendly green eyes. She pointed at herself and said, 'Harriet'. The desks were shiny and red and the chairs were attached to them so you couldn't move them.

Fröken Andersson, now back at the front of the classroom, said something again. All the pupils opened the tops of their desks and slammed them noisily. Behind the lid of her desk Harriet turned to me and smiled. I opened the book Fröken Andersson had given me and saw it had pictures with words underneath, like a baby book. Then there were dotted lines next to the words. I wondered if I was supposed to write in the book with the pencil. In my old school we never wrote in the books, even if the book told you to. But Fröken Andersson had not given me an exercise book to copy onto. I looked up. She saw me and came over to kneel next to my desk. With her face close to me, she spoke softly, but I didn't understand what she was saying. When I didn't do anything, she took my pencil and copied the first word onto the dotted line, gave the pencil back to me and nodded at the next empty line. I copied her and wrote 'äpple' under a picture of an apple. Fröken Andersson smiled and patted my back. Then she stood up sighing heavily and walked back to her desk at the front. The classroom had become very noisy again.

I think Harriet had been told to look after me. She knew

I had a sister in the upper school. She even knew her name, because at lunchtime, she said, 'Anja,' and then something else. I followed her into the canteen where we found Anja in the lunch queue. Her hair looked very blonde against the yellow jumper. We waited to be served together. I mistook the soured milk for ordinary and put it over my cornflakes. It tasted awful and I couldn't eat it. We had the oddest lunch. There was cereal, rye crackers with cheese and ham. For pudding, there was strawberry kissel. I looked around me and saw that most people had cornflakes with strawberry kissel. I wished I'd taken some because I couldn't eat anything on my plate. My tummy felt empty for the rest of the afternoon.

'It's so cool, I've made masses of friends already!' Anja said and smiled at someone across the room.

'So have I,' I said.

'Have you been to the Swedish teacher yet?'

'No, Fröken Andersson just gave me a book in Swedish and I've been trying to do the exercises in it, that's all.'

'Oh, you'll see her later today then. She's a bat!'

'What do you mean?'

'Oh, everybody knows she's a witch, just wait and see – she even has a wart on her nose!'

After lunch was over the bell sounded. Fröken Andersson reappeared and took me into a separate building opposite my classroom.

A large woman sitting alone in an empty room spoke to me in Finnish, 'Hello Eeva! Have you enjoyed your first day so far?'

Fru Jorvela was my Swedish teacher. She was Finnish like us and wore a flowing brown dress that came to her ankles, large bangles on her wrists and wooden beads around her neck. She had a moustache as well as a wart. But to me she was an angel. She was going to provide me with the key to this new world.

After my first Swedish lesson, Fru Jorvela said, 'I think you and I are going to get on! Your sister and you are so unlike each other, aren't you?' She smiled and led me back to the orange building where my class was having an art lesson. Some pupils were actually drawing, but most were chatting or clambering over desks. Fröken Andersson didn't seem to mind. She was sitting in front of the class making notes. She nodded and smiled at me when I came in.

'I'll see you tomorrow at the same time,' Fru Jorvela said, and she disappeared out of the room.

On my desk was a picture book of birds. I saw that everyone else had one too, and that some were copying from the book. Harriet was colouring in a drawing of a beautiful peacock. I took the colouring pencils Saara had given me out of my bag and started to leaf through the book. I chose a picture of a puffin to copy. Its beak had streaks of red and orange. It also had yellow tufts of hair on its head, which made it look like a blonde rock star. When I'd finished I looked at the drawing. I was pleased with it and wished I could show it to Saara. I'm sure she would have liked it too. Suddenly I saw Fröken Andersson standing in front of me. She smiled and put her hand out, pointing and nodding at my picture. I gave it to her and lowered my eyes. The classroom became quiet and everybody was watching us. Fröken Andersson gave the drawing back to me, said something in Swedish and nodded. Then she went back to the front of the classroom and the bells sounded. It was home time.

Fröken Andersson tried to get the class's attention, but nobody listened to her. They all walked or ran out of the room. I stayed behind. Anja and I were supposed to walk home together. She appeared at the door with two other girls. They wore short T-shirts and flared jeans, displaying bare tummies. They made Anja look old-fashioned and pale faced.

Harriet touched my arm, and said, 'Hejdå'.

Anja nodded to me and turned around at the door with her new friends, chatting and laughing. I realised that Harriet had said goodbye to me in Swedish and smiled and hummed to myself the whole way home. The sun was shining. I walked along the path a few steps behind Anja and her friends.

At dinnertime Pappa asked us about our school.

'It's good,' Anja said. She was picking at her food and reading a magazine at the same time.

'Put that trash away and eat your dinner instead of playing with it!' Pappa said. He had a mouthful of potato and the words came out garbled. Anja smiled and folded the magazine and put it on her lap underneath the table.

'Eeva, what was your teacher like?' Pappa said.

'She was nice, but the kids were really naughty!' I said.

'What do you mean?' Mamma said.

'Everybody shouts and throws things all the time and they don't listen to the teacher at all!'

Mamma had stopped eating and looked at Pappa. He said, 'Anja is your class unruly too?'

'No, it isn't at all!' Anja said. 'And I bet Eeva is exaggerating. She kicked my leg under the table. I looked at her and she narrowed her eyes but didn't turn to face me.

'If it's no good, we'll have to take you out of there, don't you think Mikko?' Mamma said.

'It's very good, I learned loads already.' Anja said. 'Eeva probably just misunderstood, she doesn't speak the language, remember.'

'That's true,' Mamma said.

'It is isn't that bad, is it, Eeva?' Anja said staring hard at me.

'No it's not,' I said.

'It's only the first day,' Pappa said. 'We'll see after a few weeks. Perhaps the children here in Sweden are allowed to be a bit wild at the start of the new school term. But you must tell me if it doesn't get any better, Eeva,' he said with his stern eyes on me.

'Yes, Pappa,' I said.

The next day Harriet was waiting for me outside the school gates.

'Hej!' she said and I nodded. I was beginning to understand but didn't yet dare speak.

'You say: hej,' she said when we walked along the path.

'Hay,' I said shyly.

Harriet giggled. 'No, it's HEJ!' Her eyes were friendly so I didn't mind her laughing at me. I tried again: 'Hej!'

Harriet let out a long string of words, and I knew they were good. She linked her arm with mine and we walked into the chaotic classroom. Fröken Andersson was trying to shout above the noise. When most of the class became quiet, she handed me the exercise book from yesterday. She'd marked my work and I understood her when she said, smiling, 'Very good, Eeva.'

A boy two desks along stuck his tongue out at me. Fröken Andersson went to him and told him off, wagging her index finger. He gave me a nasty look behind her back and said, 'Jävla Finne'.

I thought I must ask Anja what that means. The words sounded like those said to us by the woman in the shop, and she wasn't friendly either. I decided to ignore the boy, who looked like one of the boys messing about with their bikes outside my window. I hoped he hadn't seen where I lived.

At home Mamma was baking. It was Friday night and I felt as if I'd been going to the Lego school forever.

'I am starting school, too,' she told us. I looked at her. With her bright eyes, blonde curls and long red-and-white checked pinafore, she looked like a mother from a fairy story. Anja was reading a comic in Swedish. It had grown-up girls in it and boys with tight trousers and polished white-toothed smiles. I wanted to have a look but she'd said I wouldn't understand it.

'Can I mix the dough?' I asked Mamma.

'Of course, Eeva.'

'What school?' Anja asked.

'I'm starting Swedish lessons at the Folkskolan.'

'Does Pappa know?'

I was concentrating hard on not leaving any lumps behind as I blended the flour with the milk.

'Here, darling, put the melted butter in too. It'll make it

easier to mix.' Mamma poured the yellow, shiny liquid into the bowl.

'I haven't had a chance to talk to him yet,' she said.

Anja looked up from her magazine. She had bright blue eye-shadow on and her eyelashes had lots of black mascara on them.

'He's not going to like that,' she said and turned the page.

'Mamma, is that enough?' I asked.

'No, we need to make it a bit drier.' She poured more flour onto my mixture but it became too hard for me to mix. 'Shall I have a go for a change?' she said and took the spoon out of my hand. 'I'll just give it a quick go and then we can knead it on the table,' she said.

At that moment we heard the key turn in the door. Mamma stopped mixing and looked at Anja.

'Go to your room – you must have homework?' she said. 'And remove that eye make-up!'

Anja picked up her magazine. She slid out of the second door of the kitchen just as Pappa entered from the other.

'What's for dinner?' he said and came to kiss me on the cheek. He smelled of the outside, of a cool autumn evening.

'Pyttipanna!' Mamma said, loudly.

'Out of a packet?'

'No, a family sized can. It wasn't expensive, and I thought we could try it – it's very Swedish.'

'I know. I've had it lots of times at the factory canteen,' Pappa brushed past Mamma, tapping her on the bottom. She didn't smile, but she didn't look angry either.

'It'll be ready in ten minutes,' she shouted after Pappa.

I heard the door to our parents' room shut and a heavy

bang as the wardrobe door caught the back of the wall. Mamma started to hurry. She asked me to set the table.

'Quickly, Eeva,' she said. She took out a large frying pan and emptied the contents of a large tin into the pan.

The door opened again and Pappa shouted, 'You need to fry an egg on top!'

Mamma looked at me and shrugged her shoulders, 'These Swedish habits!'

Anja didn't like the Pyttipanna. When we were sitting eating at the round table, she picked at her food, looking at every piece of bacon and potato before she put it in her mouth. She'd separated the slices of fried onion from the mixture and put them on the edge of her plate. I liked fried eggs, so I pierced the yellow centre and let it run all over my mound of food. It didn't taste so bad after that.

'Let's have Finnish food tomorrow, Kirsti.' Pappa said.

Mamma looked up from her plate, 'I thought...'

'Just because we live here doesn't mean we have to become Swedish.'

Mamma said nothing. After a while Pappa said, 'Anyway, girls, you never guess what your Pappa has done today!'

Anja looked up from her plate, 'What?' she said, yawning.

'I've bought a car!' Pappa looked at each of us in turn.

'What kind?' Anja said putting her knife and fork down. She looked at Pappa and then at Mamma.

'Mamma, did you know?' I said.

'No, I didn't.' Mamma wasn't smiling.

'Oh, please tell us, what kind is it?' Anja said, 'or is it another Triumph?' She slumped down in her seat.

'Well, it might be, it might be,' Pappa said and smiled, 'or then it might not.' He looked at me, 'What kind of car would you like, Eeva?'

'I don't know, Pappa.'

'Oh, c'mon, Pappa, tell us!' Anja said. She was fidgeting in her chair. I started to get really exited too. What if Pappa had got one of those big American cars that you saw in films, with an open top. Then I thought that would be no good in the snow in the winter, if it ever snowed in Rinkeby.

'It's a Volvo,' Pappa said.

'What colour is it?' I said.

'Green, my little Eppu, it's dark green,' Pappa said and smiled.

'Cool,' Anja said, 'Is it brand new?'

'No,' Pappa said, 'but it looks new. It's only three years old, and the new model.'

'Wow,' Anja said.

'Now then, finish your meals, girls,' Mamma said. Then she turned to Pappa, 'Are you sure about this, Mikko?'

Pappa pushed his plate away from him and it knocked his glass of milk all over the tablecloth. He lifted his eyes up at Mamma and said, 'Hadn't you better clear that up instead of asking stupid questions.'

Mamma got up quickly to fetch a cloth. The milk started dripping down the side of the table. Anja moved her legs out of the way and looked at Pappa, 'When are we going to have this nearly new car then?'

'Tonight'

'Can I come, too?' Anja said.

'Anja...' Mamma said. She was wiping the table while Pappa picked up his Swedish newspaper. 'Alright, we'll all go!' Pappa folded the paper and got up. 'We'll leave in ten minutes. You'd better be ready,' he shouted from the bedroom.

'And you've got to have eaten all your food,' Mamma said.

'Oh, well, of course, there has to be a price,' Anja said, but not too loudly. I didn't think she wanted Pappa to hear any complaints tonight.

It was too dark to see the colour of the new car properly, even though the Volvo was parked right under the streetlight and its bonnet shone. The man who sold the car to Pappa had a grey-looking shirt. He stood by the car with his arms crossed and his tummy showing between the trousers and his top. I didn't like him, or the way he looked at Mamma and Anja. As if he wanted to eat them up. I shuddered and took hold of Pappa's hand. He squeezed it, nodded to the man, and said,

'Right then, girls in the back – see you have your own doors!' He turned to Mamma, 'You'll like the seats, they're real leather!'

Anja looked as if she'd always climbed into cars. She took hold of the door and slid inside. I tried to do the same but planted my bum awkwardly and then had to reach to close the door. The fat man hurried to shut Anja's and she smiled at him. I held my breath when Pappa turned the key. What if he didn't know how to drive a new Volvo? The Swedish man would laugh at him and us. But the engine purred softly and Pappa pulled away. He held his head upright, but leant back in the seat with his arms straight, holding the steering wheel firmly.

'The seats are nice and comfy,' I whispered to Anja.

She shrugged her shoulders and looked out of the window.

'Who would have believed it, the Linnonmaa family in their brand-new Volvo in Stockholm?' Pappa said and half turned around to catch my eye. Then he put one hand on Mamma's knee and said, 'And the new furniture should arrive next week!'

I looked at Anja. She was making a face behind Pappa's back.

Seven

MAMMA SAW the furniture lorry arrive from the kitchen window. It was parked right outside the front door of the block of flats.

'Mikko, they're here. Quick, go and tell them where to come!'

'Alright, Kirsti,' Pappa said putting on his outdoor shoes. He was smiling but not hurrying.

'I'll come too,' Mamma said and put on her coat. She was out of the door before Pappa. From the window, I saw a large bulky thing being pulled slowly out of the lorry. Mamma looked cold; she had her arms folded. Then they were both walking behind the two men and the huge parcel.

The sofa had large wide armrests and a high back. It looked soft and was dark yellow. The fabric reminded me of a teddy I'd once had. His name was 'Kultapossu' because he was made of gold-coloured velvet and had dark-brown glass eyes. I wondered what had happened to that teddy.

When Mamma unwrapped the sofa, two matching chairs

were carried in and placed opposite the sofa. They were massive. Then the two silent men from the furniture company carried in a coffee table. Pappa put his hand on Mamma's waist. Underneath all the wrapping was dark-looking glass with golden legs and knobs on top. Pappa said, 'This furniture is very expensive and you two will have to be very careful. See the glass table? It's delicate, so hands off.' Then he turned his head towards Anja and me. We were looking at the vast sofa and chairs.

'Did you hear what I said?' Suddenly Pappa was annoyed.

'Yes Pappa,' I said, and Anja nodded. I wanted to touch one of the golden balls on the corners of the table. One of the men had screwed them on. I wanted to see how they came apart. They looked heavy and I wondered if they were made of real gold.

Finally, the two men in brown overalls brought in a long parcel between them. They started untying the string holding it together. Pappa had his arm around Mamma. They were both silent, Mamma hardly breathing as the rug was unrolled and laid out between the new suite.

'It's beautiful,' she said and turned to kiss Pappa on the lips. I looked down at the swirly pattern of the carpet. It was the same colour as the velveteen sofa and chairs, with a bright blue and dark-brown design on it. I was trying to make out what it was, but could only see a large crown, or a huge shapely vase in the middle. I turned my head from side to side until I felt dizzy.

A man was holding a piece of paper and a pen in his hand. Pappa took it and read it carefully. I wondered how he managed to read the Swedish so well. He said, 'Tack så mycket,' to the man, handing him the paper and pen. The two men nodded and Pappa led them out of the door.

Meanwhile Anja had stepped on the rug.

'What are you doing,' Pappa shouted from the hall. Anja moved off the carpet.

'So it's a rug that no one is allowed to stand on. It'll go nicely with the sofa that no one can sit on and the table that can't be touched,' she said.

'Anja, please be nice,' Mamma said. She was walking towards Anja on the other side of the rug.

'Kirsti!' Pappa said.

Mamma looked back at him and realised she'd stepped right on top of the blue pattern of the rug wearing her outdoor shoes. Anja started laughing and ran out of the room.

'I'll get a cloth to wipe the table down,' Mamma said. She walked around the carpet to the kitchen.

'Take your shoes off while you're at it,' Pappa called after her. He sat on the sofa and stretched his long arms along the back of the sofa. He could nearly reach the ends with the tips of his fingers.

'What do you think then, my little Eppu? Your Pappa has bought a pretty plush sofa. Eller hur, like the Swedish boys say?' I smiled and went over and sat next to him. He lowered his arm and put it around me, squeezing hard. My eyes were level with his soft earlobe and I pushed myself closer to him. I felt safe.

Mamma came out of the kitchen with a duster and started polishing the table and the golden knobs.

'Can you unscrew them?' I asked Pappa's ear.

He looked down at me and said, 'I think so.'

'Why?'

'Eeva, the 'Why Girl',' he said, squeezing me again. The tips of his soft hair tickled my face.

'Can I try?' I said. The round shape looked so inviting. I wanted to feel it.

'Alright, but only this once and afterwards you must wipe it clean with the cloth.' Mamma said. She and I both looked at Pappa. He said, 'Go ahead.'

I was surprised how cold the little ball was. It was very stiff, but finally the whole thing came loose in my hand. The weight was more than I had imagined.

'It's solid brass,' Pappa said.

I screwed the ball back on and wiped it clean. Mamma and Pappa started talking about how to arrange the suite, so I went to my room. There was loud music coming from behind Anja's door. She'd been bought a new record player for doing so well in her Swedish exam and she was playing Abba's Waterloo. Anja bought the single on our first Sunday in Stockholm and it had Ring, Ring on the flip side. I wanted a stereo, too, although I could always hear whatever Anja was playing. Pappa complained about the noise, but Mamma loved Anja's music. I thought about the pretty clothes and shoes Abba wore at the Eurovision. We'd all watched it in Tampere on Saara's television. Mamma and Pappa let Anja and I stay awake until all the voting was over and Abba won. I felt so lucky that we were moving to Sweden then. Pappa thought it was ridiculous that a singing group should call themselves the same name as a tin of pickled herring, but he seemed proud too.

'Oho, oho,' he kept saying. 'Sweden won the Eurovision Song Contest, oho, oho.'

The two girls in Abba looked so pretty with the glitter in their hair and on their lips. They sang so well in English, too.

'It's much easier for the Swedes to learn languages,' Pappa said.

Anja said it was the first time a real pop group had won the Eurovision and that from now on it would be totally different and cool. She bought magazines with pictures and interviews with all of them. My favourite was Agneta. She wore the best outfits. She had beautiful blonde hair and blue eyes. I wanted to look like her but my hair was mousey and my eyes grey-blue. Anja said she didn't like one better than the other, but I couldn't understand how she could prefer Anni-Frid. She was old and fat and had horrible hair! She didn't suit the outfits half as well as Agneta did. How Benny liked her I didn't know.

The music stopped and I heard Anja turn the single over. I picked up a book and lay on my bed humming, Ring, ring.

'Eeva,' Mamma said, 'we're off now. I've told Anja what to cook. She can do sausages, and there is a tub of potato salad in the fridge.' She was standing in the doorway. Her hair was tied back and she had pink lipstick on.

'Where are you going?'

'I told you, we're going into town for a drink!'

I turned around on my bed and said, 'Bye!'

Just after the door shut I heard Anja turn off the music. Then she was standing at my door. 'Eeva, I've invited some of my new friends over.'

'Oh,' I looked at my watch, it was half past seven already. 'Did Mamma say you could?'

'What a baby you are, of course she didn't. Anyway, I didn't ask her so she can't say I'm doing something she's forbidden! Besides, it's Friday night, party night!'

I looked at her. She'd put on some make-up and was wearing the tight yellow jumper.

'You're not going to tell, are you?' Anja had her arms crossed. She was staring at me.

'No,' I said and went back to reading.

A little later I heard the doorbell and then Swedish voices. There seemed to be a lot of people going past my door and into Anja's bedroom. Then the music came on again, but it was different. A sound I hadn't heard before, very loud and fast. The guitar player made long jarring sounds in between a lot of drumming. There was no singing at all. I sat up at my desk and looked out. It was getting dark. I hoped Anja's friends would leave before it was time for bed and before Mamma and Pappa came home. Then there was a knock on my door.

'Hello,' a tall boy with long mousey-coloured hair said.

'Stefan, kom hit nu!' Anja shouted.

The boy smiled at me and said, 'Hejdå,' and then, turning his head, he shouted 'Ja, ja, jag kommer!' and disappeared from the doorway.

I wondered if Stefan was Anja's boyfriend. Then I smelled smoke coming from her room, and then voices moving past my door again and towards the lounge. I recognised a girl's voice as Susanna's, Anja's new friend from school. There were two other voices, both boys. Susanna and Anja were giggling a lot. The boys were talking and laughing at the same time. I heard bottles clinking. They must be sitting on the new sofa and chairs. I wondered if Anja had told them to be careful. I went to lie on my bed again and tried to read.

I kept losing my place in the book. My eyes felt very heavy and I had to screw them up and look through a tiny slit at the black words on the paper. I turned onto my side and brought the book closer to my face. But it was no use. My eyes just would not read anymore. I yawned and started to look through a Swedish magazine Anja had given me. There were pages missing where she'd ripped out a picture of something she wanted to keep. She said she was making a cool scrapbook of all the best-looking clothes. The noises from the lounge became louder and then there were murmurs. I tried to listen harder. Had Anja's friends left already? I didn't think I'd heard the front door go. I looked at the clock. It was past eleven o'clock.

'Eeva,' Anja was standing at the door. I'd fallen asleep. The room around me was dark apart from the light coming from the doorway.

'Yes, what is it?' I said getting up. Anja was holding a towel in her hand. The flat was quiet. 'Have Mamma and Pappa come home yet?' I said.

'No, but they will soon. Eeva, come into the lounge, you've got to help me.' Anja said.

'Oh, no, Pappa will kill you!' I said when I saw the sofa. The room smelled of beer and smoke. Anja was wafting the towel about the room. 'What are you doing?' I said.

71

'Susanna said waving a damp towel will get rid of the smoke,' she said.

'Open the balcony door,' I said. 'What are you going to do with the burn?' I looked at the hole on the sofa. It wasn't very big, but you couldn't miss it. The fabric had melted, making a perfectly round shape the size of the tip of a cigarette. It was brown against the golden velour.

'That was Stefan,' Anja said. Though she looked serious, she smiled when she said his name. Then, serious again, she said, 'I thought I'd put the cushion over it.'

Mamma had put the cushions from the old sofa on the new one. 'We'll buy new ones when we can afford them,' she'd said.

But the burn was right in the middle of the seat, and the cushions were placed in the corners of the sofa. I moved one cushion on top of the burn. It covered the hole but looked silly. I stared at Anja. She was still wafting the towel about. Her hair was messy from the effort, and her jumper had ridden all the way up to her chest. Suddenly she stopped and looked towards the hall. 'Quick,' she said, 'Close the door, I'll do the lights, I think that's them.'

I ran to the balcony door and then straight out into the corridor. I went into my bedroom and closed the door. I jumped under the covers in my bed, turned off the bedside light and closed my eyes. I was out of breath and my tummy ached. I listened but there was no noise of a door opening. I waited. After what seemed an age, I got up, undressed and put my nightie on. I opened the door into Anja's bedroom and said, 'Anja, are you awake?'

'Of course I am,' she said.

'It wasn't them,' I said.

'I know,' she said. There was no light in her room. I stood there for a little while and then said, 'What are you going to do?'

'Nothing,' Anja said. She sat up in her bed and put her bedside lamp on. 'They're probably drunk tonight anyway, they were going to go dancing, did you know that? And it's past eleven o'clock so they won't go into the lounge tonight.' Anja looked at me with sleepy eyes. 'Go back to bed,' she said and turned off her light.

I woke up to angry voices. I got up and went into the kitchen.

Mamma and Pappa were standing in the middle of the room. Mamma was setting the table for breakfast and Pappa was standing with a paper in one hand and pointing at Mamma with the other.

'Who else is it going to be but Anja?' he said. Then he turned around and saw me. 'Eeva, what do you know about the mark on the sofa?'

'You always think the worst of Anja. When she wakes up we'll talk to her,' Mamma said. She leaned over the table to set down the spoons she had in her hand. Mamma didn't look at me.

I went quickly back to my bedroom.

'I'm going to wake her up,' I heard Pappa say. But he didn't come into the corridor. Instead, he walked into the lounge. What was Anja going to do?

Later I heard the front door shut. Pappa was going on his Saturday morning walk. I went into the kitchen and sat opposite Mamma at the table.

'Go and wake Anja, Eeva, please.' Mamma seemed tired. She was resting her head on her hand, looking down at her empty plate. I glanced up at the clock. It was half past nine. Without speaking I got up and knocked on Anja bedroom door. It took three loud bangs to wake her.

'Mamma wants you in the kitchen,' I said. I heard movement behind the door and then Anja said in a sleepy voice, 'Alright!'

'She's coming,' I said to Mamma.

Mamma took a deep breath and lifted her eyes to mine. She didn't seem angry, just sad.

Anja appeared in the doorway. She was rubbing her eyes.

'Both of you come here,' Mamma said without looking at either of us. We sat opposite her. On the table were four bowls, and four spoons, as well as plates. There was a basket full of bread, a slab of cheese and a plateful of sliced cucumber and tomatoes. Mamma had a full cup of black coffee in front of her. She took another deep breath and said, looking gravely at both of us in turn, 'What can you tell me about the mark on the new sofa?'

I looked at Anja but said nothing. She was staring at her empty bowl and plate, fiddling with her spoon. After another big heave of her chest, Mamma said, 'Well? Pappa is going to be back soon and we need to sort this out before he does. Anja, have you got anything to say?'

'Always me, you always blame me first!' Anja said and looked up at Mamma.

'No, I don't. Are you saying Eeva is responsible?'

My heart was pounding hard. I wanted to get up and go back to my bedroom but I didn't dare in case that would show

Mamma that Anja was the wrongdoer. I didn't want to be the telltale, but I didn't want to get the blame either.

'No,' Anja muttered into her sleeve. She was leaning her head against her arms on the table.

'Anja, you must tell me what happened.'

'It was Susanna,' Anja muttered.

Mamma took hold of Anja's arm, 'Look at me, Anja, and tell me the truth.'

'Susanna came over last night and I wanted to show her the sofa,' Anja said. She had tears in her eyes. 'Then she said the new stuff was really cool and lit a cigarette.'

'She smokes!' Mamma said in horror. 'Did you smoke too?'

'No,' Anja said lifting her head higher, 'Of course not!'

'So what happened? Didn't you tell her not to smoke in our flat?'

'I did, Mamma, but I don't want to be so uncool. They all smoke at school, and if I'd told her off she would have told everyone, and then no one would be my friend anymore.' Anja rested her head back in her arms and wiped her nose on the sleeve of the dressing gown.

Mamma gave Anja a tissue out of her pocket.

'What about you, Eeva, were you there too?' Mamma was standing over me.

'No,' Anja said glancing sideways at me, 'she was in bed by that time.'

'This is absolutely what happened? You are both telling the truth?' Mamma said looking sternly at us. I didn't dare to look at Anja. She said, 'Yes Mamma. What will Pappa do?'

'I don't know,' Mamma said and sat back down, 'Let's

have breakfast! At least nobody died!' she added and went to hug Anja. 'You must promise me never to start smoking, though, Anja. It is very dangerous and only a step away from taking drugs.'

'I promise Mamma,' Anja said.

Eight

Tampere 2004

DURING THE drive from the ferry port to Tampere the sun was low in my eyes. It blinded my view of the road and danced on the lakes I passed. I'd forgotten the beauty of the lakes. Even in early spring, and still covered with wet ice, they were striking, framed with dark pine trees and rocky shores. For a few moments the scenery made me forget about Saara. And Pappa. I had a sick feeling when I thought about having to see him face to face. All I needed was the name of the hospital where Saara was and then I could go. I had no intention of staying and watching him get drunk. I wondered what his place would be like. The way he used to go on about tidiness in Rinkeby, you'd think he lived in a sterile palace. As long as he didn't have to clean it up himself!

The car in front suddenly stopped and I saw there was a queue at a narrow bridge. On either side, large earth diggers stood idle. I waited for the traffic lights to change and tapped my fingers against the leather steering wheel. The clock on the dashboard told me it was 10.40. I wondered what the visiting hours might be.

It was frustrating having to wait for other traffic so near to my destination. The roads had been almost deserted all the way from the ferry port in Turku. There was a café by the side of the road. It looked familiar. I had a faint memory of a car excursion from our summer cottage for coffee and ice cream by a large bridge. Pappa drove, of course, and Anja and I sat in the back, mouths watering at the thought of the delicious treat at the other end. Pappa joked and laughed in the car. We passed a man on a bicycle and Pappa said, 'Look girls, he's cycled so much he's lost all his hair!'

Anja and I peered out of the small rear window of the Triumph at a man peddling hard, clearly struggling with a long, steep hill ahead of him. He was repeatedly brushing aside the few, thin strands of hair falling on one side of his head.

'Mikko, honestly,' Mamma giggled in the front and touched Pappa's thigh with her hand.

Did we really drive so far just to sit by the bridge and eat ice creams? There was the view, of course. It was stunning. On both sides small rocky islands emerged out of the sea, scattered over the vast lake as if by an artist's brush. Saara had a painting of a view like this. I wondered if it still hung on the wall of her lounge.

The cars ahead moved and I drove over the bridge slowly, resting my eyes on the frozen scene around me.

The centre of Tampere seemed a miniature of the picture I had in my head. The cobbled streets were narrow, the square, red-brick buildings not so tall and imposing as I remembered them, the stone statues guarding the two bridges less grand. The people walking on the pavements had their heads bent, resisting the cold. 'The north wind from Russia could cut the nose off your face,' I remembered Pappa joke. I opened my window slightly. I was feeling sick again.

When I passed the cemetery and our old block of flats I slowed down. I tried to recognise the corner window where I sat and looked over the brick wall, imagining the dead lying under the earth, weighed down by the massive headstones. Mamma told me that you had to be from a very good and rich family to have a large plot like that.

'But Uncle Keijo said we have one!' I said, my eyes wide.

'Yes, we do,' she replied and smiled.

Now everything looked smaller, even the pine trees along the wall of the cemetery. I decided to go and visit Mamma's family grave before returning to Stockholm.

Then I thought of Yri's smiling eyes and his soft lips on mine. I wanted to talk to him so badly but decided to wait for his call rather then be the one to break and telephone him, for once.

The road towards Saara's flat was unchanged. The houses looked the same, the small group of shops just before her block was still there. Even the bingo hall Saara's friends had visited remained open. I remembered how she had scoffed at the futile pastime saying, 'At least I have my painting and don't have to sit at a table staring at numbers all day long!' Then I saw the Konditoria. It had been painted bright yellow and signs were stuck to the windows so that you couldn't see inside.

I looked up to Saara's window. It looked empty. I wished I had time to linger, but needed to hurry to see her. I'd come back to see the flat later.

I parked the car outside a green wooden house with the number 7 displayed on an old-fashioned wooden letterbox. The paint was flaking, but the copper number plate was intact. There was a long path leading up to the house. It was cold and a nasty wind blew right through me. I shivered. Then I saw a shadow move behind the lace curtains of a small window and stopped. What if he was drunk? I felt dizzy and wished Yri was with me. Or Anja. I dug my mobile out of my bag and put it into my pocket.

Slowly I made my way along the path. Around the corner I found the front door at the back of the house. There was a porch full of empty flowerpots. I stood there feeling my keys in the other pocket of my Ulster. If I kept them handy I could run to the car, start the engine quickly and escape if need be.

The door opened.

An old man with loose jogging pants and a grey, unwashed jumper was standing opposite me. 'Eeva,' he said.

I was hardly breathing. I closed my eyes and felt my heart beating fast. Was I going to faint? Then I opened my eyes and looked at him. I saw he'd lost nearly all his hair. Only a few pale-grey wisps were standing up on top of his head. Then Pappa said, 'You have grown, Eeva!'

'Yes,' I said. That's right, I am as tall, if not taller, than him, I thought. Or was it because he was stooped?

Pappa coughed and said, 'Come in.' He looked down at his stockinged feet and opened the door wide. He stood aside, gesturing for me to come in with his arm. But I couldn't move. I shivered and pulled my coat tighter around me.

'C'mon, come in from the cold.' Pappa's voice was soft. His eyes were on me.

I hadn't remembered how blue Pappa's eyes were.

I followed him into a dark hall. As he opened the door into a large living room he said, 'Here we go.' I walked in. The mid-morning light was glaring through the low windows. Suddenly I felt tired after the sleepless night on the ferry and the two-hour drive to Tampere. Pappa was standing behind me.

'Do you want a drink?' he asked my back.

'Yes please.' I looked around and said, 'Coffee?'

'Oh,' he said. Then after a pause, 'What about a beer?'

Not much has changed, I thought, and looked at my watch: it was only eleven o'clock. 'OK then,' I said. I'd have one beer and then go.

Pappa's eyes lit up. He rubbed his hands together and said, 'Coming up!' and disappeared through the doorway.

I looked at the room properly and saw the sofa. It wasn't so shiny anymore. Then I spotted Anja's cigarette burn. The upholsterers made such a hash of the repair; it became a badly concealed hole with stitches in a small square. Anja said they did it deliberately so that Pappa could go on reminding her how bad she was. I wondered why Pappa hadn't had it redone.

Now here it was, the rug too: all the familiar furniture in this strange room.

'Take a seat!' Pappa said walking in with two bottles of Karjala beer. I realised I was still standing in my overcoat. I thought for a moment and then sat right in the middle of the sofa, covering the cigarette burn.

81

'How is she?' I asked. He handed me a bottle, took a swig out of his, then looked at me. I was holding onto my beer, not drinking.

'Ah, glasses,' he said. He put his bottle down on the coffee table in front of me and went out of the room again. I looked at the table. The golden knobs on the corners were worn-out and dull-looking now. I remembered how heavy they'd felt in my hands. I thought about Anja and checked my phone again. No calls or messages. If only Yri would phone soon. Surely he must have had a moment free from meetings on the ferry by now? I shivered, thinking I was being drawn into the same trap again.

Pappa came back and gave me a tall glass. He'd brought one for himself, too. He poured the beer and I saw his hands were shaking. After a while, he said, 'How are you, Eeva? You look just the same but a lot taller!' Pappa's face looked rounder and he was almost smiling, leaning back on a chair belonging to the darkly polished dining table. That's new, I thought.

'Saara; how is she?' I asked again.

Pappa looked at me. He leant over and said, 'Not good.'

Neither of us spoke. I was sitting still, holding my breath. Please, God, don't let me be too late. I wanted to scream at Pappa, pound his chest with my arms, pull his hair, tell him it's all his fault I haven't been to see Saara before. Ask him if he feels any regret, feels anything.

I couldn't look at him and turned my head towards the window. There were some fruit trees in the sloping garden, but they were brown and solitary without leaves. An old-fashioned swinging seat stood rusting at the far end, where two or three patches of snow lay stubbornly resisting the warmth of the sun. Ice had formed around the edges where it had melted during the warmest part of the previous day. I noticed a small vegetable plot, marked off by a row of round stones. I looked back at Pappa and wondered when he had taken up gardening. Living a normal life, as if he had a right to.

He was holding his hands together, examining them with his head bent. Not looking at me, he said, 'Eeva, I'm very glad you came. Even though the circumstances...'

'Well, of course I came. I knew something was not right; it's over three weeks since her last letter.'

'Letter?' Pappa said, lifting his eyes to mine.

'She wrote to me regularly.'

'Saara wrote to you?' Pappa straightened himself up and stared at me.

'Yes, we started right after, you know, right after the...'

Pappa was still glaring at me and I thought here we go. This is the explosion.

'My mother was in touch with you all these years and never told me?' Pappa's voice quivered and I felt he might be close to tears instead of rage. Suddenly he didn't look threatening. I felt tears rise up in my eyes too. I asked quickly, 'When can I see her?'

Pappa took another gulp of his beer and swallowed audibly, 'We can go after lunch – you will have lunch with me?' There was pleading in his voice. I took a sip of beer and said, 'Why not?'

Pappa told me to park the car on the path, so I went out and brought back the shopping from the ferry.

'Koskenkorva and beer!' he said like a child who'd received sweets from an old auntie. He moved towards me when he'd put the bottles on the dining table. I took a step back and sat down on the sofa, again covering the cigarette burn, 'You still drink that then?'

Pappa gave me a quick glance and said, 'Well, not so much anymore, but sometimes…'

'When did you say we could go and see Saara?' I asked.

'One o'clock,' Pappa replied. Then he looked at me and said, 'Eeva, did you speak with Anja?' He opened his eyes wide with a worried look.

'No,' I said. This is new, I thought. I didn't think he would give a damn about Anja, or me for that matter. Pappa drank his beer in silence. Then he shifted on his seat and said, 'So you've not told her you were coming?'

I looked at him and shook my head. I wanted to ask about hotels, where I could stay, but thought it best to leave it until we'd been to see Saara.

'Pappa,' I said.

'Yes?'

'Tell me what's happening with Saara, what exactly did the doctors say? When was she taken ill?'

Pappa retold the details he'd given me on the telephone. Saara hadn't been well for years, but with medication had managed her weak heart. 'Too much butter, sugar and salt in her diet, the doctors told her.' I smiled, remembering how Saara cooked with real butter. She said margarine was for bad times and war times.

'This was her second stroke,' Pappa said. He fell silent and poured the last of his beer into the glass. His hands were steady now.

I took my coat off and Pappa darted up and took it off me. 'Lunch won't be a minute,' he shouted from the hall.

I sat still. I felt nauseous with the smell of cooking coming from the kitchen. I took another sip of beer and closed my eyes. The events of the last twenty-four hours played in my mind. With my eyes closed, I could still feel the motion of the ship, as if the sofa underneath me was gently rocking. Yri's body next to me, above me, the grey hairs of his chest touching my breasts. Then I thought about Pappa cooking for me in the kitchen, so eager to please, seemingly so delighted to see me. His body soft and slack, not strong and tense as it was in Rinkeby. I wondered what I had expected and realised I hadn't thought much about Pappa, just about seeing Saara, speaking with her. I felt lonely, having to do this on my own, and foolish for not having asked Anja to come with me.

I was startled by the sound of a key turning in the front door. I opened my eyes and heard the door close again and someone walking into the room.

In the doorway stood Anja.

Nine

I HADN'T seen Anja since the previous Christmas when she came over to Stockholm with her family. They'd been cramped in my small flat, staying for only two nights. I saw she'd put on a little more weight and cut her hair. The colour was different too, or was it her new dark-rimmed glasses that made it look brown?

Anja spoke to Pappa first, 'How are you?' They hugged in the hall. I thought I must be dreaming.

'Fine, nothing wrong with me,' he said. He lifted his glass. 'Eeva and I are having a beer. Do you want one?'

Anja walked into the room and looked at me and then at the glass table in front of me. She reached into a drawer underneath the dark dining room table and pulled out two drinks mats. She lifted my beer bottle and the glass and placed the two mats underneath. Then she smiled at me and turned to Pappa. 'Yes please.'

Pappa went back into the kitchen. Anja sat beside me on the sofa and put her arm around my shoulders.

'Eeva, I'm so glad you came!'

'Of course I did – what are you doing here?'

'Oh, I came over last night.'

'What?'

'Eeva, I've been meaning to tell you...'

Pappa came back into the room and this time remembered the mats. He placed the glass and bottle carefully on top of two mats in front of Anja. He gave her a boyish grin.

Drinking the beer next to me, and shooting a glance at Pappa, Anja said to me, 'You drove?'

'Yes.' I said. I watched her: how comfortable she was in this room. She didn't look a stranger, like me; she was in charge, in control of the situation. Then Pappa said, 'The visiting hours start at one, so I thought we'd have some lunch first and then go.' He was talking to Anja. Then, addressing the both of us, 'I've got your favourite: 'Sister Soup'!' Anja lifted her eyes sideways to me. Her lips pursed together in a conspiratorial smile. I thought she might even have made the soup – it was certainly her doing to have that on the menu. Now I understood why she hadn't returned my calls.

I wondered how long she'd been in contact with Pappa. I looked over to him. He'd finished his beer and was sitting looking down at the bottom of his empty glass. He shifted uncomfortably on the seat, and I thought he should be sitting on the sofa; a rigid dining room chair must be uncomfortable for his large frame. The sun came out suddenly and lit up the gold in the carpet. I hadn't noticed it had clouded over outside. The smell of burnt dust mixed with the oats of the beer reminded me of Rinkeby. Pappa got up with a sigh and talked into the silence, 'You two girls

87

have a chat – I'll go and warm up the soup.'

When he'd gone, Anja said, 'Don't be like that, Eeva!'

'Like what?'

'Oh, that thin-lipped expression!' Anja had always been good at shooting from the hip.

'How long have you been in touch?' I was examining my hands; I couldn't look at her.

'You've got nothing to reproach me for!'

'I'm not...' I looked up at her stern face. Then I thought Pappa could hear us and continued in a whisper, 'I'm just bloody shocked! Here I am, having psyched myself up for this meeting and you've already been here...' I choked and felt tears well up. I reached for my handbag and found, as usual, no tissues or handkerchief inside.

'Here,' Anja said and handed me a paper tissue.

'Thanks.'

'Listen, we'll talk about this later,' she said, glancing towards the kitchen, listening momentarily to the noises of pots being banged and cupboards being opened. 'I just had to come,' she said and paused. After a while she continued, 'A few years ago, after the children were born and started to ask about their Grandfather...'

'But Niklas is eleven!' I was trying to do the maths.

'Eeva, please, let's talk about this later. We're here be-cause of Saara. You want another tissue?'

'Please. I guess you know where the loo is?' I said, imme-diately regretting the sarcastic tone in my voice. Anja gave me a tired look and said, 'Just there, the door opposite.'

'Thanks.' As I passed her, I tried to give her a smile but the tears came again, so I walked quickly to the door.

There was a tiny mirror in the dimly-lit loo – a typical man's household I thought. I tried to examine my face; was it obvious I'd been crying? As I was there, I thought I might as well have a pee. The place was clean at least. I sat longer than I needed, just to let my face calm down, in the hope my lips would be a little less swollen. I found lip salve in the bottom of my handbag. After a quick dab underneath my eyes to remove the smudged mascara, I decided I looked fairly normal again, as normal as you can with a treacherous sister, estranged father and dying Grandmother. And a love affair with a married Polish dentist! I thought wildly that I could find out how to get to the hospital on my own. If I sneaked out now I wouldn't have to deal with Pappa of Anja anymore. But as I unlocked the door and stepped into the hall I heard Pappa shout from the kitchen, 'Eeva, come in, we're ready to eat.'

The kitchen was old-fashioned. There was a large wood-fired range and a small stainless steel sink with a painted cupboard over the top. It reminded me of Saara' s flat, and I had to tell myself it wasn't. I wanted to say something to Anja and Pappa but didn't. The table was laid for three people. Anja was already sitting down and Pappa ushered me into a chair next to her. She wasn't looking at me but at the view from a window next to the table.

'Did you plant any daffodils last autumn?' She asked Pappa.

'Yes,' Pappa answered, 'Right then, Eeva, say when.' He was holding a pan in his oven-gloved hand, tipped over slightly so that I could see a large ladle filled with the potato and sausage mixture. I was not at all hungry.

'Just one, please.'

As he poured some soup into my plate, hot liquid splashed onto my smart black trousers. I wiped it off with a tissue. Pappa didn't notice; he'd moved onto Anja's bowl. She asked for two spoonfuls and when he'd filled his own bowl, Pappa sat down and started eating immediately. Suddenly he stopped and said, 'Bread – I've got some rye bread for you, Eeva! Nearly forgot!'

'It's OK, Pappa, I'll get it,' Anja said and got up. She went to a cupboard to get the bread and then to the fridge for some butter. She knows where everything is kept in the kitchen, too, I thought. I felt compelled to have some bread and it was true, it used to be my favourite. The taste of genuine Finnish rye bread was bitter and less sweet than the Swedish one.

'Oh, this is good!' I said. Pappa smiled.

Ten

Stockholm 1974

IT WAS exactly four weeks after our move to Rinkeby and I was very, very excited, because Pappa was going to take me to Stockholm Stadium to see Finland play Sweden. I'd not been to an ice-hockey match since last winter when Ilves played Tappara in the Jäähalli in Tampere. My team lost to their local rivals. The boys at school who wore the black and orange Tappara scarves laughed at me. But I didn't give up my green and blue Ilves scarf just because of one game.

In Sweden, nobody knew of the Finnish league, but the annual Maaottelu was a question of pride for both teams and their countries. Pappa had been given the tickets by his boss in the factory where he worked.

'You have no idea how expensive these seats are,' he said. 'And how difficult to get hold of.' He was talking to Anja. 'And I'm not going to waste them on a person who ruins beautiful new sofas.'

Anja just shrugged her shoulders. 'It wasn't me,' she said, looking down at her feet.

'What did you say?' Pappa said.

'Hadn't you better be going?' Mamma said.

We were standing in the hall. Anja was leaning in the kitchen doorway. I was looking for my Ilves scarf. Pappa was already dressed in his grey overcoat. He held onto his brown leather gloves and black felt hat. He turned to face the mirror and put the hat on.

'He thinks you're his son,' Anja whispered to me and walked into the kitchen.

I looked at her and then Mamma. She smiled at me and said, 'Go on, you'll be late!'

I was very proud to be taken by Pappa. In Tampere, I went to ice-hockey matches with my friend, Kaija. We both played on the ice-rink two blocks from our flat with the boys from our school. To be allowed to play, we had to wait until it was clear there weren't enough boys to make up a team. One boy, Jussi, was in my class and had curly brown hair and short stumpy legs. He shouted, 'Do your figure skating in the corner, girlies!' Jussi had all the latest gear, fancy leather gloves much too large for his hands, pads for his knees and a shiny new stick, which he rolled around with one gloved hand, often dropping it with a bang on the ice. Kaija sat next to Jussi in class and said he was really sweet, but she only said that because she had a crush on him, had for ages. They lived close to each other and walked home together. She'd told me that Jussi would hold her hand if there were no other boys around. Kaija was a short girl with round face and straight thin hair. Pappa called us Pitkä ja Pätkä after a

Finnish version of Laurel and Hardy. Getting ready for the match, I decided to write to Kaija later that evening. I wondered who her new best friend might be. I'd received one letter from her but she said nothing about school in it. It was already October so she must have found someone by now. I wished Kaija was coming to see Finland play Sweden with me.

The match was played in the evening, in the large stadium in the centre of Stockholm.

'There'll be lots of people there and very few Finns, so best keep together, OK?' Pappa said as we parked the Volvo. I nodded and looked at the massive dark, round building in front of me. There were people hurrying towards it. Pappa took my hand and we started running. We were late. He looked at the tickets and then up at the signs on doors. I held tightly onto Pappa's hand while we walked up steps and then saw the vast ice rink in front of us. People had to stand up to let us in, we were right in the middle of the row.

'Tack, tack,' Pappa said and I smiled. Nobody looked directly at us. Some just nodded, but most ignored us, staring at the rink in front of them.

The players were already out warming up. They smashed the pucks against the solid white edges, snapping their sticks fast and hard.

'There's Harri Linnonmaa, look – number 75!' Pappa said, pointing at a player in blue and white with a picture of a lion on his chest. 'The Finnish Lions will beat the Swedish wimpy white-bread men,' he whispered into my ear when the players skated up to the side and disappeared underneath us. I looked at his blue eyes and smiled. Then all the players came out again in a line and stopped dead when the Swedish national anthem was played over the loudspeakers. Everybody stood up. Pappa and I were the only people not singing. After the Swedish anthem I felt awkward, knowing th words to Maamme Suomi, but Pappa sang loudly, pronouncing clearly.

'Oi maamme, Suomi, synnyinmaa,
soi, sana kultainen!
Ei laaksoa, ei kukkulaa,
ei vettä rantaa rakkaampaa,
kuin kotimaa tää pohjoinen,
maa kallis isien!'

When the singing was over and the game started, with the two attackers fighting for the puck in the middle of the rink, Pappa sat down rubbing his hands together and muttering, 'C'mon, Finnish Lions!'

The Swedish players wore their blue and yellow shirts with the three crowns. They all had long, very blond hair escaping from underneath their helmets. Pappa told me the crowns were for the three monarchies Sweden had once ruled.

'Now they don't even dare take part in wars, let alone win them, the cowards!' he said. He told me Finns had earned their emblem through having to fight for their independence. 'Like lions, we are fearless and proud,' he said.

'I think we'll win, Eppu, because the Swedes are scared,' Pappa said. 'Finland won the first leg of the tournament in Helsinki. If only they can hold until half time, they'll win.' He smiled and nudged me with his elbow.

The whole of the stadium exploded when the first goal came. But Pappa and I sat still. By half time Finland was 9 goals down and Pappa had an Elefant beer in the dark, cold hall downstairs. People around us were standing in groups laughing and smoking. They were mostly men, like my father drinking beer.

'Can I have a hot dog, Pappa?' I said. He looked at me and without saying anything gave me the money. I ran to a stall and back again as quickly as I could. Thankfully Pappa was still there when I came back. He'd finished his beer and the bell was sounding for the start of the second half.

'Never mind,' he said when we sat down. 'We still have time to come back.'

But the second half was worse. Finnish players were sent to the sin bin, leaving the Swedish blonds free to score more goals. Three more times the puck ended up in the Finnish net. The Swedish players hugged each other and the crowd cheered. Pappa said nothing. The Finnish goalkeeper hung his head, while his team mates got angry with the Swedish players. Another man was sent to the sin bin. At one time there were two Finns sitting there, holding their sticks between their knees, staring ahead at the terrible result on the board opposite them.

'Let's go,' Pappa said suddenly. The game wasn't finished yet and people looked angrily at us when they let us pass. One man with a huge belly and a round face said, 'Jävla Finnar' when I passed. I didn't look at him.

Anja had told me that the words meant 'Fucking Finns'. She said the best thing was to pretend you hadn't heard.

'That way they don't know for sure if you're Finnish or not,' she'd said.

The hall downstairs and the dark streets outside were completely empty. We heard another loud cheer. Pappa walked fast to the car and quickly started the engine. He said nothing on the way home. When we pulled into the space outside our block of flats I said, 'Can we go again?'

Pappa looked at me and said, 'No.'

Eleven

THE NEXT day I heard the boys at school talk about the ice-hockey match and I understood the final score was 13-0. Worst ever Maaottelu score for Finland. They laughed at me but I didn't say anything. I didn't tell anyone I'd been there, not even Harriet.

I was thinking about the match, and what Harriet would say if she knew I'd been there, when we were walking home from school. We were nearly at the point where the path divided in two and Harriet said 'Hejdå' and turned towards her block of flats. I'd been to her home a few times. It was a mirror image of our place. It had much more furniture but her parents were never at home. She had an older brother, Jonas, who teased her whenever he was there, which wasn't often. He was tall and thin with the same red hair, but his eyes were darker. Harriet had a round face with freckles and short legs. When I was there we ate what we wanted: ice cream out of a large tub, bread and jam with cold Oboj chocolate milk. Now she was on a diet and had just toast and salad when she got home. She told me her tummy was too big, and I looked at mine and decided I needed to eat less too.

I'd been going to my new school for a month. I could understand almost everything Harriet and Fru Sundtröm said to me, but I couldn't understand the boys when they spoke quickly, just to tease me. Today when they told me about the ice-hockey score they spoke slowly and loudly. Fru Jorvela said I was a pleasure to teach because I learned so quickly. 'You may not need to take any extra lessons next term,' she said. I was glad because I didn't like my Swedish teacher anymore. She was always ill but never away from school. She told me she had a blocked-up nose all the time, causing such terrible headaches that she needed to have an operation in a hospital. She spent the whole lesson telling me how a doctor stuck needles up her nose.

'They had to do one side first, and even though I screamed and said I didn't want the other side done, they still stuck the needle up there. Eeva, my dear, never have any-thing like that done. It was the most horrible experience I have ever had. The pain went all the way from my head down to my toes.' Fru Jorvela's bangles rattled as she moved her hand up and down her body. 'So now I just suffer the head-aches and the sinus infections, because the pain is nothing to that of the operation.'

I didn't understand why she couldn't stay at home in bed if she was feeling so poorly. Besides, I was supposed to learn Swedish with her, not listen to her talking in Finnish about her nose.

My mind drifted back to the match and I decided to tell

Harriet about it after all. It was better than thinking about Fru Jorvela and her illnesses.

'Harriet, have you ever been to an ice-hockey match?' I said.

Harriet looked at me sideways and said, 'No, of course not!'

'Oh.'

'It's what boys do,' Harriet said. She'd stopped walking and was looking at me. I tried to think of the right words to tell her where I'd been the night before. Though it was a sunny day, a cold wind blew between the blocks of flats. Sometimes it made a noise like a ghost, but today it sounded different.

'What's that?' I said.

Harriet looked at me and listened. Her unruly hair was in a ponytail. A few locks had fallen down and were caught up in the strap of her canvas bag. I wanted to tell her but didn't know the right words, so I just tapped her shoulder. She moved her head and pulled the hair out. Her eyes looked very green.

'Yeah, that's funny. It's coming from your block,' she said. We looked at each other and started running, holding onto our school bags.

Outside my block of flats there was chaos. On the ground was some broken china. A lampshade had been thrown out of a window. I looked up and saw a man standing on the fifth-floor balcony, three floors above our flat. He was shouting at a woman standing hugging her daughter, who I knew was in Anja's class. I couldn't remember her name.

There was a police car right outside the front door, where

no one was usually allowed to park, and two policemen standing by. A crowd of people stood looking up at the balcony. One of the policemen had a cream-coloured loudspeaker in his hand. I saw Mamma standing on one side of the crowd.

'Mamma, what's happening?' I said taking her hand.

'A man, Herr Lahtelainen, is very angry at something,' she said hugging me. She was looking up like everybody else. The man was now waving his arms about. There was a blanket hanging on the side of the balcony. He pushed it down and shouted something again. I recognised the man's wife next to Mamma. I looked around and saw that Harriet was talking to Jonas further back. I wondered if they knew Herr and Fru Lahtelainen were from Finland like us. Suddenly the man went inside the flat and brought out a chair and flung it over the side of the balcony. A leg broke when it landed on the ground. Mamma and I stepped back. I felt very ashamed. Next Herr Lahtelainen threw a bedside table over the rail, then another one. One of the policemen rushed up the staircase, and the other one talked to Herr Lahtelainen through the loudspeaker. There was a long silence. Everybody waited.

'Do you think the police have got him?' I asked. Mamma didn't have time to reply before a bed came crashing down. It hit the ground with a bang and broke in two. There were gasps from the people watching. I looked over to Fru Lahtelainen. She had her head bowed. Then her husband hauled a mattress onto the balcony and pushed it over. It landed on top of the broken bed. The policeman came back outside. He was shaking his head and talking to the other one in whispers. There was an odd scent in the air.

'What's the smell?' I asked Mamma. Suddenly the man put his leg over the balcony. Fru Lahtelainen put her hand out and screamed. I put my hand to my mouth. Quickly and almost silently the man flung himself off the balcony, landing on top of the mattress. Fru Lahtelainen ran to him and knelt beside his head. Then an ambulance arrived. Herr Lahtelainen's eyes were wide open when he was carried away. His wife was holding his hand. He was wearing stripy pyjamas and his hair was a mess. I looked over to Anja's classmate. She was standing alone, looking at the contents of her parents' bedroom outside the block of flats. Slowly people started to walk away. Mamma said, 'C'mon, let's go inside.' I waved to Harriet. Mamma and I walked up to our flat.

At dinner the same evening Anja told us all she knew of the family.

'Herr Lahtelainen works for LM Eriksson and he's an engineer. Satu is in my class and she has no brothers or sisters. Anyway, he just suddenly started shouting this afternoon. He had a knife and ran after Satu and her mother, so they fled. Then he went onto the balcony and started throwing things at them. Somebody must have phoned the police, who used laughing gas on him.'

'That's what the smell was,' I said.

Pappa was eating his meat soup. He had a paper folded in half on the table. I didn't think he was listening, but he lifted his eyes to Anja and said, 'How do you know all this, Anja?'

'People at the Youth Club told me,' Anja said.

'Youth Club?' Pappa said and looked at Mamma.

'It's a place where the youngsters go after school. It's organised by the teachers, I think. Isn't it, Anja?'

'Yes, yes,' Anja said, 'Anyway, the laughing gas didn't make any difference and after he'd thrown everything out he threw himself on top of the pile!'

'Poor woman,' Mamma said.

'I expect she drove him crazy,' Pappa said not looking up from his paper.

'How awful to have a violent husband,' Mamma said quietly.

'We saw him fall, it was terrible,' I said.

'They took him to a mental hospital,' Anja said and took her empty bowl to the sink. 'Satu will never forgive him for making such a scene,' she continued, coming back to the table.

'It's no wonder, the poor man had two women to cope with,' Pappa said.

Anja looked at Mamma but they didn't say anything.

'I never knew laughing gas smelled like vinegar,' I said.

'Poor woman, she's Finnish, did you say, Anja?' Mamma said.

'Yes,' Anja said and looked at Pappa. Then she got up.

'I have three women to cope with. To spend my money and ruin the things I buy, like new furniture,' Pappa said looking up from his food to Anja. 'One of these days I'll end up in the Laughing Club too!' Pappa said and smiled a little. He always made up funny names for everything but this time nobody laughed at his joke.

***

The smell of vinegar lingered for weeks on the staircase. The caretaker in the ground floor flat cleared all the furniture away. I watched him from our balcony the next evening. Another man, who I didn't know, helped him haul it all, except for the bed and the mattress, into the large bins in front of the house. Then they laid the bed and the mattress against the side of the bins. Satu and her mother went away for a while, and when they came back Fru Lahtelainen had coloured her hair black. I never saw her husband again.

Twelve

Tampere 2004

AFTER WE'D eaten Pappa drove us to the hospital. It was a little way out of town, and on the way Pappa pointed out places I should have remembered, 'There's Lake Näsijärvi and over on the other side of the road is Pispala.'

'Isn't that where Mamma was born?' I asked.

Anja turned her head and looked at me.

'No, she lived there for a while, but she wasn't born there,' she said quickly. She was sitting on the front seat, next to Pappa. At junctions, he kept asking her if the lights had changed or if there were any cars coming from the other direction. Anja knew the way to the hospital.

'There are so many new roads. I don't really know where I am anymore,' Pappa said.

He isn't the confident head of the household, I thought. He's an old man. 'But a bastard all the same,' as Anja would once have said. I smiled and looked at the vast lake by the road. It was still frozen, though you could see a few dark indentations where the ice had melted a little. There were no shipping lanes here. Then I thought of Saara and feared I wouldn't be able to hold back my tears seeing her. I remembered how she hadn't cried in front of me when we left Tampere. Now I needed to be brave like she had been then. We turned off the main road and were driving down a sandy path. A hill led to a red-brick building. There was a large car park with only a few cars dotted around it.

Pappa led us to the front door and up to Saara's ward. The corridors all looked the same, and I tried to look for room numbers and department names posted on yellow and green signs on our path. I intended to come and see Saara on my own the next day.

Pappa stopped in front of a room and paused. 'Right, here we are.' He knocked on the door and opened it without listening for a reply. 'Guess who I've brought to see you!' he said in a phony high-pitched voice.

Saara looked small lying in the raised hospital bed. Her hair, which had not been brushed, had streaks of black in it and the curls were still there, although most of it was white. Her eyes were watery and red and her arms hung bony and thin. Her face was sunken. She smiled when she saw us, although her lips were colourless.

'Eeva,' she said, reaching her hand out to me. I took it and sat down in a grey plastic chair next to her bed. I couldn't speak; I was biting my lip trying to stop the tears. My throat was tight.

'Anja, you look well,' Saara said.

'Thank you, Saara,' Anja said. She was standing behind

me. She moved towards Saara and they hugged. 'You're looking better today,' she said.

'No, I'm not,' Saara said, 'Old age is a nuisance,' she said and smiled at Anja.

Pappa came over and hugged Saara too, 'What about this new visitor?' he said and moved his head in my direction. Saara moved her eyes towards me. I wanted to go and lie down next to her and bury my face in her neck.

Anja said, 'Pappa, shall we leave Saara with Eeva for a while to catch up?'

'Yes, yes,' Pappa said. He was standing at the far end of the room. 'We'll see you in a minute,' he said.

'Oh, Saara,' I said when they had left the room. I put my forehead on her dry hand. She was half-sitting in bed.

'It's alright, Eeva,' she said, squeezing my hand. It was like a child's grip, there was no strength in it. I put my cheek against the loose skin and cried.

After a while Saara handed me a tissue and I looked up to her.

'Sorry,' I said. Saara smiled and stroked my hair, 'It's alright, Eeva, I'm just resting my old eyes on you, you have the same beautiful face, but you're just a little taller.' She had the same glint in her eyes that she had when she teased me as a child. I laughed and got up to hug her. She felt small and fragile. He bosom was soft and even, I thought. The artificial breast must have been replaced with a new modern one that matched the real one on her right. Or was it left? I couldn't remember anymore. I sat back down on the uncomfortable plastic chair and looked at Saara's face. She said, 'You noticed the new breast?'

'Yes,' I said and laughed, 'How did you know that's what I was thinking?'

Saara just smiled and said, 'Now tell me all about your life in Stockholm, and Janne, is he with you?'

I took Saara's hand between mine and told her about my pupils, about Irina and Jacob. When I spoke about Janne she looked intently at me but made no comment. I felt guilty, and thought I'd finish it when I got back to Stockholm. I wanted to tell Saara about Yri, his pale eyes and blond unruly hair, but didn't. Every now and then as she listened to me, Saara closed her eyes and rested her head briefly on the pillows. After she'd done that a few times I fell silent and watched her sleep. Her chest moved slowly up and then down and her mouth opened slightly to let out a faint sound. I heard the door open behind me. Pappa and Anja were standing in the doorway. I moved my finger to my lips and slid silently out of the seat.

We were walking back to the car. Pappa was leading the way and Anja was holding onto my arm. Nobody spoke. A nurse in a crisp white uniform walking towards us said, 'Päivää Herra Litmunen,' and smiled at Pappa. She slowed down when she saw us and lingered for a moment. Pappa just nodded to her and carried on walking down the long corridor.

'I need to check into a hotel,' I said to Anja in a low voice. Anja slowed her pace and turned to face me, 'What?'

'Where are you staying?' I said and at the same time realised. 'Of course, you're…' I'd stopped walking. She'd let herself into Pappa's house with her own key!

'Yes, of course! I don't want to leave him alone at a time like this. C'mon Eeva, he's an old man, surely you could for once think about someone other than yourself.' Anja's eyes were hard and accusing. I stared at her but said nothing. Then I lowered my head and thought of what to say. How had I become the villain here? I looked out of the window. A slope in the distance was covered in lily of the valley. There was a bench by the side of a path that followed the wood into the distance. I wanted to go over, to sit down and smell the scent of the flowers and leave the antiseptic stench behind. I thought of Saara. She would have loved the view. All you could see out of her room was another building, a red brick wall of another part of the hospital. I should have come before. It was all Pappa's fault.

'But he's a bastard all the same,' I muttered.

'What?' Anja said. She wasn't looking at me anymore but at the increasingly distant figure of Pappa, stooped and with his shoulders hunched. 'C'mon we're going to lose him,' she said and pulled my arm.

We caught up with Pappa as he was bending down to open the door of his old Peugeot. I'd been surprised he wasn't driving something flashier, or sturdier. Cars had been important to him.

'Pappa,' Anja said moving close to him, 'are you alright?' In spite of her extra weight Anja looked smaller. Even with Pappa stooped over she was a head shorter than him. Then Pappa did something I'd never seen. He pulled a handkerchief out of his trouser pocket and wiped his eyes. He wiped first one side then the other, with each movement covering half of his face.

I looked away.

The weather outside was dull. I sat in the back of the car and wished it would rain or better still snow. But the day had turned into that awful combination of cold wind and drizzle that stopped as soon as we got our umbrellas up. Anja had decided we'd take a walk around Tampere, to show me the town. The cobbled main street was slippery.

Pappa had his hands in his pockets. We were standing opposite a new bus station, waiting for the lights to change. I was trying to remember what had been there before, perhaps just a square. The buildings around it were newly renovated, the stone walls washed down. Behind us was the old church where Mamma and Pappa had been married. It looked desolate and cold under its coat of pale yellow paint and white bell tower.

I turned my head and looked at the Hämeensilta bridge. On one side there was a half-naked man holding a dead animal. Suddenly it came to me that it was a lynx, the symbol of the city. Why a lynx, I couldn't remember. On the other side was a woman, looking down, demurely pulling down the hem of her dress with both hands. Almost as if the statue opposite was about to ravish her.

Anja took hold of my arm and said, 'Do you want to go to Siilinkari?'

I looked at her and tried to think, 'Siilinkari?' I said.

'The first place to serve hamburgers in Tampere! Don't you remember, Eeva?' Anja said.

Anja looked cold, her nose was red and she, too, had her hands in her pockets. 'Is it far?' I asked.

Both Anja and Pappa turned to look at me. 'It's just over

there,' Anja said, pointing at a neon sign on the opposite side of the road.

They both seemed to have forgotten that I left here over thirty years before, I thought, and said, 'I'm easy.' I wasn't hungry at all but wanted to get out of the cold.

When I walked into the shop I did remember. The smell of fried food, of French fries lingered in the air. Anja ushered Pappa into a table in the corner and told me to follow her to the till.

'Take this,' Pappa said, pushing a fifty Euro note into Anja's hand. She took it and said, 'Thank you, Pappa. We'll eat like kings!' She smiled at Pappa and he said, 'Just coffee for me, and perhaps, a Runeberg cake if they still have them. Otherwise a cinnamon bun.' Pappa sat down with a heavy sigh.

'What about a cappuccino?'

'No, not that foreign rubbish,' he said and pinched his eyebrows together. They had gone grey and very bushy.

'A normal coffee coming up!' Anja said. She pushed past a crowd of people standing in the queue. I followed her. I had a weird feeling of the past thirty years not having existed. When we reached the glass display case and looked down at the cakes, Anja took my arm again and said, 'Isn't it good to be back here again after all these years?' Her eyes behind the dark-rimmed glasses were bright and kind.

Her smile and good humour were infectious. 'I guess so,' I said and then, 'The smell of the place is exactly the same!'

'Yes, I know,' she said. 'Do you remember, we used to beg Mamma and Pappa to take us here. And do you remember how good the burgers were? What luxury it was to eat out?'

We both laughed.

'Shall we go back to the car and drive over to Pyynikki?' Pappa said, after he'd wiped his mouth with a white paper napkin. He'd eaten his Runeberg cake with two quick bites and drank his black coffee equally swiftly. Anja and I were only halfway through our milky cappuccinos. It was strange drinking Italian coffee in Finland; Tampere really wasn't that different from Stockholm after all. Anja had talked me into having a Runeberg cake. The taste was as delicious as the ones I'd bought from Saara's Konditoria. The jam was runny, and the sponge spicy and soft. I wanted to tell Pappa and Anja, but feared I'd cry if I did.

'Yes, that's a good idea,' Anja said. In this weather we don't want to be walking about too much.' She looked from Pappa to me. She put her hand on mine and said, 'You must remember Pyynikki!'

'Of course I do,' I said. Her hand still felt cold, and I could feel her weighty rings on my palm.

Pappa said, 'If you'd rather go back to the house, Eeva...' his eyes looked watery.

I looked down at my coffee cup, 'A drive sounds a good idea.'

Pyynikki was the ridge of a valley. The road wound it's way up to a viewing tower with a café on one side and all the way back down to Lake Pyhäjärvi on the other. It was a conservation area with tall pine trees growing either side of the road. As a child I'd marvelled at the height of the ridge and the steepness of the fall. The drive to the top seemed to take an age then, but today it went quickly. I watched a family brave the cold on the walkway zigzagging the hillside. I remembered that we'd picked bilberries there when Anja and I had been little. The lake between the straight, brown trunks of the trees was frozen, with white snowdrifts running along the edge, like a scattering of icing sugar. The path was sanded, as was the road, but the ground in between, on the hill, was bare and grey.

On the top of the ridge Pappa parked his car in the empty car park and we walked over to the tower. It looked like a medieval prison, all red brick, or was it granite, I didn't know. It was Art Nouveau, or Jugendstil, I remembered. The bottom part was a larger square shape, and from that a perfectly round tower emerged. The columns at the entrance looked too grand for a mere viewing tower. The whole building looked strangely out of place on the top of a wooded hill.

Inside, I was hit by the smell of coffee and doughnuts. I hadn't realised how cold I had been until the warm air hit me. To the left there was a room with large floor-to-ceiling windows, allowing a view through the stems of the trees to the lake below. A young couple was sitting on opposite sides of a table, holding hands; their heads were bent, foreheads almost touching. The rest of the small café was empty. From the doorway Pappa said, 'There's a lift up to the top, shall we go and see the view?'

Anja was leafing through a large guest book in the little hallway. 'Eeva, write your name here!' she said. As if I was a visiting dignitary. I took the pen off her and wrote my name, 'Eeva Litmunen, Stockholm,' and the date, '11 March 2004.' Underneath my name were other people's signatures. I could only make out Michigan and yesterday's date. I wondered what someone from the States had made of Tampere in the cold and wind. In Michigan, though, they'd be used to the weather, I thought.

I was startled by the noise of a lift coming to a halt. Pappa opened the heavy door. The lift jolted up with a start and then slowly ascended to the top.

I felt dizzy at first, leaning over the open window. It was more like a porthole, and we had to step up to a ledge to see properly. Pappa pointed at the Särkänniemi tower to the north, a tall spike with an UFO-shaped disc at the top emerging from an amusement park below. I remembered how we'd eaten creamy buns and steaming cups of hot chocolate there with Mamma on Sleigh Day. There'd been no rides in the park below then, only a makeshift sled run, prepared by someone pouring bucketfuls of hot water onto the hill. All the kids in Tampere went there, but only a few parents had the money or the foresight to book a table in the Särkinniemi tower restaurant. I wondered now where Mamma got the money from; perhaps Uncle Keijo helped out? Pappa came to stand next to me and pointed to the famous revolving outdoor theatre by Lake Pyhäjärvi at the bottom of the ridge.

'It's a shame you're not here in the summer. Tampere is at its best when it's hot outside,' he said and looked at me.

I remembered seeing a play there. I'd nearly fallen asleep during it, but I hadn't told Mamma or Pappa how bored I'd been or how glad I was when I was finally allowed to leave the uncomfortable seat and go home. Saara had been there too. She'd nudged me every now and then and whispered something in my ear to keep me awake. I couldn't remember Anja

113

being with us. I turned to her now and wanted to ask about it, but saw she was gazing absentmindedly out to the lake. I decided I'd leave it be. For while we all stood there leaning over the cold stone windows. Then Pappa said, 'Oh well, shall we carry on downhill and then go over to Saara's flat?'

'Her flat?' I had my hands in my pockets; I'd forgotten my gloves at Pappa's house and my hands were frozen.

'Yes, she asked me to sort out her stuff,' Pappa said. He looked at me intently. Anja said nothing. She turned her back to me and started walking around the wall of the tower towards the lift.

We stepped outside. I followed Pappa, wiping the tears from the corners of my eyes with my fingers. The wind was stronger up on the top of the ridge and it was pushing my hair into my face. My ears were burning with the cold but I was glad of the pain. For a short moment it took away the thought of Saara's slight frame in the vast hospital bed.

Thirteen

STANDING IN Saara's lounge was strange: I remembered the dark mahogany bookcase that dominated the room, yet there were pieces of furniture I didn't recognise. A dining room table looked faintly familiar, as did one leather chair in the corner. It swung around and had a high back to it. I'd made myself dizzy in it many times when we came over to watch television. The old TV had been replaced by a new widescreen one. I looked at the bookcase again: there was a black and white wedding picture. I picked it up. The frame was silver and it felt heavy in my hands. I took the threadbare tissue out of my trouser pocket and wiped the dust off. Mamma looked beautiful and Pappa handsome. Though her lips were dark grey in the picture I knew she had red lipstick on. 'That's all the make-up I wore!' She'd told us. But I was more interested in Pappa, his hair looked dark, though I knew it hadn't been. He'd never been blond, but definitely fair. It must be the black-and-white photo, I thought. The picture didn't show their waists, but you could tell Pappa was holding onto

Mamma's from their posture. I peered into their faces and saw happy smiles. Youthful and clear expressions. It was strange seeing them together like this. I was used to the photo of Mamma alone, smiling with the bouquet in her lap. I'd never missed the groom. I heard footsteps behind me and quickly put the framed picture back onto the shelf.

'I think it would be better if we start in the cellar.' Pappa said. I didn't know if he'd seen what I'd been holding. 'OK,' I said turning around and seeing Anja standing behind him.

'The boxes are marked with your names. Either you can go through them, or just take the boxes unopened,' Pappa said when we were waiting for the lift outside Saara's flat. I looked at Anja.

'We'll see how much there is, shall we?' she said.

'Sounds like a good idea,' I said, trying to remember what boxes these were. The lift stopped a floor below ground level. There was no light but the walls were painted white. Pappa got out of the lift and pressed a large red, illuminated button that shone in the semi-darkness. As the light in the cellar came on, it buzzed, the timer on the switch kicking in. I felt a surge of fear as I had done thirty years before. The dank smell hadn't changed either. We walked silently along the narrow, cold corridor. I remembered how Saara had told us that this was a bomb shelter built after the war: the place we'd have to run to if the Russians attacked. Black-and-white film reel, showing women and children running, trying to escape an air raid, played in my head. Pappa opened a heavy steel door with his keys. This space, a large stone cold room, was divided into chicken wire compartments, numbered according to the flat they belonged to.

'Now let's see, it's right here on the left – one from the end, I think. Fifteen, sixteen…here we go: number eighteen!' Pappa stopped in front of a packed cage. Some of the ones we'd passed had been half empty, one had a whole mattress in it, lying across a discarded desk; none were as full as ours. I looked at my watch – it was three o'clock. This would take the rest of the afternoon and evening. If even one-third of this stuff was mine, I thought, I'd need to decide what to take and what to throw away – there was no way I'd be able to store it all in my small flat in Stockholm. I dug my mobile out of my handbag and saw there was no reception.

'Expecting a call?' Anja asked.

'No, I just thought I'd call work to say I'm staying another night.'

'Don't they let you take as long as you like?' She said. She'd never been able to understand my devotion to my career.

'Yes, they do,' I said, thinking, 'Please, Yri, call me, text me, do something!'

'Right, we'd better get started!' she said, looking away from me.

We helped Pappa haul a box down from the very top of the pile.

'This says Eeva,' he said and fixed his eyes on me. 'Do you want to open the lid and see what's inside?'

Then it hit me: of course, this was the stuff we'd left behind! How stupid of me not to remember. I looked up and saw both Anja and Pappa watching me. Then Pappa looked away and started to struggle with the next box. He was strong, but at the same time looked frail. I thought we ought to help him but I couldn't take my eyes off the text scrawled onto the off-white, dirty cardboard box:

'EEVA'S THINGS. SAARA OPEN AS OFFEN AS POS-SIBEL'

I took off the Sellotape, which had become yellow and loose. Then I carefully opened the flaps up and was faced with Charlotte. I put my hand to my mouth and said, 'I'm sorry, I can't...' I ran into the dark corridor, hit the red button on my way to the lift and, as I stood waiting, fumbled in my pockets for a tissue. The only one I had was black with dust from the wedding picture. I covered my face with the dirty tissue and leaned against the white wall. It was very cold against my back. I should have put on a sweater, I thought. Then I felt faint and dropped to my haunches. I heard the door open again – it squeaked now – and I heard footsteps echo down the corridor.

'Eeva, it's alright, just cry; cry it all out,' Anja said. She was now facing me and I felt her arms around me. I rested myself against her and let out a muffled groan. She stroked my hair and kept saying, 'That's it Eeva, that's it.' At some point we started rocking or perhaps I'd already been rocking before she came, I didn't know. Suddenly I was aware of noise behind Anja. I lifted my head and said, 'The lift.'

'You OK?' she said.

'Yes, well, I'll just sit upstairs for a while. I don't think I'll be able to...'

'It was stupid to think you could.' Anja was moving towards the lift and I noticed she was holding a single key.

'Pappa?' I said looking back down the corridor. Then the light went out and Anja said, while hitting the red button with the palm of her hand, 'He's just putting the boxes back

118

and locking up – we'll do it another time.'

Standing in the creaking lift, waiting for the slow ascent to the third floor, I thought of the day we'd packed those boxes.

When the lift stopped with a sharp movement first up, then down, finally coming to an uncertain halt, Anja took hold of my arm as if I was unwell, 'Here we go, Eeva. We'll just pick up our coats and get back to Pappa's place.' She opened the iron door of the lift and led me inside Saara's flat.

'Were you ever frightened in that lift when it used to do that jump at the end?' I asked her. She shot a look at me, a wary quick look to see if I was about to cry again, but then smiled, 'Yes, we both were, don't you remember? It was worse when we were smaller – and carried less weight!' She looked down at her waist. I laughed, and it felt good to be able to.

Just then I heard the lift again, and Pappa stepped into the narrow corridor. 'What about a beer?' he said. 'I think we all need drink, don't you?' He went to get our coats from the small bedroom and as he handed me my black wool coat, he said, 'Tough day, eh?' I nodded.

'Right, I'm ready for a large drink and it may not be beer!' Anja said. 'There's quite a decent restaurant just around the corner – is it still there?' she asked Pappa.

'I thought we might go into town. Eeva, you're staying another day aren't you?' he said, looking in my direction, not quite catching my eye. Anja looked at me and then away, she was busying herself with her handbag.

'Yes, I suppose so,' I said thinking this is a trap, how can I now go into a hotel? I felt angry with Anja; she had engineered this.

'In that case, why don't we leave the car here and take a taxi into town?' Pappa said. He glanced from Anja to me. I noticed his large earlobes and the kind look on his face. His mouth was curved downwards and his eyes looked watery.

'That sounds like a good plan, Pappa, I presume you'll be the banker,' Anja said and widened her eyes at me.

'Of course!' Pappa said and stretched his hand out to guide the two of us out of the door.

'I'll walk.' I said. The lift was really too old and small for the three of us and I felt the need for some time alone, however little that would be. But as I turned on the staircase, I saw Anja was behind me. I stopped and looked at her. She leaned against the banister and looked at the lift slowly moving downwards. When it passed the floor below, she said, 'I'm sorry, Eeva.'

'That's OK,' I said. I started to move down again, but she took my hand and said, 'Look, I know this is difficult, but it would mean so much to Pappa if you stayed at his place.'

I looked at my shoes and said nothing. I knew I had no choice, not really, though I wanted to run away. Run back to Stockholm to my beautiful flat, to my balcony and the view of the street below. In a rush of emotion I thought I'd take Saara with me. I could try to get a bigger flat and do more translation work than teaching, so that I could look after her. In the summer we could go for long walks in Djurgården and in the winter I could take her to Spain for a week in the sun.

'Eeva, I know it's difficult. It was for me too, at first. But, I'll be there and it'll only be the one night. He's already made up a bed for you in the attic room. Please Eeva. It'll be OK.' Anja had taken my hand and was squeezing it hard. I felt tears again, so I swallowed hard and looked at Anja's dark eyes, 'That's alright, I'll stay with Pappa.'

Anja hugged me hard. Then, letting go of me, said, 'Thank you, Eeva.'

The next morning I woke up to Anja talking to me, 'Eeva, wake up!'

'What is it?' I said. I'd slept badly. The drink the night before and the dank smell of the room had kept me awake. I'd also heard Pappa walk downstairs, and flush the loo several times during the night. I'd been dreaming of Saara during the short spells of sleep I'd had. She'd been in her flat, making meatballs. The mince had been dripping with blood. I stood next to her by the sink but I didn't say anything, just watched her roll the bloody mixture into small balls and place them into a hot pan full of smoking fat. As she lifted a small amount of mince into her cupped hands, the bright red liquid in the white plastic bowl increased until there was nothing but blood. She turned to me. Her face was the tired, grey one she had in the hospital but her body was round and large and her lips full and ruddy when she said, 'That'll be a nice drink for your Pappa.' I woke up with a start.

When I looked at Anja's sallow face I felt as if I'd been awake for a long time already.

'They've just phoned from the hospital...'

'Oh, no, Saara's worse?' I said, 'When did they phone?' I sat up in bed and tried to search Anja's face to see what she was going to say, what she knew already.

'About half an hour ago, Eeva, she...' Anja broke off and

looked down on the bed. I froze.

'No, please no.' I put my hand out to Anja and she took it and looked up at me again. Her eyes were full of tears.

'I'm sorry. She...she died about an hour ago.' Anja covered her face with her hands and sat down heavily on my bed. Her shoulders shook as she cried silently into her hands. I looked up to the ceiling and closed my eyes and tried to cry, but there was only pain, pain in my throat, in my chest, everywhere. I couldn't breath. Anja came over and hugged me. I felt the dampness of her tears against my neck and wished I could cry. She moved away, wiped her eyes with a tissue and blew her nose loudly. Then she straightened herself up and said, 'Pappa wants us all to go over straightaway. He's downstairs making coffee, and he's ordered the taxi already. It'll be here in half an hour. Can you make that?' Her face was swollen and she wasn't wearing her glasses. She looked pale and naked without them.

'Of course!' I said and took hold of her hand. She was just about to get up but I pulled her gently towards me and hugged her again. 'I wish...' I choked, there was no air in my lungs.

'Don't, Eeva. I'm going to have a quick wash and then the bathroom is all yours.' She hurried out of the room and I thought how strong she was being again. In her pink dressing gown she reminded me of Saara, waking us up to leave her flat.

I thought of how old and frail Saara had looked when I'd seen her the day before. If only I had come earlier, years earlier. I put my hand on my head and realised it was aching. We'd had too much to drink the night before. Oh, god, I had a hangover on a day like this! I looked at my mobile on the bedside table: no calls. I looked at the time on the phone: ten to six. I wondered why even Janne hadn't called – he hadn't even tried the day before. Nothing from Yri either. That was that then, just a fuck for old times' sake. I brushed aside thoughts of men; what did they matter when I no longer had Saara? My chest felt tight and I couldn't breathe. I knew it was futile thinking like this, but I could have visited so many times. I could really have been part of her life: not just the letters. She'd been so pleased, elated, to see me yesterday. As if she'd waited to see me before she died.

Anja came up the stairs. We were sleeping in the small attic room. Two mattresses were placed either side of the window in the sloping gable end.

'There's no hot water yet so you'll have to shower later,' she said. The dressing gown wasn't the same at all, but similar.

'How did Saara...?' I said.

'Sleep. She died in her sleep.'

I had my head in my hands. I felt tears well up inside me. 'You're so strong, Anja.' I looked up at her and saw the deepening lines either side of her mouth, the crow's feet around her eyes and the deep wrinkles on her forehead. We were both getting old.

Anja came to sit next to me on the narrow bed, 'It's OK. I've had more time to get used to this. To Pappa and Saara, her age. She was going to be 83 in May.' She put her arm around me and talked to me in a soft voice, 'She had a good life, you know. And she was so glad to see you before...' Her voice broke and I thought I must try to sort myself out, 'Sorry, Anja, now I've made you cry too.'

'I expect we'll do a lot of that before the day is out.' She said and wiped her eyes. She pursed her lips together and patted my arm, 'C'mon, go and get washed as well you can, the taxi will be here in a minute. Pappa needs us to be strong too.' I lifted my eyes to hers.

'Go on!' she said and got up without looking at me.

In the bathroom I saw Pappa's things on the glass shelf underneath a dirty mirror: his shaving brush and razor, both grubby, a new-looking electric toothbrush, a nearly empty tube of toothpaste, an aerosol can of shaving foam that had left a brown ring on the glass. The bath and shower looked surprisingly clean, as did the toilet pan. He must have someone who comes in and cleans the place for him, I thought. A girlfriend? I recalled how he'd hugged me last night. I'd felt tiny in his bear-like embrace. That had been late last night when Anja and I were about to go up the stairs. Throughout the evening he'd avoided eye contact. He'd chatted mostly with Anja and at times testily looked at me across the blue-and-white checked tablecloth of the restaurant. I'd learned then that Anja had been visiting Pappa about twice a year, bringing the children during their summer holidays, staying for a couple of days at a time. She must have told the children never to mention Pappa to me, I thought.

As I stepped out into the cold hallway, clutching my towel and nylon wash bag, I saw Pappa sitting at the table in the kitchen. He was hunched, with his hand cupping his chin, looking out of the window. His hair was even messier and greyer looking. The table was laid for three; how on earth did he think we'd be able to touch anything, I thought. I felt sorry for him. I moved as silently as I could towards the staircase,

124

but as I stepped onto the bottom stair, I heard him say, 'Eeva!'

'Yes, Pappa?'

'Anja told you?'

I saw he'd been crying and I felt the lump in my throat again. I couldn't look at him but held my eyes down on the floor. There were specs of dust between the first step and the floorboards.

'Yes. I'll just get dressed and I'll be down. I'm so sorry,' I said quickly and walked up the stairs. Anja was coming down and she passed me without a word. She touched my arm lightly and gave me a nod. She was wearing a black dress. I thought the only black thing I had with me was my trouser suit that I'd been wearing on the ferry and all of the previous day. I realised I didn't even know what was going to happen today. Did the body need to be identified? Surely the hospital would do that. I guessed we'd need to organise or help Pappa with the funeral.

Fourteen

Stockholm 1974

IT WAS the last Saturday in October and Mamma had promised to take us shopping. She said winter was coming and we
needed new clothes. Anja had complained that hers were
old-fashioned and too Finnish. She spent all of her pocket
money and said she didn't have enough to buy clothes. She
wanted a yellow, tightly-fitting winter coat with wide lapels.
She'd seen an advertisement in her Swedish magazines, and
she told Mamma where we needed to go to find one.

'When we get off the Tunnelbana at Centralen, we go
towards Hötorget.'

'I know.' Mamma said quietly.

We were walking to the bus. There were just two stops to
the Rinkeby Tunnelbana station. A large Gypsy woman was
sitting on the pavement by the bus stop. Her huge black
velvet skirt and white lacy petticoat spread around her like a
deep pond. We stopped talking; Gypsies in Sweden were

always Finnish. She might start to talk to us, beg money or try to sell something. Or then she'd probably want to tell our fortunes. It was bad luck not to buy something from a Gypsy if she offered. She had a dark-skinned face and gold looped earrings dangling down to her shoulders. Her hair was woven into one long black plait. When we came close she gave me a dark look. I turned my face down to the ground.

When the bus arrived the woman got up. She sighed loudly and Mamma, Anja and I waited while she slowly got up the steps of the bus. She spoke Finnish to the driver who angrily replied in Swedish. Eventually she paid and went to sit in a disabled place at the front, taking up two seats.

'You've got to watch out for the Gypsies,' Mamma told us. 'Even the women hide knives among their vast skirts.'

I looked at the skirt – she could have hid a small child in there. I'd never seen a Gypsy woman carry a handbag. Sometimes the men would have a plastic carrier bag from one of the ferry companies – always Viking Line, the cheaper one. The bottles of vodka clanked when they walked drunkenly around town. Those Gypsies frightened me even more than the women. I felt I had a large sign on my forehead: 'I am Finnish and understand everything you say.' I tried not to make eye contact, ever, but once, about a week after we'd arrived in Stockholm, and I was walking home alone from school a young Gypsy boy spoke to me.

'Hei Suomentyttö, anna pusu!'

Though horrified, I'd not been able to hide my smile. His Finnish was poor, he must have lived in Stockholm for a long time and he looked harmless in his high-waisted pants and lacy cotton shirt. He was missing their usual waistcoat or short bolero jacket, which is why I didn't immediately realise he was a Gypsy. Ever since, I'd been afraid of meeting him again, especially when the evenings got dark. A kiss was not all he'd want, I knew that much.

Going past the old Gypsy woman, I kept my eyes firmly on the floor of the bus. As we all had passes we didn't have to talk to the driver. I showed my card to him and he nodded. Mamma pointed at three free seats at the back of the bus. Anja sat next to a dark-haired man, and Mamma and I shared a double seat on the other side of the aisle. The bus was very crowded. Most of the faces were foreign. The few Swedish people looked unhappy and fed up. Perhaps they were frightened. The loudest nationalities were from southern Europe. You could always tell them by the smell of garlic, too, or the dark hair and brown skin. Mamma started to talk to Anja, but when the bus stopped at the Tunnelbana station and we were getting ready to leave, Anja whispered to her, 'Just remember, not a word in the Tunnelbana. Not even in Swedish, they'll be able to tell you're Finnish from your accent.' Mamma didn't reply.

The Gypsy was the last person to leave the bus, and she walked down the stairs to the underground platform last. The Rinkeby station was made of grey concrete and had splashes of yellow and blue paint on the walls, as though a child had been allowed to play with tins of paint. A wind blew through the platform, and the moulded plastic seats were too cold to sit on. People stood with their hands in their pockets. Then I saw the Gypsy starting to talk to people closest to her, 'Tell fortune? Little children home...help poor Gypsy woman!' She did know some Swedish after all. When she came close to us, she looked at Mamma's face and stopped dead. She took hold of her arm and said in Finnish, 'Don't worry, the black clouds will shift soon. Be strong and you will be happy.' Mamma looked at her for a long time and said nothing. Then the Gypsy woman moved away.

Anja crossed her arms over her chest and shrugged her shoulders. She looked away and pretended not to have understood the Gypsy. I turned my face up to Mamma and she shook her head.

Just then a bright blue train zoomed in and stopped in front of us. The doors swung open and we stood to one side, letting people leaving the train come out. We found four free seats together. Anja and I sat opposite each other by the windows. I watched the dark tunnels go by, and the stations, counting the ten to Centralen. Closer to the last stop there were more Swedish people.

'The rich Swedes live either in the city centre, or on the north side. Never south of the water,' Pappa had told us. 'Unless it's in the expensive villas in the small islands around Stockholm.' Pappa had driven us around the city in the new Volvo and showed us the beautiful large houses.

At Centralen, Anja walked in front of Mamma. She nearly ran past all the people. It was hard to follow her. Mamma took my hand. 'One day we will live in a nice house,' she said.

'That will be nice,' I said and smiled. Mamma squeezed my hand harder.

There was a big Hennes and Mauritz on Kungsgatan with three floors of clothes. Anja went straight to the winter coats, which were in the basement. They were hanging in round, low rails. All the coats on one rail were one colour. There were yellow, blue, red, brown, black and white coats. From the top of the stairs the shop floor looked like one of Saara's paintings.

'I'm having a yellow one, you can't have one as well,' Anja said when I looked at coats with her.

'But I don't know which colour I want,' I said. There was too much choice. 'Brown would be good because it'll go with everything,' Mamma said. 'These yellow ones will show every bit of dirt.'

Anja looked at Mamma but said nothing. She was pulling out coat after coat in the colour of a tiny furry chick.

I looked over to the brown coats. They looked very dull.

'What about red?' Mamma said. 'There, those are nice,' she said walking towards a rail at the back of the room.

'Kirsti,' a woman with red lips and black hair said to Mamma. She kissed Mamma noisily on both cheeks and then hugged her too. Mamma said, 'Oh, Irena.'

'This your little girl?' the woman said in a funny jerky accent. I smiled but hoped she wouldn't kiss and hug me too.

'Yes,' Mamma said in Swedish and then to me, 'Eeva, this is Irena from my Swedish class.'

'You say to the girl I your best friend, yes?' Irena said.

'Yes, yes,' Mamma said and laughed. They started talking at the same time. They waved their arms a lot. Mamma laughed and then said in Finnish, 'Irena wants to go for coffee. Where's Anja?' I looked around and saw she was still trying on yellow coats. We went over to her. Irena smiled and nearly kissed Anja too. She bent forward when Mamma said,

'This is Anja,' but Anja gave her a hand and Irena took it and shook it for a very long time.

'I don't want to go for coffee, 'Anja said. 'Can we not stay here and meet you on Sergelstorg later?'

Mamma looked at her, and then at her friend.

Irena said in Swedish, 'What is it?' Mamma just smiled and touched her arm. 'Alright, but you must stay together,' she said to Anja.

Anja was very good at clothes shopping. She'd always think of things that went together and knew what suited me, and what didn't. She chose a pair of red jeans and a T-shirt with a swirly pattern on it for me. For herself she took flared green cords, and a white hippie top with stitching on the front and a tie-up neck. Then she handed me several T-shirts and jumpers in different colours and said we needed to queue up for the changing rooms.

'But Mamma said we would just buy winter coats,' I said.

'Not in Finnish,' Anja hissed, and then she said in Swedish, 'We can try on, can't we? Besides Pappa gave Mamma 500 Krona this morning.'

'Did he?' I said. Ever since we'd been in Sweden Pappa had given Mamma money every Saturday. I didn't know how much he usually gave her but 500 seemed a lot. Pappa said he was earning much more than he was in Tampere so we could have nice things.

The changing room was packed. One large space had mirrors all around it. There were lots of girls of Anja's age and older, giggling together. I felt embarrassed getting undressed in front of everyone, but luckily Anja found a corner behind a pillar. I put my clothes next to the wall and my back to the pillar. No one else seemed to mind being naked, but then they all looked grown-up and thin. Anja pulled her sweater over her head and took her jeans off. Then she put on the hippie top and looked at herself. She had nothing but knickers on her bottom half. Her legs looked long, brown and skinny. The hippie top gathered just above her chest and made her breasts look very large and her body long and thin. I took my shirt off and quickly replaced it with the T-shirt. I was wearing my flower-patterned bra, my very first one that Mamma had bought me in Tampere. Then I took my jeans off and put on the red pair. I looked at myself in the mirror. I looked very trendy. The red jeans were very tight. Anja had put on the green cords and she was doing up the zip on a pair of platform boots.

'I've got to have these,' she said and smiled at herself in the mirror. Her hair looked more blonde and curly and she had green eye shadow on.

'Are these too tight?' I said in Swedish.

'No,' she said after a while, 'they're cool.'

I looked at myself and decided to go on the same diet as Harriet. We tried on the jumpers and T-shirts and I liked everything. I decided red was going to be my colour.

'Let's go and meet Mamma and see if she can buy these for us,' Anja said when we were back on the sales floor.

When we got to Sergelstorg, Mamma wasn't there yet. The sun had come out, so it was warm and we sat down on one of the stone benches. Anja took out a packet of cigarettes and lit one up.

'Mamma will see you!' I said, looking down Sergelsgatan and Drottninggatan for Mamma's brown coat. Any minute now she'd spot us and then she would know it was Anja who burned the sofa. And she would know I had lied too.

'Keep an eye out then, if you care so much,' Anja said.' I'm nearly sixteen and can smoke if I want to.' Anja had had her fourteenth birthday just before we left Tampere. I looked at the floor. Sergelstorg was made of blue-and-white checked tiles, just like a bathroom, not like a square or a street at all. The ones under my feet looked dirty and some were chipped, but from a distance it looked like a large chessboard. Anja sat next to me, her legs crossed, puffing on her cigarette. I wondered if I'd want to start smoking when I was as old as Anja. The smell was quite nice as it drifted past my nose and up into the air. Mamma and Pappa would never allow it, I thought.

Suddenly I saw Mamma and Irena walking towards us. They had their arms linked and they were smiling and laughing.

'Mamma's coming!' I said to Anja, and she stubbed the cigarette out against the back of the bench and dropped it behind her.

'Hej girls!' Mamma shouted in Swedish. Irena said goodbye with kisses for all of us. She smelled very nice, of flowers and cigarettes. When we'd waved to her, Mamma turned to Anja and sniffed.

'You've been smoking!'

'No I haven't,' Anja said.

'Has she?' Mamma said, turning to face me.

'No.' I said.

'Well, I'm telling you, Anja, if I catch you smoking I will tell Pappa and you know what that means.'

'There's no need because I have not been smoking. Anyway, it's probably that mad woman whose smoke you're smelling,' Anja said. She was standing upright, her chest pushed out.

'Well, yes, Irena does smoke, but she's a grown-up.' Mamma said.

'That's alright then, isn't it?' Anja said. They looked at each other and then Mamma took a deep breath in and said, 'So, did you choose your coats?'

Anja said, 'Yes.' She was sulking.

'And Eeva, have you decided which colour you want?'

'Yes,' I said, 'A really cool red coat.' I thought that's it now, we won't get any of the other clothes, but when we got the Hennes and Mauritz, Mamma bought us the trousers and Anja the hippie top as well as the swirly T-shirt for me.

When we were back in our flat and Mamma was cooking dinner I asked her where Irena was from.

'She's Polish,' Mamma said, and she smiled at the potatoes she was peeling at the sink. A dill meat stew was cooking on the stove and the smell of it made me hungry.

'She seemed very nice,' I said. I heard Pappa cough in the bedroom.

'She's really funny. She's a dentist and very clever. Her husband is a doctor, but they can't work here until they've finished the Swedish course. They escaped from Poland, you know.'

'Why?'

'It's a Communist country and people aren't allowed to

leave and move somewhere else,' Mamma said.

I thought how awful it must be, and imagined a country with high wire fences and police walking on the streets arresting everybody and throwing them into jail. Then I caught the smell of the stew again and asked, 'How long till food?'

'Yes, how long is it going to be? I'm starving,' Pappa shouted from the bedroom. I could see his feet on top of the bed. Mamma said, 'Half an hour. Eeva, can you set the table?'

I got up and opened the cutlery drawer. Anja was never around when the table needed laying. It was always me who had to do it. I took out four knives and forks and put them on the round table. It was already dark outside though it was only a quarter past four. I took out plates and glasses and set them down as well. When I'd finished the front door opened and Anja came in. She was wearing her new clothes. The yellow coat had a tie-on belt. She went through the kitchen and past Pappa on the bed.

'Dinner is ready soon, Anja,' Mamma said.

'Oh, the wanderer returns!' Pappa shouted. Then I heard him get up with a groan. He stood at the kitchen door, scratching his head. The hair was standing up and his beige knitted cardigan was buttoned up wrongly.

'Your buttons are drunk!' I said. I was sitting at the table, leaning on my elbows. Pappa looked down at his tummy and said, 'So they are!' He came over to me and ruffled my short hair. Then he sat down opposite me with a heavy sigh. 'When is this food finally ready? You've had all afternoon to cook the bloody thing!'

Mamma was stirring the meat stew. She said, 'Good sleep?'

135

'I work hard during the week so surely I'm allowed a little nap on Saturday afternoon?'

'I didn't mean...'

'Oh yes you did, I heard it in the tone of your voice,' Pappa said.

'You'd better get Anja,' Mamma said to me. I got up and went into Anja's room. She was lying on the bed on her tummy, listening to Abba.

'Food's ready,' I said from the door. She looked at me and tapped the bed. I sat down on the side of it.

'They're arguing again,' I said.

'Great,' Anja said. 'What about this time?'

'Oh I don't know. Pappa thinks Mamma didn't want him to have a nap.'

'Well obviously, because he's a lazy pig.'

'No, he's not,' I said.

'Oh yeah? He never does anything but drink vodka and have naps.' Anja said, sitting up next to me. I said nothing for a while. Waterloo ended and the needle made a scraping noise. Anja got up, lifted the record up and turned off the player. 'We'd better go in. If he's in a bad mood we'll get told off too,' she said.

Mamma was dishing up meat stew to Pappa when we walked into the kitchen. They weren't looking at each other.

'Glad you decided to join us,' Pappa said. He cut a cooked potato in half and then pierced a piece of meat. With his mouth full, he said to Mamma, 'Not enough salt. How bloody difficult is it to put a bit of salt into the food?'

'The salt is on the table,' Mamma said, 'but eating too much salt isn't good for you.'

'Feminist bullshit,' Pappa said and sprinkled salt all over his food.

Mamma winced. 'How many potatoes, Anja?'

'Jag är inte hungrig,' Anja said in Swedish.

Mamma looked at her and said, 'Even if you're not hungry, you have to eat something,' and gave her two potatoes.

'Oj!' Anja said and slumped in her chair.

'Speak Finnish!' Pappa said.

'Oh, so now it's wrong to speak Swedish when we're fluent!'

'We are Finnish and at home you speak your mother tongue!' Pappa was looking at Anja with angry eyes, but Anja didn't seem to mind. She said, 'Just because you can't learn it…'

'Anja,' Mamma said, 'do your friends like your new coat?'

Pappa looked at me and then started eating again.

'Yes. And guess what, Mamma?' Anja said. 'Susanna's got exactly the same one as me in green! Isn't that amazing?'

'You don't mind?' Mamma said.

'No, we look just like a fruit bowl when we're together, and then we can swap coats because we're exactly the same size too.'

'Are you?' I said. 'Harriet is much smaller than me, though she thinks she is really fat and is on a diet.'

'Really?' Anja said, 'What kind of a diet?'

'Is this your sofa burning friend? I thought I told you not to see her again?' Pappa had stopped eating and was looking at Anja again. He had a fork with a piece of meat in his hand. Sauce was dripping on his plate and on the tablecloth.

Anja looked at Mamma, who shook her head.

'We talked about this,' Pappa said.

'I can't help seeing her at school. Or are you going to forbid me from going to school now? That would be cool!'

'Anja, please.' Mamma said. 'Mikko, do you want some more meat? Anja, you haven't eaten anything.'

'Yes I have,' Anja said and put a tiny piece of potato in her mouth.

'I'm warning you, Anja. If I see that Susanna in this house there will be trouble.' Pappa said.

'Let's not talk about it at the table,' Mamma said.

'Peace at the dinner table would be a fine thing with three yapping females,' Pappa said.

'We're only talking about our friends,' Anja said and lifted her eyes to Pappa.

'Nonsense. That's what you're all talking, nonsense.'

'No we're not!' Anja said.

'Yes you are, and if you don't have anything sensible to say, be quiet.'

'Anyone for some more meat?' Mamma asked.

I shook my head. Everyone ate in silence. Except Anja, who pushed her food around the plate with one hand, while leaning her head against the other one. I wanted to ask Mamma about Irena, but didn't. Finally, Pappa got up from the table with a grunt. He went to the living room and I heard the TV being switched on.

'I have homework,' Anja said. Her plate was still full of food but Mamma said nothing. Anja took her plate to the sink and emptied it into the bin. I looked at Mamma. She got up and sighed, 'Will you help me clear up, Eeva?'

Fifteen

THAT SATURDAY I went over to Harriet's flat. Her parents were away and we sat and talked in the kitchen. We made a salad, because Harriet was still on a diet. There was a different smell in her kitchen, a sweet chocolaty smell, which I thought came from the Oboj chocolate powder Harriet put in the milk. It never smelled of cooked food like our kitchen. Though Harriet never cleared up after herself, the kitchen was always tidy when I came over. 'Let's take the bowls to my room,' Harriet said and got up from the table.

I looked at the cutting board and the dirty knife by the sink. There were bits of lettuce, tomato and cucumber left on the side. Two dirty spoons and glasses and an opened packet of Oboj stood next to the wooden chopping board. 'Will your Mamma not be angry when she comes home and sees the mess?' I said.

Harriet laughed. Her red curly hair shook as she said, 'You worry too much. I'll clear up later. Mamma and Pappa won't be home until I've gone to bed.'

'Where are they?'

'At work.'

'On a Saturday?'

'Yes,' Harriet said and took my free hand. I was holding my bowl of salad in the other. 'C'mon let's go and see if the boys are playing outside!'

I wondered about Harriet's parents when I was walking home. Their flat was full of nice things, like colourful vases of flowers. The sofa and chairs in the lounge, which we never sat in, looked old and expensive. Harriet had the latest clothes and pencil cases, and a brand-new set of colouring pencils. The tin case was shiny and though she let me borrow the pencils during art lessons at school I still envied her the set. There must have been twenty different colours in the case. I wondered whether we too would be rich like Harriet's family if we'd always lived in Stockholm.

I turned the corner of my block of flats and stopped. The Gypsy boy I'd seen the week I started school was standing further away along the path. I stood still for a second. Then I started walking again with my head down, watching him come closer to me from the corner of my eyes. He was wearing ordinary clothes, but I recognised his dark hair and eyes. I looked around. There were no other people about and it was getting dark. I couldn't breathe. When he came closer I heard him whistling. My front door was on the other side of the block; if I ran he'd catch me before I could reach it, I was sure of that. I carried on walking.

'Suomentyttö,' he said and stopped in front of me.

I looked at him. I had to strain my neck because he was much taller than me. 'Hej,' I said.

'Where are you going?' His voice was low and croaky, as if he had a sore throat. I looked around. He looked at me and then around us too, 'You waiting for someone?'

I realised he was talking in Swedish and that he didn't look that frightening. 'No, I'm going home,' I said and pointed around the corner.

'Ok, see you.' he said and continued walking. I heard his whistling all the way to the front door.

When I came home our kitchen smelt different. Mamma was at the sink with her checked apron on. She was peeling potatoes.

'Hello, Eeva, I'm glad you're home. You'll help me, won't you?'

'Yes Mamma,' I said. I went into my bedroom and looked at the clock on my bedside table. It was only just past three o'clock.

'You're cooking early,' I said, stepping back into the kitchen. There was a delicious smell coming from the stove. 'What are you baking?'

'A cake for the party! You remember, I told you,' she said and pushed back a strand of hair that had fallen on her face.

'A party tonight?'

'Eeva, I told you, I've invited Irena and her husband Lew and my teacher, Nils, and his girlfriend.'

'Oh,' I said, 'Does Pappa know?'

'Of course he does,' Mamma said and turned to look at me.

'Where is Pappa?' I said looking down at the floor.

'He's gone into town to get some drinks for tonight. Now Eeva, can you finish peeling these potatoes while I see to the cake.'

I took the knife from Mamma and started peeling the round thick-skinned potatoes. Mamma had taught me to take the skin off thinly. It would be difficult with these ones, I thought.

I looked around the kitchen. Though there were pots everywhere, it looked very clean. The floor shone. The hall had been gleaming, too, when I stepped inside, I now realised.

I thought about the Gypsy boy. I couldn't wait to tell Harriet about him. That day we'd listened to her records and talked about boys. Harriet liked a lot of boys in our school and had already had a kiss from one boy in our class. His name was Tomas and all the girls loved him. He made jokes in class and didn't care if Fru Andersson heard him or not. I didn't tell Harriet but I liked him too. He smiled at me once when his bag brushed against mine on the way out of the classroom. He said, 'Akta dig söting.' I knew 'Akta dig' meant 'watch out', but I had to ask Anja about the other word as soon as I got home. She laughed and said Tomas must love me. She teased me and didn't translate it for me for a long time. Only when I gave her two Krona did she tell me it meant 'cutie'. I'm not sure if she lied, although she swore she hadn't.

'Come on, Eeva, the guests are coming at five o'clock and I haven't even made the meatloaf yet,' Mamma said, going past me into the lounge.

I started peeling quickly and thought how typical it was that Anja wasn't at home. She always knew when to be around and when to disappear. It was strange, preparing for a party in Stockholm, though. We'd had lots of parties at Saara's place, and sometimes in our small flat too. Pappa had his friends over and they drank vodka until very late. I'd listen to their laughter and smell the smoke creeping in through the door while lying in my bunk bed. The next day Pappa stayed in bed until late and we all tried to be quiet so as not to wake him.

Saara's birthday party in the summer ended in dancing. She rolled the carpets to one side and pushed the sofa and chairs against the walls of her living room. Then the adults did the tango, the waltz and polka. A friend of Saara's, a man with round, red cheeks played the harmonica. He smiled and beat his foot in tune with the music. Anja and I hid in the kitchen until Saara came to fetch us to dance too. I preferred the polka. Uncle Keijo was a good partner and I didn't have to think about the steps at all. He danced so fast that I felt dizzy when the music stopped. When everybody sat down and had a drink out of a large glass bowl, the adults started laughing and joking about boys and about how pretty Anja and I would be when we grew up. That was very embarrassing.

The food Saara cooked was delicious. She started preparing it days in advance. Mamma and I helped with the sandwich cakes and the biscuits, as well as the plaited buns and tarts. Saara made the punch in a lilac-coloured bowl. It had a matching ladle made out of glass too. Anja and I were allowed only a taste of the punch because it was so strong. During the party Saara kept filling it up with vodka, juice and ice. Because it was a summer party, Saara put strawberries in the punch too. I had one but it tasted different, and I had to spit it out in the kitchen. Only Anja saw me and laughed.

Having a party for just four people didn't seem like a party to me at all. At Saara's there were lots of people and not enough seats. Anja and I were told not sit on any but to save them for the adults. I sat on Pappa's knee until he said, laughing, I was getting too heavy for him. He was in a good mood at Saara's party.

'Eeva, are you finished with the potatoes?' Mamma said.

I looked around and realised I'd stopped peeling.

'Nearly,' I said.

'When you have, can you help me set the table in here? I'm going to do a smörgåsbord in the kitchen and drinks in the lounge.'

Mamma was spreading a red cloth on the round table. It was the best one, with large rosebuds. I hadn't seen it since we'd left Tampere. It looked freshly pressed.

'Does Irena's husband have a harmonica?' I asked Mamma. She was now standing next to me, mixing the meatloaf mixture with her hands. She looked up at me and said, 'It won't be like Saara's party, Eeva. I don't know if people here play the harmonica at parties.' She was smiling.

I helped Mamma fill the cake with jam and tinned pineapple and top it with whipped cream. She let me decorate it with a second can of pineapple rings. I cut them in half and fanned the pieces out to make a flower. I put chocolate buttons all around the edge.

'That's very pretty, Eeva' Mamma said.

'I need something green for the stem,' I said.

We heard the front door open and Pappa walked in with two plastic bags that clanked. He put the bags down and took his coat off before coming into the kitchen and kissing Mamma on the cheek.

'What a lot of people there were at the Systembolaget!'

he said and patted me on the head, 'You helping your Mamma with the party?'

'Yes, I am Pappa,' I said. He was humming to himself when he went to put the bottles in the fridge. Then he turned around and rubbed his hands together.

'I think that deserves a beer,' he said and took a bottle of Elefanten out of the fridge.

'Do you want to start before the guests arrive?' Mamma said looking at her wristwatch.

'Perkele,' Pappa said, 'if a man is not allowed to have one beer on a Saturday afternoon...'

Mamma looked at me and then at Pappa and said, 'I just thought...'

'Well, don't think, just cook.' Pappa turned around and went to sit in the lounge. I heard him bang the bottle hard on the new coffee table. I looked at Mamma to see if she heard the bang and worried about the table breaking, but she was looking down at the sink.

I helped Mamma set the table. She was very quiet and told me in a hushed voice which cutlery and plates to use. 'The best ones, of course,' she said.

Pappa came to the door of the kitchen with an empty bottle and took out another.

'Please, Mikko, don't get drunk before the guests arrive. They've never even met you before and...' Mamma said, but was interrupted by Pappa.

'That is the point, isn't it? Your new fancy friends, they are the most important thing to you, aren't they?' Pappa looked very large and angry.

'I'm sure you'll like them too, especially Nils.'

145

'Your lover boy, you mean?' Pappa took hold of Mamma's arm, 'Tell me what's going on, you'd better tell me, you little…'

Mamma looked at me and said, 'Mikko, please, remember Eeva is here. And no, he's bringing a girlfriend, I told you that.'

Pappa let go of her hand and turned his back to us.

'I believe that when I see it!' Pappa said and went back into the lounge. He didn't seem so angry any more.

Mamma took a deep breath and said, 'I think we're finished here. I'm going to go and get changed.' She went into the bedroom and I followed. She showed me what she was going to wear: a green cotton dress with large yellow and pink flowers on it. When she put it on it came just to her knees and made her legs seem longer. It was sleeveless and fitted snugly to her body.

'You look nice,' I said. I was sitting at the end of the bed, watching Mamma. She was at her little dressing table made of dark wood, putting on pink lipstick. I wished one day I'd be as beautiful as Mamma.

'Go and tell Pappa the guests will be here soon,' Mamma said, turning around to look at me. She was brushing her hair now. The blonde locks gleamed.

When I went to Pappa he was watching ice-hockey on the TV. He scooped me up with one arm and started tickling me. His breath smelled of alcohol.

'Mamma says…the guests…are coming soon,' I said between giggles. My head was buried in the sofa and my legs were up in the air. Pappa let go of me and said, 'Well, I guess I have to attend to the honoured guests.' He got up and left me lying on the sofa. Mamma came in and said, 'Get up, Eeva. Look at this mess.'

She'd put on black high-heeled shoes. She looked very elegant. She picked up Pappa's empty beer bottle and a newspaper, turned off the TV and straightened the swirly rug with her feet. She smoothed the back and the seat of the sofa with her hands and put a cushion over Anja's cigarette burn. Then she put chairs in a straight line opposite. I looked down at what I was wearing and wondered if I should get changed too. Before I had time to ask Mamma, the front door bell sounded.

'Right, Eeva, you know Irena, be polite and a good girl now. I'll go and let them in. Wonder which couple it'll be?'

But it was neither. Anja had forgotten her key.

'You look all posh, what's going on?' She said.

'The party!' Mamma said. 'Will nobody remember that we're having a party tonight!'

Anja said nothing, just looked at Mamma and went straight to her room. Then the doorbell went again and this time it was a tall blond man.

'Nils,' Mamma said and smiled. 'Come in.'

'Tack,' the man said and coughed. Pappa came into to the hall and said, 'Mikko Litmunen.' He took the man's hand. He said, 'Nils Karlsson.' Then nobody spoke for a very long time. Finally Mamma gave out a small laugh and closed the front door. She gestured with her hands towards the man's coat. Mamma hung the coat up and said, 'Kom in, kom in.'

'Very good,' Nils said and smiled at Mamma. But Pappa was standing in the middle of the hall.

'Mikko,' Mamma said and opened her eyes wide.

'Ah,' he said and moved across towards the kitchen. Mamma walked behind Nils into the lounge. Pappa stayed in the hall, scratching his head. Then he turned around and came into the lounge.

'My daughter, Eeva,' Mamma said and Nils took my hand, 'Hello Eeva, how old are you?' He smelled of aftershave and had a very bony hand with long fingers. He was a bit taller than Pappa and much thinner. His eyes were wide and kind and his thin lips turned upwards like he never stopped smiling. He had lots of lines on his face and he was wearing a red stripy shirt, which was unbuttoned at the top.

'I'm twelve,' I said and lowered my eyes. Nils's gaze was very piercing and I wondered where his girlfriend was. Why had Mamma not asked him? Perhaps she didn't know how yet.

'Your eldest daughter?' Nils said.

'Anja, yes, Anja is...' Mamma was pointing towards the corridor to Anja's bedroom but Nils looked puzzled. Then the doorbell went again and Mamma hurried to it.

Pappa said, 'Drink?' making a gesture of drinking out of a cup with his hand.

'Yes, please,' Nils said.

Pappa went into the hall. I heard Mamma and Irena laugh, as well as a deeper voice. Then Pappa said he was getting the drinks and Mamma came into the lounge with Irena and her husband. Irena kissed Nils on both cheeks and then came over to me and kissed and hugged me. She was wearing a red dress with floaty sleeves and hem. She had a flower in her hair and wore bright red lipstick. I felt the wet of her kiss on my cheek. She got hold of her husband and said something in a very strange language, then in her broken

Swedish, 'Lew, this is Eeva, Kirsti's young daughter. Can you believe? She has one three years more!' Irena was pointing at me.

'Anja is two and half years older than me,' I said. Irena's husband came over and took my hand between both of his soft hands. He smiled. He was a small man. Irena was taller than him in her black shiny shoes. His hair was fair but not blond. I liked him, but he didn't say much, only 'Ah,' and then he let go of my hand.

Mamma said, 'Eeva, go and fetch Anja.'

'You send Eeva away?' Irena said waving her arms about. The fabric of her dress made her arms look like wings. She reminded me of an actress in a play. I smiled and went to Anja's room. She didn't want to come to say hello at first.

'There is this man, Mamma's Swedish teacher, and he is very nice, and then Irena has a really wild dress, you've got to come and see. Besides, Pappa will be angry, I bet, if you don't,' I said. She was lying on her bed reading a magazine. I was sitting next to her.

'I'm not allowed to have a party, so why should I care about theirs?' she said but got up and walked with a straight back out of the room. When we stepped into the lounge Irena got up. She stretched her arms, taking both of us into her dress. I closed my eyes and felt her arm tightly squeezed on one side of me with Anja on the other. Then she let go and went behind us, putting her arms around both of us, 'Look beautiful Kirsti daughters!'

Nils said, 'Hello,' and smiled. He was sitting on the sofa talking to Irena's husband, who turned around and smiled shyly and made a little wave with his hand. Pappa was sitting in one of the chairs. Mamma wasn't in the room. Everybody held a tall glass with red liquid in it.

'Girls, drink?' Irena said looking at Pappa.

'No, no, we have homework,' I said.

'No we don't,' Anja said, smiling.

'Anja, huoneeseen!' Pappa said. Anja stopped smiling and turned on her heels.

Nobody spoke for a while. Irena looked at Pappa and then said, 'She done wrong?'

Pappa said, 'Eeva, go to your bedroom, too,' in Swedish. He didn't even look at Irena or reply to her.

I smiled and said, 'Yes Pappa.' I was glad to leave because Pappa didn't look at all happy to be having a party. Perhaps he was still tired, I thought.

I stopped by the kitchen door. Mamma looked busy. She was moving from looking into the oven to putting hot potatoes into a bowl to taking the wrapping away form the sandwich cake. I hoped there would be some left when all the guests had had their helpings. It was my favourite. At least the way Saara made it. When you cut into her oblong cake, layered with rye and white bread and filled with different ingredients. Ham, Italian salad of peas and cooked carrots in mayonnaise, liver pâté with pickled cucumbers with dill, chopped, hard-boiled eggs with butter. Mamma had made hers with prawns, dill and mayonnaise. She said it was a finer version and prawns were much less expensive in Stockholm. She also made it out of white bread, because you couldn't get dark rye in Stockholm. I couldn't wait to have some of the sandwich cake. The decoration was so pretty too. There was chopped dill on the sides and lettuce leaves, prawns and lemons slices on the top. It looked like the cake we had on the ferry.

'Eeva,' Mamma said, 'everything alright in there?'

'Yes. The sandwich cake looks nice.'

'You can have some after,' Mamma said. She had her back turned to me and I went to my bedroom.

On my desk was a drawing I'd started. At school, Fröken Andersson had pinned my puffin picture on the wall and put a gold star in one corner of it. I didn't think this one was that good yet, but then it was a copy of my favourite book, Anne of Green Gables. It was harder to draw people than birds. The dress Anne was wearing was very complicated too: it was made of lace, and the sleeves were puffy and there was a difficult pattern on the front of it. I wanted to redo Anne's arms. They looked too straight and unreal. I picked up an eraser and started to rub off the drawing.

Later in the evening the noises from the lounge became louder. Above it all I heard Irena's laughter. I imagined she was standing in the middle of the swirly carpet, throwing her head back and waving her arms about. I also heard Mamma's steps going back and forth between the kitchen and the lounge, and sometimes Pappa's too. In the background, I heard Nils Karlsson's shy voice and his perfect Swedish accent. He sang the words as if he were one of the members of Abba.

A little later, I crept into the kitchen, which was empty and dark now. The food was still laid out on the round table, covered with bowls and kitchen towels. I took a plate from the cupboard and helped myself to some. I poured a glass of water and took it all back to my room. There was a strong smell of cigarette smoke in the hall. Everybody was laughing in the lounge, including Pappa and Mamma. Passing Anja's room I heard music. She was singing along to it. I went into my room and put the plate of food on my bed. I crossed my legs and picked up my book. I looked out of the window at the tops of dark pine trees and felt very lonely. I wished we were in Tampere having a party at Saara's place.

Sixteen

THE NEXT morning I woke up very early with a tummy ache.

In the kitchen the curtains were still drawn and the food from the party was left on the table. The sink was full of dirty dishes. I went into the lounge, which smelt of cigarettes and alcohol. There was a full ashtray on the glass table and some of the stubs had fallen onto the swirly carpet underneath. It was Pappa's ashtray and I used to play with it. It was round and had a lever at the top, which, when pushed, opened up the two round blades, dropping the cigarette stub and the ash down to the bottom. But when it got too full, as it was now, there was no room for the blades to move and it would just make a mess, pushing the ash and stubs up again.

I cringed at the horrible smell in the room. There was an open bottle of vodka on the table and dirty glasses everywhere. I opened the Venetian blinds and saw there were empty beer bottles on the balcony. I unlocked the door to let in some fresh air. It was cold outside. I pulled my dressing gown tighter around me and went into the bathroom.

I was sitting on the toilet when the door opened. I'd forgotten to lock the second door.

'Perkele, Eeva, you have to learn to lock the door,' Pappa said and closed it with a bang.

Pappa had never said a swear word to me before. 'I'm sorry, Pappa,' I shouted. I couldn't move, though. There was blood on my pants and on the bottom of the pan and I didn't know what to do. I hoped Pappa hadn't seen it. It was my period starting but it was far too early. Anja hadn't started hers yet. Tears rolled down my cheeks. Pappa was waiting outside, wanting to come in so I had to hurry. I wiped my face and stuffed layers of toilet paper in my pants and went out.

'Was it you who opened the balcony door?' Pappa said. He was sitting on the sofa drinking beer. It's the morning, I thought.

'Yes,' I said. I was afraid he'd tell me off because the room was very cold by now. Even standing back in the hall I could feel the draught around my legs.

'Are you trying to freeze us? Go and close it!' he said. His hair was standing up and he had stubble on his chin. His dressing gown was open so that I could see his large bare tummy and the loose pyjama pants underneath. He was sitting with his legs apart looking down at his toenails, which were long and yellow. Mamma told him off for picking them on the sofa. 'Something like that should be done in the bathroom,' she said. But Pappa just grunted and said she was too 'fiini'. Pappa joked that Mamma thought her family was better than his.

When I'd closed the balcony door, Pappa looked up at me again. His eyes were red and he looked very angry and tired.

I smiled at him but he just grunted and didn't smile back, 'Bloody women, too many for one man to cope with.'

I hurried past him to Anja's room. I never woke her up unless Mamma told me to on school mornings. Today was Sunday but I needed to talk to her.

It took a long time to stir her. Eventually she sat up in her bed and said, 'What did you say? Your period has started! Already!' Her eyes were wide and large.

'Yes,' I said. I felt proud and ashamed at the same time. 'I woke up with a tummy ache and then in the bathroom it happened,' I said. My tummy hurt again and I felt a warm flush between my legs.

Anja rubbed her eyes. 'What have you got in there?' She was looking at the area below my waist.

'Toilet paper.'

Anja got up and took a green plastic packet out of her drawer. She tore it open and said, 'Here you go, take these.' She handed me two pads, the size of small towels made into tight rolls. They looked like cotton wool covered in muslin netting. I couldn't imagine putting those between my legs and still being able to walk. They wouldn't fit inside my new red jeans, I thought. What would I wear to school tomorrow?

'They sell them in the Pressbyrå. You'll have to ask Mamma for some money and go and get them later. I'll come with you, if you like. But now I'm going to sleep.' Anja laid back down under the covers in her bed.

'Ok,' I said.

I got up, holding the pads.

'Eeva,' Anja said when I was at the door.

'Yes?'

'You're a woman now,' she said and smiled. Then, throwing her head back onto the pillow, she turned her back to me and said, 'Make sure you close the door behind you.'

In my room I changed my bloody pants and tissue for a clean pair and wore the pad. It felt as if I had a whole roll of toilet paper down there. I got back into bed and tried to sleep. The pain in my tummy came and went. It was mostly just sore, as if someone had jumped up and down on it all night long. I felt like a child who'd eaten too many unripe berries, not like a woman at all. I closed my eyes.

I woke to angry voices coming from the kitchen. Pappa used swear words and I thought he must still be in a bad mood. Mamma's voice sounded shrill. I couldn't hear what they were saying. Then the door to my bedroom opened and Anja appeared in her pink dressing gown. She came to sit on my bed, pulling her feet up. 'How's your tummy?' she asked.

'Oh, a bit sore. What time is it?' I said and sat up in the bed.

'Half past ten.' Anja was leaning on my poster of David Cassidy but I didn't mind. A deep but muffled voice came from the kitchen, and then, straight afterwards, a high-pitched, 'No, Mikko, don't.'

'They're fighting again,' Anja said into her dressing gown. She had her head resting on her knees. Her arms were around her long thin legs. There was blue nail varnish on both her fingers and toes. They made me think of Agneta in her blue satin jumpsuit.

There was a loud noise, like glass breaking. Then I heard Pappa's angry voice.

'What are they saying,' I asked.

Anja looked at me and shook her head, 'It's about last night I think.'

'Didn't they have a good time?' I asked and then thought about Pappa this morning, in a bad mood and drinking beer. 'Pappa was angry with me this morning. It was so embarrassing. He came into the bathroom when I was in there.'

'Didn't you lock the door?'

'I forgot to lock the other one,' I said. 'But when I came out he seemed OK. He was drinking beer on the sofa, looking at his toenails. Perhaps he cut them on the sofa and Mamma is angry with him.'

'It sounds more like Pappa is angry with her, as usual, the bastard,' Anja said. She'd tipped her head forward in between her knees.

We didn't speak for a while, just listened to the voices from the kitchen going up and down. Then it sounded as if a chair had been knocked over. I thought of Herr Lahtelainen. But Pappa wasn't like him at all, he'd joked about the Laughter Club Herr Lahtelainen had been sent to. I listened carefully but now there was silence in the kitchen.

'Let's go and see what's going on,' Anja said. I was frightened and didn't want to go but was ashamed to admit it to Anja. She'd only laugh and call me a coward.

The kitchen was clean and tidy. Mamma was standing by the sink washing dishes. Anja went over to her and hugged her, putting her head on Mamma's shoulder.

'You want some breakfast?' Mamma said. She looked tired and her face was white without any make-up.

'Hello Eeva, you've slept a long time this morning,' she

said, looking at me. I was usually up at the same time as Mamma. It was Anja and Pappa who slept in at the weekends.

'I had tummy ache,' I said and went over to the drawer and took the knives out. Then I reached up to the cupboard and took out two plates and two glasses. Anja sat down at the table and Mamma brought over bread and cheese and a carton of orange juice. We never used to have juice at breakfast in Tampere but in Sweden everybody did. Mamma said it was good for us because it had the vitamins we needed. The carton was white with a picture of half an orange on it. A drop of juice was dripping from the flesh of the fruit.

'Are you better now?' Mamma said and sat down next to us at the table.

'Her period started,' Anja whispered.

'Eeva,' Mamma looked towards her and Pappa's bedroom and then got up and gave me a big hug. 'When did it happen?' she said quietly.

'This morning,' I said. Mamma smiled and whispered, 'My little Eeva is a woman already!'

Anja said, 'Did you have a nice time last night, Mamma?'

Mamma turned her head quickly and again looked towards the open door of the bedroom. She got up and went back to her dishes and said, 'Yes, it was nice. I think they all enjoyed themselves.'

'Oh, yes they did,' Pappa shouted from the bedroom. 'Especially your dear Mamma.'

'Eat up now girls,' Mamma said turning to us. Then she said, 'Eeva I expect you need to go and get some more things, or are you alright?'

Anja said, 'I'm going with her to buy them at the Pressbyrå. But we need money.'

'Is that girl after money again,' Pappa shouted.

'It's not for me, it's for Eeva!' Anja shouted. Pappa didn't reply.

I looked at Anja and whispered, 'Don't tell Pappa!'

Mamma shook her head at Anja and said, 'You get dressed girls. I think I might come with you. I could do with the walk.'

Pappa appeared at the doorway. He was wearing his pyjamas but the top was only half-tucked into his pants. One side was hanging over the top of his trousers. His feet were bare. He sat down at the table and said, 'Where's the coffee?'

Mamma got up without saying a word and poured a cupful for him. Anja and I sat still. Then Pappa looked up from his cup and said, 'What's this, a silent movie?'

I looked at Mamma. She came back to the table and said, 'We're going for a walk. Eeva needs something from the Pressbyrå.'

My cheeks felt hot when Pappa looked at me. 'Bloody women,' he said, 'with a son I'd never have this trouble.' Then he got up with a grunt and went back to lie on his bed.

I liked walking to the shops. Today, though, it was a cold, wet November day. The pad between my legs felt funny and I had to walk with my legs a little apart. I was glad my new coat came down to my knees in case it showed. I hoped I didn't smell. I was too embarrassed even to ask Anja or Mamma if I did. Anja told Mamma the whole story of the morning but left out the unlocked door part and Pappa shouting. Mamma said there was no need to tell Pappa, 'This is something that concerns only us girls.' I was glad about that and slipped my hand in hers.

When we were going up the steps to the little square of shops Mamma said, 'Why don't we get some ice cream to have with coffee?'

'Yes, please,' Anja said and hugged Mamma. 'There is a really cool new flavour, Coca-Cola. Can we get that, Mamma?'

'That sounds good, don't you think so, Eeva?' she said. The three of us had our arms linked as we came to the top step. All the shops, apart from the small newspaper kiosk, were shut on Sundays. There was a queue of people outside the Pressbyrå. A group of boys from Anja's year stood by the corner, smoking and laughing. I saw one of them was Stefan. Anja took her hand away and went over to talk to him. Mamma and I stood at the end of the queue. Mamma watched Anja standing in the middle of the group of tall boys but didn't tell her to come back. She looked slim in her yellow coat and platform boots. As soon as Anja was with the boys she pretended not to notice us. She stood next to Stefan, who kept flicking his hair off his eyes. I'd seen him at school. He always wore a red jumper and grey flared trousers. I wondered what he would say if he knew I'd started my period and was a woman already but Anja wasn't. Would he call me over and laugh and talk with me, too, then? I wondered if I could go and see Harriet on the way home but didn't know if I dared. Her parents might be there. I couldn't wait to tell Harriet about my period.

'What would you like?' the woman at the kiosk asked when it was our turn.

Mamma asked for the ice cream and then pointed at

some pads on the shelf. The woman put the packet into a brown paper bag. I could feel my cheeks burning when Mamma handed me the bag and paid. Anja and the boys laughed. Was that aimed at me? Had Anja told them? I turned away from the Pressbyrå, keeping my eyes on the ground. Mamma said, 'Anja, we are going,' in Swedish.

'I'm staying here,' Anja replied. Her accent was perfect; you'd never guess she hadn't been born a Swede.

'Anja, can I talk with you,' Mamma said in Finnish. She stood there in the middle of the little square, not moving, looking at Anja. At first Anja didn't shift, but seeing Mamma wasn't going to budge, she came over, slowly, dragging the worn-out hems of her jeans on the floor.

'What is it?' she whispered in Finnish.

'Who are those boys?' Mamma said.

'My classmates, of course,' Anja said. Her eyes were wide and blue.

'Are there going to be any girls coming over?'

Anja opened her mouth and looked pityingly at Mamma, 'Why are you asking that?' She had some very shiny lip gloss on. Whenever I put some on I couldn't speak normally. I wondered if Anja had practised a lot because she didn't seem to have any trouble at all.

'You know full well, Anja. If there aren't any girls there, which I don't think there are, you are coming home with me, or else...'

'Or else what?' Anja said. She pursed her lips and made her eyes even wider.

Mamma said nothing. She just looked over to the boys. They weren't looking at us. One boy was stubbing out his cigarette while two others were bending their heads down, lighting another one. Stefan, wearing the red jumper, was cupping his hand around a match, while the other one, with long thin hair, had the unlit cigarette in his mouth. I heard him swear when the light went out.

'Well, Anja?' Mamma said.

Anja turned around and waved and smiled at the group of boys, 'Hejdå,' she said. They nodded. Stefan smiled.

All the way home on the path past blocks of flats and the school I kept thinking about that smile. Did he smile at me, or Anja? Anja and I were walking either side of Mamma, arms linked with her. Anja taught us to walk in a pattern, so that all our right feet would turn right at the same time, then do the same with the left. I found it hard with the pad, but didn't say anything. We laughed and walked so much my tummy started hurting again.

At home, Pappa was sitting on the sofa. He had got dressed and was reading the paper. He was lying down and when we came in, he said, 'You're being jolly, girls.'

I felt very grown up together with Mamma and Anja.

'We've got Coca-Cola ice cream for coffee,' I said.

'I'll put it on,' Mamma said and went into the kitchen. I took my coat off and went into the bathroom, making sure I locked both doors. I washed myself and changed the pad. The new one was a lot thinner and I worried it might not last long. When I came out I saw Anja was sitting on one of the comfy chairs in the lounge.

The room was tidy now and smelled of furniture polish. The ashtray was empty and clean and placed on the bookcase where it belonged.

'So Coca-Cola ice cream, eh?' Pappa said. 'I bet that was your idea,' he said to Anja.

'As a matter of fact it was,' Anja said and smiled.

'Good, good.'

'Why don't we play a game of Monopoly, while we are having the coffee? Please, Pappa, please,' I said. I wanted to go over and sit on his lap and tickle him to make him promise a game, but didn't in case the pad slipped, or he noticed what I was wearing. I was glad he was in a better mood.

'Yes, please Pappa,' Anja said.

Pappa rubbed his hands together and said, 'Alright then, if you two want to be thrashed again.' He was smiling and his voice was soft.

I went quickly over to the drawer in the bookcase and pulled out the game. Pappa had bought it soon after we'd moved to Stockholm. He said it would teach us girls how to handle money, but we always lost to him. I loved playing it all the same. Once Anja nearly beat Pappa. Mamma was always out first. Pappa said, 'That figures.'

Mamma came into the room, and I said, 'We're playing Monopoly!' She looked very serious.

'C'mon, Kirsti, let's play, both the girls want to,' Pappa said. For a while they didn't say anything and I was afraid there was going to be another fight. At last Mamma turned to go back into the kitchen and said, 'I'll bring the coffee then.'

I thought the argument must have been about the toenails because Mamma still seemed to be angry with Pappa. She'd soon forgive him when we started playing and Pappa made us all laugh with his jokes and stories. My tummy wasn't hurting at all anymore.

Seventeen

Tampere 2004

'YOU GIRLS wait here,' Pappa said. He was hunched over and looked as if he was going to collapse any minute. He was wearing black trousers, a white shirt and a brown jumper. He hadn't put on a tie – had he forgotten? His outdoor coat looked shabby and it didn't quite fall right, it looked longer in the front than the back.

'We're alright,' Anja said. She'd taken hold of Pappa's arm. 'Aren't we?' she said and looked at me. We were standing in a shiny clean hospital corridor waiting for the doctor to see us. A man was walking purposefully towards us through the empty space. Anja said, 'Eeva?'

'Yes, of course, we'll all go,' I said.

'Herra Litmunen?' The man said. He had a bright blue shirt and a darker spotted tie showing underneath the open white coat. He had wavy dark-brown hair, unruly looking. He had a plain, youthful face. 'I'm sorry,' he said and took

Pappa's hand. Pappa looked at his hand first then at the man but said nothing.

Anja said, 'Thank you.' The man nodded and stretched out his hand to Anja in turn. Then he took mine and nodded as he lightly touched my fingers. He held my gaze for a moment, but I had to look away. I didn't want to be the first one to start crying again. He led us to a room furnished like a kitchen: there was a pale birch table with four chairs. On the table a green vase contained white chrysanthemums. They were fresh. Someone must buy those every few days, I thought. Wilting flowers would give the wrong kind of air to this place. A small window had colourful, stripy curtains. This room is supposed to cheer us up, I thought. Two green chairs with wooden armrests stood half facing each other against a wall. The doctor indicated that Pappa should sit down in one of the chairs and he sat in the other. Or perched. He was leaning forward with his elbows resting on his knees, facing Pappa. Anja and I sat down in the chairs by the table.

'Herra Litmunen, as I said on the telephone, your mother died very peacefully.'

Anja looked at me, then took a tissue out of her large handbag. She removed her glasses and wiped her eyes. There was no make-up on them. I felt ashamed I'd put on some mascara. I hadn't thought. I did what I always did every morning, just two or three strokes on each set of lashes. The doctor looked up at Anja and continued, 'Rouva Litmunen merely fell asleep. She had an emergency button next to her bed but it had not been pressed.'

Anja said, 'Who found her?'

'The nurse on her first rounds.'

'And how long had she been…?'

'Well, we don't know exactly, not yet. That's what I need to talk to you about.' The doctor looked at Pappa, judging how much information he could take, seeing if he'd be a problematic relative. He's done this many times before, I thought.

'Post-mortem?' Anja said quickly, 'But why?'

'No, no, we just need to have a look at the data and determine the time of death exactly. Hospital policy,' he said, turning to Anja.

The data, I thought, Saara has become 'data'.

'I don't understand,' I said.

'We just need to keep her here for a little longer, and we need to make arrangements…' the doctor looked directly at me. A strand of hair had fallen on his face and he brushed it aside with a flick of his head.

'So can I ask, what happens now then?' Anja said.

'That's what I need to discuss with Herra Litmunen,' the doctor said looking at Pappa, who was not moving. He was looking out of the window, leaning all the way back in the chair. His hands were resting loosely on his lap and his shoulders were hunched. Anja shot a look at me and I nodded, 'Can we see you outside for a moment?' she said to the doctor. Pappa still didn't react.

'Of course,' the doctor said, moving up from his chair. Anja went over to Pappa and whispered something in his ear, touching his arm slightly with one hand and rubbing his back with the other.

***

In the corridor, where noises echoed against the shiny floor, Anja and I faced the man who looked too young to be a doctor.

'I don't think our father is taking all this in,' Anja said. 'Could you tell us what the...' Anja looked at me and put her hand on my arm. Then she looked down onto the floor for a moment. A noisy group of women walked towards us. They were laughing. As they came nearer, they stopped talking. The doctor nodded to them when they passed us in silence, leaving us like an island in the middle of the passageway. We were like statues, unable to move.

I put my hand on Anja's arm and looked at the doctor's brown eyes and said, 'What happens now?'

He took a deep breath in and said, 'We'll need the morning to establish that the cause of death was natural. All indications point to that, but we have to confirm it, obviously.'

'Obviously,' I said. I was still holding onto Anja's arm. We were now leaning against one another. The doctor continued speaking. He sounded as if he was in a tunnel. My hearing seemed to have worsened suddenly.

'Then we will take the body down to the morgue,' the doctor continued.

Anja, or I, I couldn't tell, swayed a little at the last word. There was a long silence.

'Can we see her?' I said. Anja took her arm away from mine and looked up at the doctor again, 'Yes, can we?'

'You'll need to contact a hautaustoimisto, and they'll...'

'Now,' Anja said. 'We want to see our grandmother now.'

The doctor said nothing for a while again. He looked from Anja to me and said, 'What about your father, will he be up to it?'

'Yes, he'll be fine,' Anja said and moved over to the door of the room we'd been sitting in.

'I need to make a phone call,' the doctor said and hurried away.

At the sound of the door opening, Pappa looked up at us. He was still sitting in the same chair. He didn't say anything and his face was blank. His eyes were a watery colour, but he didn't meet my gaze – he was looking at Anja. I looked away. The curtains in the room were too bright and the light from the window hurt my eyes. Anja went over to Pappa and said, 'We can go and see Saara. Eeva and I spoke with the doctor.'

'Jaha, jaha,' Pappa said and got up.

'We'll have to wait for the doctor,' Anja said and put her hand on Pappa's arm. He sat down again with a heavy thump. I looked at Anja and she shook her head.

Saara looked peaceful, as if she was sleeping. Her hair was tidy around her face and her eyes were closed. She looked like she did when I left her the day before; still it wasn't quite her. I stared down at her face for a long time. Was she really no longer there asleep, was the one thing missing her spirit? And where was that spirit, her soul now?

I didn't cry but Anja did. She made whining noises behind me. I saw Saara's dry hands. They'd been placed either side of her, palms down. Or perhaps that's how she had been when they found her, I didn't know. I leant closer to Saara's face and whispered, 'Hyvää yötä.' Saying 'goodnight' to Saara felt right, but I didn't want to touch her in case she was cold. I wanted to hold onto the memory of her child's grip, not of a stiff, lifeless hand. I stepped away and Anja, arm in arm with Pappa, moved forward. Anja was still sniffling when we left Saara alone.

Walking back along the corridor I saw through the window the white lilies and the bench set against the slope. It looked empty and lonely now, not inviting as it had done the day before. Then I thought about the flowers for Saara's funeral; I decided they'd have to be lily of the valley. But they would be too plain on their own; Saara liked colour. She needed bright shades, cornflowers or sweet peas, but nothing too artificial. I wondered if you could get summer flowers in Tampere in March. Surely they came from Holland or somewhere in Africa? Then I thought about the church, and where she would be buried? The closest church was Kalevan Kirkko, but I knew Saara had always disliked the modern design of the building. Perhaps she would be buried in the Cathedral, where we used to go for a service on Christmas Eve. I thought back to her letters. She had never mentioned going to church in them. Perhaps she wanted to be cremated, so many people were nowadays. I shuddered at the thought of sending Saara into the flames.

On the way to Saara's flat no one spoke. The taxi was a gleaming white Mercedes, and at first the driver whistled happily. Then, seeing our faces, he became silent and kept his fat white hands on the wheel and his small eyes on the road. Pappa sat in the back with Anja while I chose the front seat. I wanted to be on my own and watch the city as we drove through it. People were hurrying to work and it was still raining. The inside of the car was black leather. The smell was overwhelming. I opened the window slightly. The driver was startled by the sudden noise from the passing cars and buses on the road and glanced sideways at me but said nothing. We were driving past Siilinkari and then Stockmann's department store. At the Kalevan Kirkko crossroads I wanted to ask about the service but didn't. The cobbled street made the ride bumpy. Anja told the driver the address and directed him to where Pappa's car was parked. I paid him when we stopped behind Pappa's Peugeot.

'Shall I drive?' Anja said when we stood on the pavement by the car.

'Perhaps you ought to,' Pappa said and gave his keys to her. Then he walked around the front to the passenger seat. I sat in the back as before. The car looked different to me. It was cold and damp inside. I saw the window had been wound down and rain or mist had made the other side of the back seat wet.

In Pappa's car I thought about going back to Stockholm, to my clean, bright flat and Janne's risotto. The thought of Janne startled me. I must phone him. I took my mobile out of my handbag and looked at the small screen. Then I glanced up at Pappa and Anja. They were concentrating on the road ahead. I saw I had missed calls: from Yri? I dialled the voicemail number and got Janne's concerned voice, 'Can't get an answer from your flat, and at the school they say you're away. Can you please call me?'

The sounds of my mobile had alerted Anja. She was throwing glances at me through the mirror.

'Janne,' I said.

Anja nodded, her eyes dark and wide.

There was a message from Harriet too, 'I've had Janne on the phone. He told me you've gone away, something to do with your grandmother. What's going on? Give me a call!'

These voices from my life in Stockholm were from another world. Although it had been just over 24 hours, it seemed to me an age since I'd spoken Swedish. The language seemed too jolly, the words too plentiful. Then I thought about Yri, how he promised to call, and hadn't. How was I going to explain all of it to Janne? I pressed my head against the cold window and closed my eyes.

When we got to Pappa's house, he said, 'Anyone for a drink?' I looked at my watch and thought it's getting earlier and earlier, but nodded. I knew he didn't mean just coffee, though Anja went straight over to the percolator and started loading the machine with water and spoonfuls of strong ground coffee. Pappa got a bottle of vodka out of a cupboard and placed it on the table.

'A little bit of strength for us all,' he said and sat down in front of the bottle. His face looked a bit brighter. Anja put one cup in front of him and the two others around the table. Pappa unscrewed the top off the vodka and poured half a cupful out for himself. I watched him gulp it down in one go. He held the open bottle up, and looking at us said, 'Anja, Eeva?' His eyes were lifted and he looked from one to the other. Anja shook her head and said, 'I'll wait for the coffee.'

'Me too,' I said.

Pappa poured a second helping into his cup and left the liquid there. His head was bent down, as if he was examining the bottom of his cup through the clear vodka. The percolator started making gurgling noises and we all looked at it.

'Nearly ready,' Anja said and glanced at Pappa. It was as if she was talking to a child. Then the coffee maker was silent and Anja got up, holding onto the table with both of her hands. She sighed and poured coffee for us all. Without asking, Pappa sloshed vodka into our cups. 'C'mon girls, this will help a bit,' he said and lifted his up. The scent of the alcohol mixed with coffee made me wretch, but I swallowed half a cupful.

'Now I need to talk to you two,' Pappa said after another round of coffee and vodka. His eyes had a determined look and he had his arms resting either side of the cup and saucer. His slender hands were crossed. I was sitting opposite him while Anja was looking out of the window. She had her hands on her lap, her fingers playing with her wedding ring. I wanted to touch Pappa's hands but didn't dare.

'Saara decided everything before she fell ill. She's going to be buried in the Kangasmaa cemetery and the service will be in the chapel there. You know, where Vaari was buried.' Pappa added, looking at me, 'Though you are too young to remember my father, Eeva, aren't you?'

'He died before I was born,' I said. I couldn't believe Pappa would not remember that.

'Of course, so it was,' he said and looked old and frail again for a moment.

'Anyway, she told me she spoke with the pastor there, so I'll phone and make the arrangements. You needn't worry, it's all taken care of,' Pappa said looking up. Our eyes met and I touched his hands and said, 'OK, that sounds right.'

'Yes,' he said. His eyes filled with tears, and he coughed

and took his hand away. 'It may be a couple of days before the funeral can be arranged. I need to contact her one living cousin. Then there is her neighbour, and…anyway, she's left a list for me. So you girls can go and take care of your families,' Pappa looked at me and added, 'or jobs and things. I'll let you know when the funeral is and then you can make a trip here again for that.'

Eighteen

THE VODKA warmed my body. Pappa had been right; it helped. I can see how you can become an alcoholic, I thought, as I looked around the attic. The two mattresses on the floor were about a metre apart, but Anja's had edged towards mine and was lying at an angle. I went over and straightened it. We hadn't had time to make the beds in the morning, not even with just a loose sheet covering the mattress and a pussilaka-na covering a thin blanket. I wondered about the Finnish word; directly translated it meant a 'bag sheet', which de-scribed it precisely. Except for the ones Pappa had given us. The blanket was far too small for the duvet cover. The ends hung loose on the floor.

I'd told Anja and Pappa that I was coming upstairs to lie down, but instead I sat on an old 1960s office chair. It squeaked when I swivelled around in it, and the orange fabric was worn out on the armrests. I could hear voices from the kitchen, Anja's calm tone interrupted by Pappa's baritone.

I took my mobile out of my handbag and thought I ought

to phone Janne. I pressed the arrows and scrolled along the familiar names in my directory. The last on the list was Yri. I had not called him since he told me it was over. He said he had to try and repair his marriage and I didn't want to pester him, or his wife. Many times during the last few years, coming across his number on a busy day I nearly deleted it. More often since I'd met Janne. But I wanted to keep something of Yri, a memory. The number was evidence that he existed.

Strange, I thought now, that he never left even as much as a toothbrush in my flat. When he stayed the night, the one wonderful night, he had an overnight bag, which he packed meticulously when he was getting ready to leave in the morning. I watched him fold his jumper and his white, soft cotton boxer shorts in the bottom of the worn-out leather holdall. In the bathroom, he picked up his shaving gear and toothbrush, and the little plastic comb he used to try to control his unruly hair, and placed them one by one in a small dark-green wash bag. I leant against the doorframe of the long bathroom in my flat, watching him. I was wearing a white cotton dressing gown. Yri zipped up the wash bag, and I watched his gaze move from my eyes down to my throat and follow the edge of the dressing gown past my waist to my bare thigh. I pushed one knee further out to reveal more of me and felt the ache for him again.

Next day Yri told me he had been in trouble at home for being so late back.

I looked at the name on the telephone and at the green button with a small picture of a receiver. I needed to talk to Yri so badly. Surely he'd understand this was an emergency?

What the hell, I thought, he can pretend it's a wrong number if he can't talk.

I could feel the dampness of perspiration under my arms as I listened to the ringing tone. I practised what I'd say, 'Hi, it's me.' That's how we always started our telephone conversations. Suddenly I wondered what time it was and looked at my watch: five past five. I panicked at the thought that he'd be at home already and was just about to hang up when a voice said, 'Hello?'

'Hi, it's me.'

There was a silence at the other end and I half expected to hear the disconnected tone next. Was he angry I'd called? What a mistake this was, I thought. I should have waited for him to contact me. I wasn't playing the game, wasn't following the rules. Then he said slowly, 'Eeva, how nice to hear from you.'

I was trying to read his voice, but felt dizzy with hearing it. The low, almost whispering sound made me hold the small mobile phone tighter. My hands were burning.

'How are you?' I said with the little breath I had left in my throat.

'Good, good...'

I could see him nodding, the loose wheat-coloured curls bouncing on his forehead. He spoke Swedish as if it was Polish and I imagined him saying instead, 'Tack, tack'.

'Yri, I'm still in Finland.'

'Oh'

'Yes, but it's not good.'

'Not good?'

'No, my grandmother died today.' When I said the words

I felt as if someone else was speaking them, or as if I was acting out a part, the part of a mourning granddaughter. I struggled with the lump in my throat again.

'Eeva, how terrible for you!'

'Yes, Saara was old, but...'

'It's very sad for you, Eeva.'

'Yes,' I managed to say, avoiding the lump. Then I swallowed hard and said, 'Yri, when can I see you?'

Silence again. I hadn't planned to say that. It sounded so needy. But it was what I wanted to say, and it just came out. Again I had a surreal feeling, as if this was not truly happening. As if the lovemaking on the noisy ferry, in the narrow, uncomfortable bunk, hadn't happened either. I bent my head. The mobile felt hot and sticky against my ear but I didn't dare to move it to the other side of my head in case I'd miss what Yri said. I wished I'd taken another cup of vodka and coffee upstairs with me. I wanted the warm feeling of the alcohol in my chest. Instead I had a dread in there, a fear of the terrible mistake I was surely committing. Something I would torture myself with at night. But I wanted to shout the words again. I wanted to say, 'Please come to me here, I want you here.' I said instead, 'Yri, please.'

'OK, Eeva, I'll come and see you. When are you back in Stockholm?' His voice was dry and formal.

My mind was racing. Could I pack my bags now and leave Tampere with the night ferry? Anja would think me selfish, again. I could hear her say, 'Pappa has just lost his mother. He needs us.' If I left it another twenty-four hours Yri might change his mind. I heard footsteps on the creaky wooden staircase.

177

'Yri, can I call you back?'

'Yes, but not today, tomorrow.'

'OK, bye.'

'Bye, Eeva.'

I felt as if I was floating. He'd said he would come and see me. Did that mean he was free now? Then I remembered he said not to call today, issuing warnings just as before.

I heard footsteps again on the staircase and Anja came into the room. She slumped down on the other chair in the attic. It was one of the comfy chairs belonging to the golden velour suite downstairs. It was dirty now, and the middle was sagging.

'What a day!' she said and took off her short, black boots. Her toenails were painted pink and shone through her stockinged feet. 'How was Janne?'

I said nothing just shrugged my shoulders and fiddled with the mobile in my hands. My chair squeaked.

'How's Pappa?' I said.

Anja looked at me for a long time before answering. Her eyes were accusing at first. Then they started to soften and fill with tears. She came over and sat on one of the mattresses on the floor and took my hands in hers, 'What a bloody mess!'

'I just can't, Anja, I can't forget,' I said. I realised I'd started crying. The tears just came and ran down my face as I looked at Anja sitting uncomfortably on the low bed.

'I know, Eeva, it took me a long time too.' She got up and put her arm around my shoulders. 'The thing is, Eeva, it's easier if you do.' She was speaking to a space above my head. I felt as if we were on a stage, both looking at the audience sitting somewhere in the darkness in front of us.

'Easier for Pappa, you mean,' I turned to look accusingly at Anja. She removed her arm and went to sit on the velour chair again. For a while, neither of us spoke. We could hear Pappa walking around downstairs, then talking to someone, on the telephone I presumed. I didn't hear what he was saying. Anja got up and gave me a tissue.

'Thanks,' I blew my nose and wiped my face. Then I looked up at her. I was startled by what I saw. She was the image of Saara. I'd never noticed the similarity before. That was probably why I thought she'd been wearing Saara's dressing gown that morning. Perhaps it was her round shape and her large bust, or the new brown colour of her hair, nearly as dark as Saara's. Her eyes were blue and not hazel, but there was something of Saara in the curve of her mouth, in the slant of her eyes when she looked down at me. I wondered if it was true that the soul of a person enters someone else when they die. But I'd always believed it entered a new born baby, not a grown woman, even a grand-daughter. I must not let my mind wonder like this, I thought and shook my head.

'What is it?' Anja asked.

'Nothing,' I said. She looked hurt, so I quickly added, 'I had a crazy thought because you really reminded me of Saara the way you looked at me just now.'

Anja smiled and said, 'She was our grandmother so we are both bound to look a little like her.'

'Yes, I guess so.' I said and smiled too, 'But I thought her soul had entered your body, that was the crazy bit.'

Anja put both her arms around me and hugged me hard. 'Eeva I'm sure she's in both of us. Now let's go and see what

179

arrangements Pappa has made. I need to phone home and tell them what's going on.'

'OK,' I said and got up. Tomorrow I can talk to Yri again, I thought, as I followed Anja down the narrow stairs.

The vodka had made Pappa more energetic and composed. He looked taller as he ushered us into the living room where Anja and I sat on the sofa, facing him as he sat at the dining room table as before. He told us he'd spoken with the pastor and the funeral directors and that the date was set for next Saturday.

'It's all sooner than I thought. You can stay here, all of you. I'm sure we can fit in,' Pappa said, looking at Anja first and then me. I said nothing, just nodded.

'We can worry about that later,' Anja said. She smiled at me and put her hand on mine, 'Isn't that so?' she said. I nodded again.

'I'm going to cut some keys for you so that you can go and see what you'd like from Saara's flat whenever you want to,' Pappa said. 'Unless you already know what you want?' Pappa didn't look at us but at a notebook he had in front of him. 'There's money in the fund for your travel, and if need be hotel bills...'

'Fund?' I said.

Pappa looked at me, pulling the corners of his mouth up, almost smiling at me. 'Saara planned her funeral well; she saved up for a fund. I helped her when I could, and now it's there, available for us to use.'

Then he straightened himself and said, 'I haven't really

got any food in the house. We'll have to go out again tonight.'

'What about the pizza place around the corner?' said Anja. 'They deliver, don't they? I don't know about you two but I'm not very hungry. Besides, they do quite good side salads too, so we could just have two pizzas and share?' Anja was looking questioningly at Pappa, then at me. I wondered if motherhood always made you worry about food and eating, or was it just in Anja's character. I could just drink neat vodka for the rest of the evening. Becoming an alcoholic, I thought. 'That sounds fine,' I said.

'We can go out, it's not that...'

'No, really, pizza is good. I like pizza.' I said squeezing Anja's hand.

'Pappa?' Anja said.

'What?' Pappa said. He seemed to have nodded off, his eyes wide open, looking at something on the bookcase.

'What kind of pizza would you like?' Anja said. Her voice was soft, soothing. She'd moved off the sofa and was leaning close to Pappa.

'I don't want any of that foreign rubbish!' he said. His tone was different and it made Anja stiffen. She turned her face to me and her expression was tense. Her look carried a warning.

Pappa stared at both of us, 'You two have got into that American culture, just like...' he stopped speaking for a while and tapped his fingers on the table, looking down at his long fingers. 'You should learn to eat proper Finnish food,' he boomed.

Anja came over and sat next to me on the sofa. She looked close to tears.

Then Pappa laughed a dry laugh; it was just a sound, more like a cough.

'You have what you like. I'll pay,' his voice was softer and he was looking at us with his head bent, like a little boy who had misbehaved.

Neither Anja nor I spoke.

'You never know, I may just fancy it when it arrives,' Pappa said with a sigh and got up.

We ate at the kitchen table in near silence. Pappa drank more vodka but Anja and I just had Karjala beer. Pappa ate nearly a whole pizza on his own. When he went to take the last slice, Anja gave him a hard stare, but said nothing.

I was imagining, wildly, how I would ask Yri to attend the funeral with me. If anyone asked, I would say he was my boyfriend. No one in Tampere would know he was married. Besides, I couldn't think who'd know me either, apart from Saara's neighbour, Marja. But, of course, Yri wouldn't be able to come with me – what would he tell his wife? I was already regretting my phone call, but pushed the feeling away. What did it matter anyway that I phoned him? He owed me that much, to be there when I really needed to talk to someone. Meeting him again on the ferry seemed like fate; we were fated to be together. But the feeling that I was acting like a foolish schoolgirl kept playing on my mind. Yri didn't love me, the other voice told me, but I pushed that thought away too. I had more important things to worry about.

'Is Janne going to be able to come to the funeral?' Anja said.

'I don't know,' I breathed. Was Anja reading my mind? I looked at Pappa. Was he going to ask who Janne was? But Pappa was still munching on the pizza, looking out of the window. It was dark now and all you could see were the streetlights and occasional shadows of dog walkers hurrying past. Pappa's fingers were around a small glass of vodka, which he brought to his lips and sipped once in a while. At least he's not gulping it down, I thought. I looked at my watch: it was nearly seven o'clock. Only some fourteen hours ago the nurse had found Saara sleeping but not breathing. Yet it seemed to me an age ago.

'I've put the sauna on,' Pappa said.

'Right,' Anja said. I looked at her. She had her eyes cast down at her plate. She was still angry with Pappa, I thought.

'Will you have a sauna?' Pappa asked me, his blue eyes carefully meeting mine. I looked at Anja.

'Anja, are you going to have one?'

'It's a wood-fired one, supposed to be better than any of the Swedish saunas you two are used to,' Pappa said.

Anja looked up and straight at Pappa, 'Our sauna in Sundsvall has a combination stove, both wood-fired and electric, and it is the best sauna you can buy. Both Bengt and I know a lot about how build a sauna.' Anja had straightened her back and looked a head taller than Pappa sitting opposite. Her eyes had become black and round.

'Yes, yes, I forgot, Anja, yes, of course, I forgot,' Pappa said. 'That Bengt, he is a very clever man, you've done well there,' he said. 'For a Swede, at least,' he added. Now his eyes had laughter in them and Anja couldn't help but smile.

'Pappa!' she said.

'Yes, yes, I know,' he said and then, 'Will you two have a sauna? I had one yesterday, so if you don't, the heat will be wasted...'

Anja looked at me and I nodded.

The sauna was a separate building in front of the house, which I had thought was a garage. The dressing room was cold but once I stepped inside the sauna, a soft, wet heat hit every part of my body. It was so very different from the sauna I had every week in the gym in Stockholm, where you had to wear a swimming costume and the heat came from a small electric stove. I was the only person who threw any water on the stones and then somebody always complained that it was too hot.

As soon as Anja and I had climbed onto the wooden bench, she picked up the bucket and threw two ladlesful of water onto the stones. The steam rose following a slow hissing sound and caressed our bodies.

'Aah,' I said, 'this is wonderful. I'd forgotten what a real sauna feels like,'

Anja smiled, she was leaning against the wooden wall, her large, round body relaxed. How strange it was that we were sisters and yet were built so very differently. I felt like a wiry, dried-up old spinster next to Anja. She was so much more feminine, with her painted nails and coloured hair.

'You must come and sample Pappa's perfect sauna more often,' Anja said.

Back in the house Pappa was still sitting drinking at the kitchen table. He hadn't even cleared the plates away.

'A beer?' Anja said. She'd gone straight to the fridge and was now showing me the bottle.

'Yes please,' I said and thought it would help me sleep. The feeling of cleanliness after the sauna had relaxed me too.

Pappa leaned back in his chair, 'Good sauna, Eppu?'

'Yes,' I said and sat down.

'So what's this about some junkkari you have, Eeva?' he said, looking directly at me.

'Junkkari!' Anja shrieked. 'I haven't heard that expression since, well not for a very long time!' She was smiling.

Pappa winced wearily. He looked pleased with himself. 'Isn't that what he is, this Janne, isn't Janne his name?'

I looked at Pappa and said, 'Janne is my boyfriend, yes.' I got up and took my plate to the sink. When I sat back at the table I gave Anja a hard look.

'Oho, I see,' Pappa said. He looked down at his empty plate and took another sip of vodka. 'You girls should drink some of this proper stuff; that beer will just make you wee all night long,' he said, lifting his eyes to us.

'It's alright, this is nice beer,' Anja said.

I looked out of the window and decided I'd like something stronger. 'I'll have some,' I said.

Pappa opened his eyes wide and tried to get up, but decided against it halfway. Anja said, 'I'll get you a glass. Do you want something with it, what have you got, Pappa?' Without waiting for a reply, Anja looked in cupboards but found nothing more than an old bottle of flat Coca-Cola. 'Must be from our last visit,' she said and smiled at Pappa.

'I'll have it neat, that's OK,' I said.

Anja poured some vodka into two glasses. I took a sip and nearly gagged at the strength of it. I was used to snaps, flavoured vodka served ice cold with sill or at crayfish parties, but drinking neat Koskenkorva out of water glasses seemed very Finnish, almost Russian to me. The Finland I didn't belong to. But today I just wanted to get anaesthetised.

Pappa lifted his glass up and said, 'To Saara!'

'Saara,' I said and fought the tears again.

'Saara,' Anja said. Her voice shook and we knocked our glasses together. The sharp clink hurt my ears.

'And where did the Finnish soldiers defeat the Russians?'

'Pohjanmaa!' Both Anja and I said. I looked at her and she nodded, as if to say, 'Yes drink it all. It's medicine, it'll make you feel better.'

It was as if acid was making its way from my throat down to my guts. The taste was vile, like drinking lighter fluid, but the feeling afterwards gave me a strange buzz, a surge of energy.

'I'd forgotten about that saying. You used to make that toast a lot at Saara's parties!' I said.

'Yes,' Pappa said, his eyes gleaming with the alcohol, you remember that?'

'It's handy, it means "bottoms up" as well,' I said.

'We Finns have always been inventive with our language,' Pappa said proudly.

'Especially when it comes to words linked with drinking,' Anja said.

We all laughed, then fell silent.

Pappa got up, sighed and said, 'How about another round, girls?'

I looked at Anja and then up at Pappa. He sat down again and without waiting for a reply refilled our glasses. Anja shook her head, but when she looked up her eyes were gleaming too. I thought we must all be quite drunk by now. I felt my body relax and I started wondering if I could phone Yri again. Surely he could go to the bathroom or something to talk to me?

'So, Eeva, is this Janne coming to the funeral?' Pappa was looking directly at me.

'I don't know,' I said, 'I may not want him to.'

I took a large gulp of vodka. It didn't taste so bad anymore.

'Well, it's about time you settled down,' he said.

'I'm not sure I'll be bringing the children,' Anja said.

'What did you say?' I said. My eyes were fixed on Pappa. He looked away.

'I'm just saying, it's no fun being on your own.'

'What, you're asking me to feel sorry for you now, are you?' I said. I felt such a surge of anger that I wanted to get up and tell Pappa how I really felt about him, what he did to Mamma. How it was his fault I never came to see Saara, how I'd missed her all these years.

'No, Eppu, I'm just saying I know how sad it is not to be able to share a life with someone.'

'Eeva can make her own choices in life,' Anja said. 'Besides, what's wrong with boyfriends, I wish I was still free. Marriage isn't all a bed of roses, you know.' Anja touched my hand and patted it.

'Yes, I do,' Pappa said and leant back in his chair, crossing his hands over his large chest.

'Oh yes, he does. He made a hell of a job of his, didn't he?' I said and went to stand up. My movement was too quick and the chair fell over. The clatter startled everybody.

Both Anja and Pappa looked up at me. Anja said, 'Don't Eeva, please.'

I nearly ran up the stairs. What right had Pappa to ask

me about my private life? And to call Janne names. Did he use that expression on purpose, the one reserved for Anja's unsuitable boyfriends?

Up in the attic I sat on the orange chair and hit the worn-out armrests. My hands hurt from the impact. There no cushioning between the frame and the fabric anymore. I replaced my hands gently on the armrests and squeezed it hard. Pappa had no right even to be talking to me, or have me here, staying in his house. Not after what he did. How could Anja have forgiven him just like that for everything? I thought of what I should have said to them downstairs: 'I can't pretend anymore, play happy families,' as Anja used to say in Rinkeby. 'Or have you forgotten how you were then, Anja?' I'd stare hard at her. 'I used to admire you, the way you stood up to Pappa. Now, look at you, "Pappa this, Pappa that", as if he was a bloody invalid.' I'd turn to Pappa and say, 'And you, don't you dare call me "Eppu", and don't give me advice on how to conduct my life when you ruined it in the first place!'

I put my head in my hands and wished I could talk to Saara. She would have understood how I felt. I wondered what version of events Saara had been given. We had never mentioned either Pappa or Mamma in our letters. Now I wished we had. I hadn't wanted to upset her with the past.

All day I'd been feeling sorry for Pappa. He had seemed as before, before Rinkeby, but then the outburst about the pizzas and he was back to the monster he'd become in Stockholm. I realised I was shaking. I looked at my bed but had no desire to lie down and sleep in it. I took the thin duvet off my bed and wrapped it around myself.

The anger was slowly withering away and I was glad Anja was going to be sharing the attic with me. I decided to sit up and wait until she came up before changing into my nightie.

Nineteen

ANJA WOKE me up by placing a hand on my arm. I sat up in the chair and rubbed my neck. It ached from the position I'd been dozing in. My mouth felt dry.

'What time is it?' I said.

'Late,' Anja whispered. Her breath smelled of alcohol. She was wearing the pink dressing gown that had reminded me of Saara. But now she didn't look anything like her.

'I'm sorry about earlier,' I said.

'Eeva, you need to sort it out with Pappa. He's our father; neither of us can help that.' Anja was now sitting on her mattress. She had propped a cushion from the velour chair behind her back and was holding a paperback novel. On the cover were two women in sixties-style frilly bikinis throwing a large beach ball to each other. It reminded me of the sunny Nivea adverts when I was a child.

'I know, but...'

'But what?' Anja looked at me over the book cover. She was wearing her dark-rimmed glasses.

'That night was horrible, Anja, don't you remember?' Though I tried to stop them, tears filled my eyes again. Anja continued to look at me over her glasses, 'It was a long time ago. He's changed.'

'Oh really, has he?' I couldn't keep the sarcasm out of my voice.

Anja put the book down on top of her blanket. 'Listen to yourself, Eeva! You're acting like a twelve-year-old. And I do believe you're a grown-up woman of forty-two, not a child anymore. It's about time you gave Pappa a chance. He's not perfect; he's just a man. We all make mistakes. And it was all much more complicated than you know.'

'What do you mean?' I'd stopped crying and had wrapped my blanket tighter around me and pulled my legs up on the creaky chair.

'Well, I don't know. I had better things to do then than worry about Mamma and Pappa.' Anja gave me a sideways look.

I stared at her. She picked up the book again and her eyes were fixed on a page. What was she telling me? I put my hands on my forehead and tried to think clearly, but couldn't. The alcohol had scrambled my brain.

'What are you saying,' I said finally.

Anja turned to face me and said, 'Nothing. I'm just saying everything was complicated then.'

'Complicated?'

'Yes,' she wasn't looking at me but on the page of her open book.

'Anja, I think if there is something you know, you should tell me,' I said slowly. I could feel that my voice was shaking.

Anja placed her book down on the floor next to her, slowly folding a corner of the page she was reading. She took in a deep breath, flaring her nostrils. 'Look, Eeva, you've got to talk to him. I can't mediate between the two of you. All I'm saying is that what we saw as children may not have been the whole picture.' Then she lowered her voice and said softly, 'Pappa loves you very much, you know. He's always asking about you.'

I put my head on my knees and looked sideway at Anja. She smiled and said, 'I've got to go to sleep now; it's past two o'clock. C'mon, Eeva, come to bed. We'll talk more tomorrow.'

I thought it was the middle of the night when I woke up, but through the window I could make out the tops of the apple trees in Pappa's garden. We'd forgotten to draw the curtains. Anja was still asleep next to me. I got up carefully, so as not to wake her, and went downstairs.

Pappa's hair looked as if it had been ruffled up in a salon with a fine comb. He reminded me of a troll. He was sitting by the window at the kitchen table drinking out of a small china cup. He looked up and said, 'Couldn't sleep, eh?'

'No.' I shook my head and looked at a wall clock. It was just past six o'clock. I felt embarrassed about the night before, being drunk and acting up.

'Coffee?' Pappa said and got up. He was wearing a pair of baggy pyjama bottoms and a brown cardigan over a grey-looking cotton vest. He scratched his chest with one hand while filling the percolator with spoonfuls of coffee with the other.

'Won't be a minute,' he said, and he placed a cup and saucer in front of me.

It was getting light outside. I watched the darkness fade for a while. Pappa was sitting opposite me, with his eyes downcast and his large, round shoulders hunched. Slowly the smell of fresh coffee filled the room. Pappa put his hands on the table, palms down and made a noise with the effort, as he pushed himself up.

'You don't take sugar or milk, do you?' he said when he poured the black, hot liquid into the tiny cup in front of me.

'No.' I could smell his musty scent, of sleep, old alcohol and sweat.

'Oho,' Pappa said when he splashed some of the coffee onto the saucer.

'It's OK. Thank you.'

When Pappa had sat down heavily again, I said, 'The arrangements for Saara's funeral…'

'Yes?' Pappa lifted his eyes to me.

'Do you need any help? I could organise the flowers, or drive you to see the pastor, or whatever.'

'No, no,' Pappa said quickly. 'Anyway, there's not much to do, she did it all herself long ago.' He got up again with a sigh and filled the table with food for breakfast.

I looked at the rye bread and the cheese and ham sharing a saucer. The edges of the meat touched the tablecloth. I wondered how long it had covered the table. It didn't look that clean. Pappa wanted to cook scrambled eggs, but I couldn't face any.

'But it used to be your favourite, Eppu!'

'What about a boiled egg?' Pappa was standing in the

middle of the small kitchen, holding a frying pan. A carton of eggs stood open on the work surface. It was strange seeing Pappa fuss about food.

'I'm sorry, I'm not hungry,' I said. I couldn't remember when I had last enjoyed eating. It was tasteless, just some texture I knew I had to consume to keep going.

'Morning,' Anja said. She'd appeared behind Pappa. She kissed him on the cheek and went to get some coffee. 'Want some?' she said to me, lifting the glass jar towards me.

'Please.' I lifted my cup up. Anja poured the coffee for both of us. Then she squeezed Pappa's shoulder, 'Did you sleep at all?'

Pappa looked at her and then me and said, 'I'm fine, don't worry.'

I wondered how long he'd been sitting in the kitchen when I came down. Looking at his lined and grey face, I guessed most of the night. Had he been sitting here thinking of the past and feeling guilty? Or mourning Saara and thinking of the happy days in Tampere. He must have found happiness here again after everything... Living in this house, being so close to Saara, seeing Anja and his grandchildren. Was it true that he had changed, that he regretted the past? I watched Pappa making scrambled eggs after all, though no one had said they wanted any. He put plates, knives and forks down at each place. For once, Anja sat down and let him do everything. She looked tired. She shot a glance at me over her coffee cup, but said nothing.

'Here we go.' Pappa divided the egg mixture onto the three plates. When he put a portion onto mine, he said, 'You don't have to eat it, but try.' His eyes were pale and kind.

194

'I'm going to go into town today,' I said, considering the plateful of food.

'What for?' Anja looked up at me. As if I was making an escape.

'I need to check my email.'

'Pappa has a PC in his bedroom. You could use that. Couldn't she?' Anja said to Pappa.

'It's less complicated if I find an internet café somewhere in town and do it that way. I want to have a little look around Tampere anyway.' I hoped I sounded determined. 'Is there anything I can get you Pappa? Anja?'

Anja looked at me and said after a while, 'No, I'm fine. We need to go to the florists today, don't we?'

'Yes, yes,' Pappa said. He'd started reading a newspaper.

I looked at him and wondered if he refused my help because Anja was already helping, or did he think I couldn't cope?

'We could all go together, of course.' Anja said.

'Let Eeva go and do her shopping. We won't be long anyway,' Pappa said over the rustling of the paper.

Anja crossed her arms over her chest, 'Anyway it's far too early yet. Shops and cafés don't open until nine at the earliest.'

'I'll take a chance,' I said and left the kitchen. I was being suffocated in this house and had to get out.

The town wasn't busy. I drove past the train station and found a parking place one street from Stockmann's. The old department store had been refurbished and I hardly recognised it inside. The coffee shop was still upstairs though. I found a table by the window. The interior was new, but the smell was the same – expensive perfume and coffee. I bought a cappuccino from a friendly girl at the till and a bar of Fazer chocolate and then sat watching the people and cars passing on Hämeenkatu. The train station opposite looked small. The clock tower, a very modern, tall square column of concrete, stood at one side of the building. I looked at the clock. It was only five past nine, just past eight in Stockholm. I wouldn't be able to phone Yri until nine his time. That meant I had an hour to kill. I drank my coffee slowly and decided to have a look around the station.

The station building hadn't been refurbished. There was a small kiosk selling magazines and tobacco, and a line of ticket booths as before. There weren't many people inside. I remembered the dank smell and the noise of the trains above. The tunnel to the platforms was as dark and cold as it had been when I was a child. To a twelve-year-old it had seemed endless and mysterious. In a few strides I was at the steps of platform one. Two Gypsy girls were sitting and smoking cigarettes on a bench. They looked very young, but wore the traditional heavy black velvet skirts and white cotton blouses with intricate embroidery at the sleeves and neck. Both had dark hair done up in a single plait. The hair on the girl closest to me came past her waist. Their dress was feminine, but their posture anything but. Both girls were leaning forwards, with their legs far apart and elbows on knees. Before I'd stepped onto the otherwise deserted platform, the girls had been talking and laughing, but fell silent as soon as I appeared. They were both looking at me. I wanted to flee back downstairs, out of the building, but didn't. The girl closest to me spoke first.

'What are you staring at?' Her eyes were dark and threatening.

I noticed a bottle of clear liquid with a white screw top on the floor between the two girls. The label was worn away. Home brew, I thought. They can't be any older than fifteen. I could be their mother.

'What are you doing?' I said. 'That stuff can make you go blind.'

Both the girls blinked and the one standing opened her mouth, but said nothing. Then she turned to look at her friend, who was still sitting on the bench.

'Do your mothers know you're here?' I said.

'What's it to you?' the girl sitting down said, stretching her neck to speak to me from behind the vast skirt of her friend.

'How old are you?' I said, thinking I had no idea what I was doing. I knew I should have turned around and left but I couldn't help but think that these girls needed help. I must be very tired and losing my mind, I thought. In Stockholm I would have been knifed by now, and it never occurred to me to intervene in anything anyone did on the street or in the Tunnelbana there. So what had got into me?

'Fifteen,' both the girls said at the same time. Then they looked at each other and laughed. 'You going to tell on us?' the girl standing up said. She was serious now. I noticed her eyes were perfectly blue, dark blue, and that she was very beautiful. Her hair had a few loose curls framing her face, accentuating her high cheekbones.

'What's your name?' I said. I realised I could report them

to the police. Not only were they underage, probably even younger than they had said, but they were also drinking home brew. That was serious. At least it had been when I was young.

'Sini,' the girl said and flicked her cigarette end onto the train track.

'Mie olen Tuula,' the other girl stood up, too, and walked up to me. This is when the knife comes out, I thought. But Tuula gave me her hand. It was a slight white hand and I noticed her nails had been bitten short, almost non-existent stumps at the end of her small fingers. The accent wasn't from Tampere, but I couldn't place it, perhaps from Eastern Finland.

'Nice to meet you, I'm Eeva, 'I said and then asked, 'You're not from Tampere, are you?'

'No, we're from Imatra,' Sini said and came to shake my hand too. 'We're just waiting for our train.'

I looked around the platform. We were the only people on it. 'When is it due in?' I said.

'Don't know,' Tuula said.

'Are you sure there will be a train today?'

'Oh yes, there always is, every day.'

I looked at the two Gypsy girls. They didn't seem too drunk, just happy to be with each other. I decided I'd check the board downstairs for the time of the next train to Imatra, and leave them be.

'You want a swig?' Tuula said, reaching out for the bottle.

'No, I'd better be going. I've got the wrong platform, I think.'

'Oh,' she said. 'Where are you going, then?'

I looked at the girls again. 'Nowhere. Be careful with that stuff, it can kill you if you have too much.' I gave what I thought must have been a stern look and left. When I was walking down the stairs I heard first giggles, then laughter. The sound of the sniggering made me feel old and weary. The lack of sleep was getting to me.

Twenty

'HELLO, YRI, it's me.'

'Ah, can I call you back?'

I looked at the time on the phone: a few minutes past ten.
'Yes. I'll be around for the next half an hour.'

'Great, speak to you soon. Hejdå.'

I was sitting in my car. It had started raining and I didn't
have an umbrella. I started the engine and drove up
Hämeenkatu, out of town. A bus showing Pispala as its
destination was in front of me and I decided to follow it. I
wanted to see the hill of mismatched workers' cottages, which
had become a conservation area. When Mamma was a girl she
lived there. She told us it was where poor people moved after
the war. Each family was allowed a small plot to build on.
There was no planning on the hill, and the result was a
cluster of wooden houses of all shapes and sizes, with narrow
winding streets and lanes in between.

'But the view of Lake Näsijärvi is breath taking,' Mamma
said, 'so now the rich people want to live there.'

She was right. Even in the drizzle you could see far out to the frozen lake. The houses looked well kept with expensive garden lighting and shiny cars parked in front of them. I drove all the way to the bottom of the hill and up again. It was a long time since I'd been in Pispala, I was trying to think why we used to come with Mamma. There was an old auntie, a friend of Saara's perhaps, whom we visited. She lived in an old yellow house with a sauna in the cellar. I parked the car at the top of the street, opposite an expensive-looking house with a large terrace around it. The clock on the dashboard was a little slow, showing it was twenty-five past ten. I checked my mobile to see what time I'd called Yri. Two minutes past ten. I'd forgotten how much I hated waiting for his calls. In the car mirror I saw the vast empty space of the grey-white lake behind me. I looked at the dashboard again: it was now 35 minutes past ten. Perhaps he wouldn't call. Perhaps he'd already changed his mind about seeing me. Perhaps he had a new girlfriend. I'm a fool, I thought, and started the car again.

Driving back wasn't easy. I ended up on a motorway, and although I recognized the place names I had no idea where they were in relation to Pappa's house. I decided to follow signs for Tampere city centre and retrace the road I'd taken into town. The rain had stopped and once in Hämeenkatu again, I changed my mind about going back to Pappa's house and parked the car instead.

Stockmann's was busier now and I strolled around the rails of clothes, fingering the fabrics. I lifted up a beige blouse on its hanger. It was made out of a silky fabric and had frills at the front, reminding me of the Gypsy girls' outfits. But where would I wear something like that? I moved onto a velvet jacket and thought it would go very well with the blouse. From the corner of my eye I saw a sales assistant looking at me, and I walked away from the clothes. I checked my phone: no calls. I was tired and wanted to sit down. I needed more coffee.

At last I felt the buzz of my mobile in my coat pocket.

'Eeva, it's me, Anja.'

'Hej,' I said. Please get off the line, I thought.

'Listen, you'd better get back here!'

'What's happened?'

'Janne's here!'

Janne looked different. He was sitting on the sofa, on the cigarette burn, exactly where I usually sat. His light cotton trousers were crisp and he was wearing a blue shirt, unbuttoned at the collar. I hadn't noticed it before, but he seemed very Swedish.

When I walked in he stood up and kissed me on the mouth, taking hold of my arms with his hands. I felt safe in his embrace at first, then remembered Yri's urgent, demanding hold of my body and froze with guilt.

'We were beginning to worry about you,' Anja said in Swedish.

I felt rigid in Janne's arms.

Janne took his lips away from mine and pulled me even closer to him. I relaxed a little and leant on his chest. He smelt nice. 'Eeva,' he whispered, his voice fresh and masculine.

Pappa coughed.

I sat down on the sofa next to Janne. I was still wearing my Ulster. I took it off and put it into Janne's outstretched arms. He placed it carefully on the arm of the sofa. Anja sat down on one of the velour chairs and looked at the coat and then up at me. There was an awkward silence. I looked at Pappa. I didn't know how much Swedish he spoke now. He cleared his throat and said, 'Does Janne want something to drink?' Then he turned to Janne and said, 'Dricka?'

'Yes thank you.'

'Beer?'

'Er,' Janne said and looked at me. I nodded. 'Thank you,' he said.

Pappa got up. Anja said, 'I'll go and help.'

'Are you OK?' Janne asked me, taking hold of my hand.

I wanted to cry. I put my hand on my forehead and sighed. I didn't want to look at him. How could I explain to Janne about Yri? What if he phoned now? Then it occurred to me that I hadn't told Janne where I was.

'How did you find me?' I moved my hand out of his grip.

'I saw your note.'

'My note?'

'In the kitchen. I was so worried, no one knew where you were and you weren't answering your phone. Did you get my messages?'

'No.' I looked down at my shoes. They were scuffed from walking around the cobbled streets.

'Really? I must have left at least ten on your mobile.' Janne's eyes were on me.

'Oh, sorry, I haven't looked,' I said breathlessly. I crossed

203

my legs and looked into the hallway. I could hear Anja and Pappa washing dishes in the kitchen.

Janne was silent for a moment. I felt his gaze boring holes into my story. Then I realised something. 'You went into my apartment?' I lifted my eyes to his.

'Yes,' he said and glanced away quickly. 'You gave me the key, remember?' Again there was a silence.

'I was worried,' Janne said and leant forward and put his hand on my knee.

'I know,' I said and tears filled my eyes.

I heard the clink of beer bottles from the hall and then Pappa and Anja stood in the room with a tray of sandwiches and glasses and bottles.

'I thought you might be a bit hungry,' Anja said and smiled at Janne.

While we ate, awkwardly balancing the plates on our knees, I felt like a teenager bringing a boyfriend home for the first time. Everybody was far too polite and well behaved. I wanted to take Janne away and talk to him alone. When I watched him sipping from a glass of beer and eating, being careful not to spill anything or talk with his mouth full, I realised I was glad he was here. I'd missed him. Pappa was biting into his sandwiches in silence, watching Janne. Anja had engaged him in a conversation about world politics and I guessed Pappa had difficulty following the Swedish.

'Beer tastes good,' I said to Pappa in Finnish.

He smiled at me. He looked sad and stately somehow today. He was wearing his dark trousers and a white shirt with a black tie. Mourning clothes.

'Did you organise the flowers?' I asked.

'Yes, Eeva, we did. And the pastor was here too.'

'Oh, was he nice?'

'Yes, well, you know I don't go much on that stuff but for man of the cloth he was a decent sort of a jätkä.'

I laughed. It was just like Pappa to call a pastor a 'bloke'.

'What's funny,' Anja said in Swedish. I hadn't noticed their conversation had stopped. Janne was looking at me too.

'Oh, just something Pappa called the pastor,' I said.

Both Anja and Janne looked gravely at Pappa. He coughed and looked embarrassed.

'Oh, nothing bad, just you know, Anja,' I said. 'Never mind. Janne, would you like to look around town? I've got my car here. How did you get here by the way?' How strange that I hadn't asked that before.

'I flew with Finnair. Straight from Arlanda to Tampere.'

That must have cost him a lot of money, I thought. 'Pappa, I thought I'd take Janne to see Tampere,' I said in Finnish.

'Why don't you show him Saara's flat as well?' Anja said.

I looked at her. She was looking smart too. She wore a long red cardigan over a pair of black trousers and black boots. I thought I needed some more clothes. If Janne was to stay until the funeral, there was no point in me going back to Stockholm.

'You two could stay there, you know,' Anja said in Finnish. 'What do you think Pappa? Don't you think Saara would have wanted that?'

We were all silent for a while. I was thinking about the cellar and the lift and then about Saara by the window in the kitchen. Janne glanced from me to Anja to Pappa. I patted his hand and shook my head. Finally Pappa raised his eyes to mine and said in Finnish, 'I think Anja is right, but it's up to you, Eppu. I'll pay for a hotel room if you prefer. I can see how you can't stay here,' he added and smiled his sad smile again.

'What's up?' Janne said.

'It's OK,' I said to him in Swedish and then to Pappa, 'I'll think about it. It would be lovely, but I'm not sure if I can...'

Pappa got up from his seat and dug in his pockets for a key. He handed the small piece of metal to me. It felt as if it weighed a ton in my palm. I closed my fingers over the key and looking up at Pappa said, 'Kiitos, Pappa.'

'No need to thank me, just do what feels right, I will not be angry or upset either way.' His blue-grey eyes smiled at me. I wondered if he would always make me feel like a little girl. Had it been the same for him with Saara? I put the key in my jeans pocket and squeezed Janne's hand, 'C'mon, let's go.'

The drizzle had stopped and Tampere looked prettier than it had that morning. I drove past the Näsinneula tower, showed Janne Pispala, the view of the Lakes, then drove into the centre of town and pointed out the Finlayson factory, the rapids and the statues. I took him to Stockmann's and bought him a coffee in the cafeteria.

'Over there is the train station and it smells like piss inside,' I said. We were sitting at a table next to the one I'd sat at a few hours before. Now the place was half full, with people chatting and laughing with each other. A few people glanced over to us when they heard Swedish being spoken. Janne looked at me over his coffee cup and smiled, 'Piss, eh?'

I looked down and smiled, 'It's true.'

'It may be true, Fröken Litmunen, but that word is not one I've ever heard you use before. I bet you don't teach that to your pupils at the Language Centre!'

I leant across and kissed Janne on the cheek. He took hold of my face and kissed my lips instead.

'I've missed you, Eeva,' he said when he released me from his grip. He smelled freshly shaven, though he couldn't have been. He was clean-looking, and with his fair complexion even a little stubble looked downy, as if he was still a teenager, not a man over forty. I wondered why he had never married. How strange that we had never discussed such things. I sat back down opposite him and smiled, 'Me too.'

My chest felt tight with affection for Janne and I said, 'Do you want to see Saara's flat?'

Janne's green eyes flashed a warning, 'You sure?'

'Yes,' I said and put my hand on his, 'Pappa gave me a key.'

'OK, if you're absolutely sure.'

'Yes I am,' I said and put my Ulster back on.

Twenty-one

Stockholm 1974

'IT'S ALREADY the fifteenth of November. In Tampere we would have snow by now,' Mamma said. She was leaning over the kitchen table looking out of the window at the trees growing on an island of rocky ground in the distance, between the blocks of flats. She was wearing a red jumper and a brown skirt, which made her look very slim.

I was sitting at the table reading a letter from Kaija. Mamma was right, I thought, it did look cold out there. The leaves were still yellow, though many had fallen off and been taken by the wind.

'But we're not in Tampere now and it's not that cold,' Anja said. She was standing in the kitchen, dressed in her yellow coat and faded jeans.

'Anja, please wear the hat as I ask,' Mamma said.

'But nobody else will be wearing a hat!' Anja looked miserable.

'Your friends have lived here all their lives and are used to not wearing a hat. You're not, so you will catch a cold if you don't wear a hat.' Mamma sounded less angry now.

I looked at the parking lot outside. It was nearly empty. Most of the men, who drove the cars, were out at work. It was midday on a Friday and Anja and I had the day off school. I couldn't understand why Anja was arguing, I knew as soon as she was out of the flat she'd take her hat off anyway. She always did in Tampere, even when there was snow on the ground and the wind was so cold that it burned your ears. I had never had flu, but then I was stronger than Anja. Once she had a temperature so high that Mamma called the doctor out. Anja had shivered and said she was very cold. Mamma had given her three blankets but they hadn't been enough. The doctor had listened to Anja's chest and Mamma had looked worried. For a long time afterwards Mamma kept asking Anja how she was feeling. She'd only have to say she had a headache and Mamma would send her to bed and let her stay home from school.

Whenever I had a headache Mamma just gave me an aspirin and said the walk to school would do me good. I wondered if it was because of being ill that Anja got whatever she wanted from both Mamma and Pappa. I turned my face back to the kitchen and heard Mamma say, 'Alright Anja, but take the hat with you, just in case.'

Anja slammed the door shut and I picked up my letter, 'I'm going to write a reply to Kaija straightaway,' I said.

Mamma had started peeling potatoes. She was singing along to a Swedish pop song on the radio. Kaija's letter was very short. It was written on one sheet of blue paper with a picture of a horse and its foal eating grass in the upper corner.

'Hei Eeva,

I heard about the ice-hockey match. It was a terrible result, but next time we'll win! Or do you support Sweden now? Here it snowed last week but the snow has melted now and it's wet and horrible. I'm wearing my winter clothes already. Does it ever snow there?

Kaija.

P.S. Everybody at school says hello.

K.'

I sat down at my desk and took a pad of letter writing paper, which Mamma had bought before we left Tampere. It had no pictures on it, just thin lines to show where to write. I looked out of the window. The boys on their bikes were out. They were not wearing hats either, and their hair blew off their faces in the wind. I saw one of them was Tomas. He was with two other boys from my class, Mikael and Stefan. Mikael had stuck his tongue out at me on my first day, but since then he'd not teased me so much. I watched them while thinking about what to write to Kaija. Then Tomas looked up, smiled and waved to me. I waved back, my face feeling hot. I went to lie on my bed to be out of sight. Had he seen me blush? I heard the boys shout and laugh through an open side window. I couldn't tell what they were saying and was afraid to get up. They'd see me again through the large window and think I was doing it on purpose to attract their attention. After a while, when the voices had trailed off a bit, I sat up on my bed and slowly got up to look out. The path was empty. I put my elbows on the table and rested my head in my hands. I wished I could tell Kaija about Tomas, but didn't know how to in a letter.

'Eeva, I'm off now,' Mamma said. She was standing in the doorway. She had on her brown coat and her hair was tied back. She was wearing red lipstick.

'Where are you going?' I said. I had a pen in my hand and had managed to write two lines:

Dear Kaija,

I don't support Sweden. Not yet anyway. It hasn't snowed here yet. Mamma says it usually does but not always. Today it's cold.

'I'm off to my Swedish class and then we're going to the cinema to see a Swedish film,' Mamma said. She was looking down, fiddling with something in her handbag. 'I forgot to remind Pappa, but I've peeled the potatoes. They're in a pan of water on the stove. You can have them with sausages. Anja can cook it for you and Pappa.'

'Hejdå,' I said and turned back to my letter.

'Hejdå,' Mamma replied.

I was alone in the flat. I went into the kitchen and looked at the pan full of peeled potatoes and water. The table was laid out, too, for three people. I looked at the clock and saw it was already four in the afternoon; Pappa would be home in an hour. I wondered what time Anja was supposed to be back. I'd forgotten to ask Mamma.

The living room looked large and empty. I went to sit on the sofa, at the end closest to the TV where Pappa usually sat. I put my arms along the back of the seat as he always did, then pulled my feet up and lay across the sofa, with my legs dangling over the armrest. I saw the ceiling was painted very white and had a thin crack along the middle. I imagined the people upstairs in their sitting room, on their sofa. What if the ceiling gave in and they came crashing down on top of me? All that concrete! Dust and people's legs and arms. Screams would fill our silent flat. Then there'd be a gaping hole. Perhaps the small boy, who I'd often seen on the staircase, would peer down at me and at the mess.

The front door opened and in came Anja.

'What are you doing?' she said, taking off her boots and coat in the hall. She came and stood over me. She smelled of cigarettes and the cold outside.

'Nothing, just…' I sat up.

'Where's Mamma?' she said walking into the empty kitchen. I heard her lift the lid on the pan of potatoes just like I had.

'Language class and then cinema.'

Anja came back into the living room, 'Cinema?'

'Yes, she said to tell Pappa and that you'll cook for us.'

Anja was staring at me, 'What time is she back then?'

'I don't know, she didn't say. Anyway, I'm writing a letter, Mamma said there are sausages too.' I left Anja standing in the living room.

I was on my fourth sheet of writing paper. Three unfinished letters were crumpled up in my rubbish bin under the desk. There was so much that I wanted to tell Kaija, but I didn't know where to begin.

'Hello, Eeva!' Pappa said. He was standing at the door in his socks and work clothes, blue shiny trousers and a blue shirt. I jumped up. I hadn't heard him come in.

'Hello,' I said.

'Where's everybody?' Pappa sounded hoarse and his eyes were small and angry.

'Anja is in her room.'

'And Mamma?' Pappa had straightened himself up and crossed his arms over his chest.

'Oh, she's gone to the cinema after her Swedish class,' I said. Pappa didn't say anything, just glared at me. 'She forgot to tell you,' I said and coughed. My throat felt dry and I wished Pappa wouldn't stare at me like that.

'What about food – who's going to cook?' Pappa said after a while.

'Mamma said Anja would.' I felt as if I wanted to cry.

'She's left the house in a mess, there's dust everywhere, it's like a pigsty in here!' Pappa was nearly shouting. I didn't say anything, just looked at the floor and at Pappa's socks. After a long time, Pappa turned around and banged my door shut. I heard him open Anja's. Without knocking. Mamma and I always knocked before we went into her room. She said it was her right to decide who she talked to. Pappa never came into our rooms, so I guess he didn't know about the knocking.

I heard Pappa say something about food and Mamma to Anja but I didn't hear her reply. Then Pappa shouted, 'Get off that lazy backside of yours and do as I tell you.' There was a silence and then he said, 'I'm warning you Anja!'

'Cook your own bloody food,' Anja shouted.

'That's it!'

'What's that?' Anja shouted even louder. Then I heard her door slam shut.

'No dinner for you then!' Pappa shouted in the corridor. My hand shook and I put the pen on the table to stop it knocking against it. 'And don't even try to come into the kitchen to help yourself! You are to go without food today. That should teach you a lesson!'

'Ja, ja' Anja shouted from inside her room.

Then I heard Pappa walk down the corridor. He took something out of the kitchen and went to sit down on the sofa in the lounge. I listened for sounds of cooking, but there was nothing. Anja was playing music in her room. It was her latest favourite, Ted Gärdestad. I liked him too. He was a new Swedish pop star and he was only eighteen. There was a picture of him on the album sleeve. He was smiling, his hair flowing in the wind. He had his hands in the pockets of his bomber jacket. Anja said he was born in Dalarna, in northern Sweden, but he lived in Stockholm now and was very rich and famous.

'And he doesn't have a girlfriend yet!' Anja told me.

I heard Anja singing the words of the song. I wondered if I should try to do the food instead. That might calm Pappa down a bit. I got up from my desk and knocked on her door. She turned the record player off.

'Oh, it's you,' she said and went to put the LP on again.

'Who's going to cook?' I said closing the door behind me.

'I'm not hungry,' she said and started singing again. She was sitting on her bed, reading the words from the back of the LP cover. Ted Gärdestad in his bomber jacket was smiling at me, hiding Anja's face. 'Close the door,' she said when I turned to leave.

I went into the kitchen. It was getting dark outside and

the room was empty. I put on the lights and turned the electric plate on underneath the potatoes. Then I went to the living room. Pappa was sitting on the sofa drinking Koskenkorva vodka out of a coffee cup. His large shoulders were bent over his knees. He looked up at me but said nothing.

'I've put the potatoes on,' I said.

'Oh,' he said and went back to staring at his cup. He hadn't even changed from his work clothes.

I found the sausages in the fridge and put on a pan of water for them. There was cucumber too, so I cut it up in neat slices and put a little vinegar and dill on top of them. I'd helped Mamma and Saara cook many times but I'd never cooked a whole meal before. The potatoes were boiling fast. When I lifted the lid it was hot and I dropped it. I found the oven mitt and picked up the lid again. The potatoes looked ready, so I drained the water out. It was very hot and I burned myself when a little of the liquid splashed over my bare wrist. It hurt and I ran cold water over my arm.

Pappa appeared at the kitchen doorway, 'Oh, you're cooking?'

'Yes Pappa,' I said. I felt very grown-up not complaining about the pain and cooking for him.

'Can you do it?' he said. He looked from the pan of potatoes to the table.

'Yes, I can. I've seen Mamma do it many times,' I said.

'That's no guarantee!'

Pappa turned his back to me and I heard him say, 'Saatanan akka.' He must be drunk, I thought, to swear in front of me like that. Or perhaps he didn't think I'd hear him call Mamma 'a fucking woman'. Saying the words in my

215

mind made me feel hot on my cheeks.

'Anja is not allowed to eat,' he shouted from the lounge, 'so take away her plate.'

I put the sausages in the other pan of boiling water and waited five minutes. I looked at the table and the three sets of plates, knives and forks. It felt bad to take Anja's away. Perhaps she'd eaten something at her friend's house, or at the youth club, or wherever she'd been that afternoon. I hoped she'd been telling the truth when she said she wasn't hungry. I called out to Pappa that food was ready.

Pappa never talked much while he was eating. But he was even quieter with just the two of us sitting at the round table, looking at the rain outside. It was dark now, but you could see the drops against the orange glow of the street-lights. He'd brought his cup and the bottle of vodka with him to the table. I asked him if he wanted a beer with the sausages.

'Mind your own business, I'm drinking what I'm drinking,' he said. He didn't look at me, just at his plate of sausages and potatoes. He was eating with his fork, not bothering to use the knife even to cut up the skin of the sausages. Mamma would have told him off for that if she'd been eating with us, I thought.

I didn't dare to say anything, though. I wasn't at all hungry but ate what I'd put on my plate in case Pappa would be angry to see me waste the food.

Halfway through his plateful he said, 'Salt, did you put any salt in the potatoes?'

I couldn't remember so I said, 'No, I don't think so, Pappa.'

He got up and said, 'I suppose your Mamma told you not

to! You bloody women always cook without salt.' He looked at me with small eyes when he sprinkled a lot of salt on his potatoes. I didn't say anything. 'She doesn't know how to cook either, your Mamma, saatanan akka!'

'Yes, Pappa,' I said. I wished he wouldn't swear so much. And I wished he'd stop drinking the vodka before it made him ill.

'Saatanan akka!' he said again. I looked at my plate and not at him.

During the rest of the meal he didn't speak, he didn't even say anything when Anja came in and took a carton of milk from the fridge and poured herself a glass. He just looked at her angrily. I felt sorry for her then.

After he'd eaten, Pappa got up. He took the coffee cup and the vodka bottle with him and went into the lounge.

'You might as well do the dishes, Eeva. And don't stay up late,' he said. His voice was very deep.

I heard him put the TV on when I started to clear the table.

I didn't hear Mamma come home. I'd already gone to bed, but later I had a bad dream. Someone was chasing me and I screamed but couldn't run. My legs didn't work. All I could manage was a slow walk. I didn't see who was behind me, but they were running fast. I woke up with a start.

There were noises coming from Mamma's and Pappa's bedroom. I got up and tiptoed to my door. It was slightly ajar. There was a light on somewhere in the flat. I opened the door wider and listened. I heard Mamma's voice. She sounded

217

upset. Then the light flickered and I heard a crash.

'Please, Mikko, please don't,' Mamma said. She was crying. I opened the door and slowly crept along the corridor. Anja's door was shut, but the door to Mamma's and Pappa's bedroom was open wide. I looked at the crumpled sheets on their bed; the blankets were on the floor. I heard Mamma's cries and followed the noise to the living room. The scene made me freeze. Mamma was lying on the swirly carpet. Her hair was a mess and her nightie was ripped at the neck, revealing a bare, pale-coloured shoulder. Pappa was on all fours on top of her, holding tightly onto her wrists above her head. Mamma didn't notice me, her eyes were closed and she was sobbing. Pappa was doing something with his flies. A scream escaped from between my lips. Suddenly I felt Anja behind me. She took hold of my arm. Mamma, too, was startled by the noise. Quickly, so quickly that I couldn't remember how it happened afterwards, Mamma, in her torn night gown scampered out from underneath Pappa and fled into the bathroom. Anja and I followed, and once inside, Mamma quickly locked the door, while Anja took two leaps across the bath tub to turn the key on the second entrance to the toilet. Anja was wearing her pink dressing gown and the back of her hair was knotted.

Mamma sat down on the toilet seat. She was shivering. The bright light hurt my eyes. 'What's happened?' I said. Half of Mamma's face was red, her left eye was swollen and she had a deep cut on her bottom lip. Blood was slowly trickling from the cut.

I started crying.

'Shhh, it's alright, Eeva, rakas,' she said hugging me.

Anja stood in front of us, arms crossed over her chest, her long hair loose around her pale face, 'What you need to do is phone the police.'

Mamma was stroking my head on her lap, 'It's the middle of the night.' I saw there were black marks on the inside of her thigh.

'Just go and phone. I'll defend you if he comes close,' Anja said.

I looked at Anja. She was behaving like a grown up.

Suddenly, there was a thud on the door.

'What are you all doing huddling inside a bloody toilet?'

Mamma looked at Anja, I felt her tummy muscles flex. She was squeezing me harder against her. I stopped breathing.

'Is it a feminist conference?' Pappa was shouting through the door. There was a pause, and then, 'saatanan akat!' Mamma covered my ears. Her hands were shaking.

'Go away, you bastard!' Anja yelled. Mamma looked at her and moved her head slowly from side to side. Anja stared back but said nothing. Then we heard footsteps in the hall. Then it was quiet again. Anja sat down on the floor, wrapping her pink nightie tight around her knees. She looked cold and thin. Mamma stood up and took a large towel from a hook on the back of the door. She wrapped it around Anja.

'It'll be alright, it'll be alright, rakas,' she was saying to Anja, hugging and rocking her like a big baby.

Then we heard footsteps in the hall again and the clang of a coat hanger. The front door slammed shut.

'We'll wait for ten minutes,' Mamma said. Anja had her wristwatch on, and we all watched the little arm move second by second. When the time was up, Mamma opened the door and went outside. Anja and I waited. We were both squatting on the floor. Mamma came back and said, 'Go to your rooms and get dressed. And pack a bag, we are going to stay at Irena's for the night.' Mamma picked up the phone in the hall. The blood on her face had dried.

We were standing under the canopy of the front door downstairs waiting for the taxi Mamma had ordered, when Anja asked how we could afford it. Mamma said she'd got some money from Pappa.

'What, you took it out of his wallet?' Anja said. Her eyes were wide.

'Yes,' Mamma said and smiled for the first time that night.

Outside it was still raining and very cold. I had my canvas bag slung across my shoulders. I'd never been to Irena's house. I wondered what her home looked like and what she would think of us all arriving in the middle of the night. I'd not been out this late since the night we arrived in the flat. It seemed a very long time ago. I looked over to Anja. She had her arm around Mamma.

'Promise me you'll never let Pappa do that to you again,' she said.

Mamma didn't have time to reply because just then a car pulled in front of us.

Twenty-two

THE TAXI driver left us standing in the dark outside a strange block of flats.

'What if she's not at home?' I said.

Mamma looked at me and pressed a button on the door. We waited. Then a woman in rollers and a long green house-coat came down a staircase. She peered through the glass in the door. I didn't see it was Irena until she opened the outside door and was hugging Mamma and Anja. Mamma moved away from her when she came close to kiss her.

'My God! Kirsti, what has happen?' Irena said in her funny Swedish. She moved away from Mamma to get a better look at her.

Mamma looked at us and then at Irena. She said nothing.

'Come, come,' Irena said and pushed the three of us towards the staircase and then through an open door on the first floor. Irena's flat looked the same as ours but was smaller. The living room was open to the hall here too. But there were even fewer pieces of furniture in Irena's lounge than there were in ours. Irena fussed with our bags in the hall and then said, 'Go in there girls.'

Both Anja and I went into the lounge and stood in the middle of the dark room. The only light was a lamp with a wide-brimmed yellow shade in the corner.

'Sit, sit,' Irena said. Then she took Mamma's arm and led her out of the room.

'Where do you think we'll sleep?' I asked Anja.

Anja looked down at the shabby sofa she was sitting on. 'On this, I guess,' she said and took a deep breath. Then she yawned, opening her mouth wide. Looking at her made me want to yawn too. I felt very sleepy and leant back into the sofa. It was covered in a stripy woollen fabric, which I was sure would itch our bare legs and arms if we had to lie on it in our nighties. The other piece of furniture was an old leather chair in the corner of the room. On the wall opposite were shelves full of books. Next to it stood a glass cabinet containing vases and tumblers made of coloured glass. One large bowl looked as if it was crystal, because it shone in the dark. On the wall next to us was a large wooden cross. Next to that was a picture of a woman in a headscarf.

'That's the Virgin Mary,' Anja said.

I was surprised to find Irena had a cross on her wall. She didn't seem like the people who went to church every Sunday in Finland. They were serious and didn't laugh like Irena did all the time. And they wore brown or grey clothes, not red dresses with high-heeled shoes. I thought if you were religious you weren't allowed to wear make-up either. Irena always wore lipstick.

'Girls, you sleep here, Ja?' Irena said. Her Swedish was

still very bad. Mamma said it was because Polish was a very difficult language to translate into Swedish. Irena was carrying sheets and blankets in her arms. Mamma was behind her. She had a glass in her hand and she looked less sad now.

'You'll be OK here. You can make up a "Sisterbed" just like at Saara's', she said in Finnish. Irena looked at her and Mamma explained in Swedish, 'They are OK.'

I looked over to Anja. She'd taken the bedding from Irena and was spreading a sheet over the sofa. I thought she'd complain, but she said nothing, she just gave me a blanket and said, 'Put the duvet cover over this, and here's the pillow-case.'

'We'll be fine here, don't worry,' she said in Swedish and smiled at Mamma and Irena.

'You're good girls, I'll come and say goodnight later. The bathroom is there in the hall,' Mamma said and followed Irena into the kitchen.

I realised Mamma must have been to Irena's place before. Just like I went to see Harriet after school, I thought. I looked at the sofa, it was smaller than Saara's, but Anja was already lying at one end.

'It's just one night, Eeva, c'mon, it'll be alright.'

'Are you not brushing your teeth?' I said.

'No, I already did them at home,' she said. She closed her eyes and then opened them again. 'Can't you sleep?' she said.

I looked at her. She didn't look at all sleepy, her eyes were bright and blue, and her face looked angular and very pale. Her hair wasn't a mess anymore. She must have brushed it before leaving the flat. 'Let's sleep,' she said.

'Mamma said she'd come and kiss us goodnight,' I said.

'Oh, she's probably forgotten.'

'Anja, what did Pappa do to Mamma?'

'You saw her face, he hit her.'

'I saw red marks on her thighs.'

Anja said nothing for a while, just looked at me.

'And you said to Mamma not to let him do that again, why did you say that?'

'Because he's been doing it for ages, that's why!' Anja sat up in her end of the bed. She leant closer to me and whispered, 'I can't believe you haven't noticed. He gets drunk and then hits her or worse...'

'Worse?' I whispered.

Anja looked over to the hall where you could see the light from the half-open kitchen door. I heard voices, too, but couldn't make out what Mamma or Irena were saying. 'Pappa raped her!' she whispered. Her face was very close to mine now and I felt the hot air from her mouth on my face when she spoke.

I stared at her. I'd seen a documentary on television about prostitutes in Stockholm. The reporter said they had been raped. I didn't really know what it meant. The women had marks on their bodies so I thought they'd been beaten up, but then they said the men had forced the women to have sex. It was very frightening, but the women were walking the streets at night. I'd never heard normal people being raped in their homes. And Pappa? How could Pappa be so horrible? He wasn't a monster like the men in the programme.

'Tonight?' I said.

'Yes, tonight and before.'

'When?'

'Oh, a couple of weeks ago, after the party, remember?'

'But are you sure?'

'Yes.' Anja gave me a quick look and yawned again. Then she lay back onto the sofa and said, 'Let's sleep now, I'm tired.' She closed her eyes.

I couldn't sleep. I looked at the picture of the Virgin Mary. I wondered if she could protect us. Perhaps that's why Irena had her hanging on the wall to protect her from being raped by Lew. The voices from the kitchen were like listening to a record, one of the slow songs Ted Gärdestad sang.

I woke up to someone kicking me. First I didn't know where I was and then I realised it was Anja's foot next to my thigh. I looked around the room. It was different in the morning light. There was a shape lying on a mattress on the floor. It was Mamma lying with her back to me, a blanket wrapped tightly around her. The blonde hair was lying neatly around her head. I looked closely at her. She wasn't moving! Or breathing! Then I saw her back lift slightly. She was breathing slowly in and out. I closed my eyes and thought about what Anja had told me. What had happened to Pappa? Had he turned into Herr Lahtelainen? Would he too start throwing furniture out of our flat and be sent to a mad house? And was that what he had done to Satu's Mamma? I opened my eyes and looked over to Anja. Perhaps she'd misunderstood, or was making it all up. That wasn't the first time.

I looked around the room. There were photos in picture frames on the shelf with the books. A man with a little boy was smiling at me. It was Lew, with their son. Mamma told me he was five and very clever. Then I heard voices from a room next door. A woman was talking to a child. The language was strange, it had a lot of s-sounds and Irena spoke it very quickly. The little boy answered with one or two words. Then I heard him giggle.

'Eeva, are you awake?' Mamma whispered. She'd turned around and was leaning on her elbows. Her face caught my breath. The left cheek and eye were very red and swollen. It must be so sore, I thought, and looked at Anja, still sleeping at the other end of the sofa.

'Yes, Mamma,' I whispered and tried to smile.

Mamma got up, took my hand and led me into the kitchen. It was exactly where our kitchen was, between the hall and a long corridor. The table was square and smaller. From the window you could see out to the sea.

'Lew and Irena are taking us to Djurgården later. If it doesn't rain, we'll have a picnic in the park there,' Mamma said.

We spent two nights sleeping on Irena's sofa. On the Saturday, after we came home from Djurgåren, where we'd had a picnic and I'd skimmed stones across the large pond with Lew and the little boy, Kiran, Mamma phoned Pappa.

'Mikko, it's Kirsti,' Mamma said.

'Eeva, let's go outside to play on the swings,' Anja said.

'No, we're staying another night,' I heard Mamma say when we closed the door. She was holding the telephone a little away from her ear and her hands were shaking.

'What do you think Pappa will do?' I asked Anja. We were walking slowly down the stairs.

'He can't do anything. If he does it again, Mamma will phone the police,' she said. She was leaning against the wall in the stairway.

'Do you think she's finished by now?' I said after we'd been standing there doing nothing for a while.

'Yep, let's go back in,' Anja said. She was looking very serious again. She'd been different ever since last night.

When we rang the doorbell, Irena came to the door. Lew and Mamma were sitting in the kitchen and I saw Mamma had been crying. Half of her face still looked red, although some of it was more blue than red. Lew looked at Anja and I and said, 'You want watch TV?' He smiled when I looked at Anja and saw her nod. When Lew left the kitchen, Anja went over to Mamma and said, 'You'll phone the police if he does it again, won't you Mamma?'

Mamma nodded and started crying. Anja put her arms around her. She made very little noise and I went over and hugged her too.

'Mamma, let's not go back to the flat. Let's stay here!' I said. Both Mamma and Anja looked at me.

'We can't do that, stupid!' Anja said.

'Shh, Anja!' Mamma said. She patted my hand and said, 'Eeva, rakas, we can't stay here. Irena and Lew have been very kind to us but there isn't enough room for us here. Besides, there are all of our things, and...' Mamma started crying again and put her hand over her mouth.

'See what you've done now!' Anja hissed.

I started crying. 'I didn't mean to,' I said.

Mamma looked up to me and said, ' Don't worry, Eeva, everything will be fine.'

'Girls help you, ja?' Irena said. I hadn't noticed that she'd come into the kitchen too. Mamma lifted her head and looked at Anja first and then me. She patted our arms. 'Yes, they are good girls,' she said and nodded at Irena. Then she dabbed her eyes and said, 'It'll be OK, you'll see.'

Anja turned around and went to the lounge. I followed her and we watched TV for the rest of the evening.

On Sunday morning Lew drove us back home in his light blue Lada. Irena sat on the front seat and chatted to Mamma all the way to Rinkeby. On the fast road from Sundbyberg other cars were overtaking us all the time. I wished we'd been in Pappa's new Volvo. When we pulled up to the car park and got our bags from the back of the car, Irena said, 'You want me to come too?' She pointed at the covered walkway. Our front door was the fourth one from the staircase. I saw Pappa's car, which was parked in its usual place. Mamma had her scarf tied around her face. It hid the marks around her eye. 'No, Irena, we'll be OK,' Mamma said. They hugged and Irena went back to the car. We waved as they drove away.

Anja, Mamma and I walked up to the second floor. I wished Mamma had let Lew and Irena come with us. Mamma opened the front door with her key. Inside there was silence. Both the doors to the bathroom were open wide and there was a smell of burnt dust. The sun was shining into the lounge from the large window. There were dirty cups and plates on the glass table and the ashtray was full. The bottle of Koskenkorva was empty.

'I think we'll need to have a clear up,' Mamma said.

'Is Pappa at home?' I said.

'I don't know,' Mamma said and walked into their bedroom.

Anja went into her room.

'He must be having a walk,' Mamma said and went into the kitchen. She put on her apron and started washing up. I went into my room and lay on the bed. I was very tired. I kept waking up at Irena's, with Anja's kicking and the strange sounds of their flat. The little boy had cried in the night, and both Lew and Irena had gone into his bedroom. They sang a song, which made me fall asleep again, but I woke early when I heard the boy and Irena giggle in the kitchen. I wondered what was going to happen when Pappa came home. He would be sorry for the horrible things he'd done to Mamma when he saw her face.

I went to sit at my desk, hoping to see Tomas and the other boy outside, but instead I saw Pappa walking up the path towards our block. I was suddenly scared. He was carrying a plastic Systembolaget bag. That meant more vodka. His face looked dirty and he had stubble on his chin. His hair was a mess and it blew across his face. He didn't look up at me. I followed him until he disappeared behind the corner of the house. Then I got up and went into the kitchen. Mamma wasn't there. I looked over to the lounge; she wasn't there either. She must be in the bathroom.

The front door opened and at the very same time Mamma came out of the bathroom.

'Ah, the Gypsies have returned,' Pappa said. He didn't look at me. He took his coat and shoes off and went into the lounge with the plastic bag. Mamma said nothing. She wiped

229

her hands on her apron and went back into the kitchen. Pappa sat down on the sofa and took a newspaper out of the bag. He put his feet on the glass table and started reading. I stood at the doorway and watched him. He looked up and said, 'What do you want?'

Pappa looked as if he hadn't washed all weekend. His socks were the same ones he'd been wearing the night I cooked for him. They were thin and shiny. One big toe was nearly showing through the worn out end.

Mamma came out of the kitchen and went into their bedroom. I could hear her opening cupboards and drawers. I went over to see what she was doing. She had her pillow, two rolls of clean sheets and some blankets in her arms. I couldn't see her face and she didn't see me, so I stepped aside when she came out.

'Ah, Eeva, can you help me, please. Take this,' she said and handed me the sheets.

'What are you doing?' I said in a low voice. I didn't want Pappa to hear us.

Mamma just passed me and went into Anja's bedroom. Anja was lying on her bed reading a magazine. She go up and said, 'I've cleared a space on the floor, Mamma.'

'Good girl,' Mamma said.

Anja's bedroom had never looked so tidy. All her schoolbooks were neatly stacked on her desk and her LPs and singles were arranged next to the record player on the floor. None of her clothes were thrown about as they usually were.

'Are you sleeping here?' I asked Mamma.

Anja said, 'Yeah, stupid.'

Mamma turned to look at me and said, 'Just for a couple of nights.'

I didn't want to ask anything more. I was embarrassed to talk about what Anja had told me. What if she hadn't told the truth? Mamma would be angry with me for using such words about Pappa. And she would be sad that I'd think Pappa would do such a horrible thing to her. I looked at Mamma making a mattress out of two blankets and covering it all with a sheet, then placing her pillow at one end and folding the upper sheet neatly underneath a third blanket.

'This will be just fine for me,' she said. Just like camping, isn't it girls?' She smiled at Anja and then at me.

That week there were fewer fights. Pappa was out a lot, Mamma told me he went for walks. I saw him coming back but he didn't look up at my window, not even once. The rest of the time he sat on the sofa reading a paper and drinking Koskenkorva. I didn't dare to speak to him. Neither did Anja. She came home from school and went out to the youth club in the evening. At least that's what she told Mamma.

When Pappa came home, Mamma asked me if I wanted to go for a walk. We went out whether it was raining or not, whether it was warm or cold. I got to know all the paths around our block of flats and they looked less frightening, even in the dark. Mamma asked me about school and I told her about Tomas, Harriet and Fröken Andersson. The class was as unruly as ever and when I told Mamma about the pupils throwing things at Fröken Andersson, Mamma said, 'You don't do that, do you, Eeva?' Her eyes were wide and sad. I said, 'No, of course I don't, Mamma.'

She didn't talk about Pappa or the Koskenkorva he was drinking. I didn't talk about him either. But she talked to Anja, because I could hear their voices in the evening when we'd all gone to bed, leaving Pappa alone on the sofa in the lounge. In the morning, Mamma cleared up the cups and bottles from the lounge after Pappa had left for work and before she went to her language class.

On Saturday morning, after I'd had breakfast on my own in the kitchen, I saw Mamma and Pappa sitting opposite each other in the lounge. I was on my way to Harriet's house. I jumped up when I saw them. I didn't think anyone else was up. They both looked at me, and I said, 'I'm going to Harriet's.'

Pappa looked away and said nothing, but Mamma smiled a little and said, 'Alright, Eeva.'

When I came home the flat was empty and I went into my bedroom to read The Building of Jalna by Mazo de la Roche. I'd started reading the book after coming home from Irena's. I'd found it on the bookcase in the lounge. Mamma said there was a series of Jalna books and when we next visited Tampere we could buy more of them.

In the afternoon Mamma came to my bedroom and said, 'Can you come into the lounge, please?' She looked very serious. I followed her down the corridor and into the lounge where Anja and Pappa were already sitting. Mamma sat down in one of the comfy chairs and for a long time no one said anything.

Then Mamma said, 'You can start, it was your idea.'

Pappa looked at her in disgust. I was sitting on the plush sofa, with my feet touching the brightly coloured carpet. Anja was next to me, leaning against the high back of the seat. I looked over to the balcony where I'd seen Anja smoking. She'd been doing it every day since coming home from Irena's, after school when Mamma was out at her language classes and before Pappa came home. I thought he must smell the tobacco, but Anja told me she didn't care what Pappa said or did. 'He's a bastard, why should I listen to him?'

'Right. What we've decided to do is,' Pappa began. He shot an angry look at Mamma. She'd been crying. Then he continued, 'Mamma and I are going to be divorced.'

'What a surprise,' Anja said.

'Thank you, Anja! That may have decided it for you, then.'

'Decided what?' Anja said. How I admired, and feared, her courage. Pappa could explode any minute and hit her across the face, and then me, and then Mamma, again.

'Mamma and I...'

'Not me, this is not my idea,' Mamma interrupted.

Pappa didn't look at her, but said, 'We want you to decide which of us you want to live with.'

Silence.

Mamma and Pappa were looking at Anja. She was sitting twiddling her fingers and admiring her red-and-white platform boots. You could see the stripy heels underneath her flared jeans. Before the fight, Pappa had forbidden Anja to wear clothes like that. He said her jeans were too long and had dirty hems. 'You look like a bloody clown and a beggar,' he'd told her. That had started another row because Mamma had given Anja the money for the clothes.

It was nearly dinnertime on a Saturday afternoon in November. The sun was out but weak and only a few thin strips of light came through the Venetian blinds. Specs of dust were dancing in the rays. I wondered if Pappa was going to complain about the state of the house, or whether he'd not bother now they were divorcing.

'Well?' he said, looking challengingly at Anja. 'You're the eldest; you go first.'

'I'll live with Mamma,' Anja said quietly.

Now Pappa turned to me, smiling, 'And Eppu – are you going to live with Pappa?'

I was trying to remember when he stopped calling me 'Pappa's girl'. I didn't dare look at him now. I couldn't speak. I looked sideways at Anja. She had her eyes on her boots. Mamma was in one of the comfy chairs. She held a piece of toilet paper, worn to shreds, and was fiddling with the pieces. She lifted her eyes and they met mine. She nodded to me, and I whispered, 'Mamma'.

There was another silence, then the sound of Pappa sucking in a breath. The whole of his body moved. First his large chest lifted and then collapsed.

'Well, you've done it now,' he said. 'Don't come running to me when she can't look after you, and you're on the streets with no money to your name. And you needn't think you can stay here – this flat is paid for with my bloody hard work – she'll have to find a hellhole for you somewhere else.' He got up and left. I heard him sit heavily on the bed in his room. Anja straightened her back on the sofa and looked up to Mamma. Mamma shook her head, silencing her. I just wanted to cry but there were no tears. Mamma went to the kitchen. I followed Anja down the corridor to her bedroom, the room furthest from where Pappa was. I didn't dare look in as we passed the open door. But from the corner of my eye I could see his feet at the end of the bed.

'It'll be so cool to live with Mamma,' Anja said when we were safely in her bedroom.

'What's going to happen?' I asked.

'He'll have to leave.'

'But, he said…'

'Oh, he'll have to – it's the law.'

'How do you know?'

'I just do. Anyway, I'm out of here, I'm meeting Susanna at the club.'

This was my cue to leave. Anja had turned to her mirror and started to apply more cosmetics to her already made-up face. Her eyelids looked like a peacock's tail. I knew I'd be accused of ogling if I stayed. I got up from the bed and quickly slipped out of the room.

In my bedroom I wondered which pieces of furniture we'd be allowed to keep. My large drawings on the wall looked childish and pointless to me now. Besides, they were just copies of the covers from my favourite books, Anne of Green Gables and Little Women. Childish stories. I'd take my poster of Abba, though. The drawings would stay when I left. I flung myself on the bed with its terrycloth bedspread and picked up The Building of Jalna. At least in this series of books real life happened. Life I wanted to belong to. I heard Anja's door slam and then the heavier thud of the front door closing. I was lying on my bed trying to find a way to get into the magical house in Canada, pretending to be one of the children in that happy home, where fathers chopped wood and mothers cooked dinner on the stove. I was startled by heavy footsteps in the hall and then the bang of the front door. Then I had to turn on my bedside lamp. My tummy felt a pang of hunger and I knew it must be dinnertime.

I saw Mamma sitting at the kitchen table only after I'd switched on the lights. She was looking out of the window at the dark street below.

'Mamma! What are you doing?'

'Oh, Eeva, nothing, just thinking.'

'Where's Pappa?'

'He went out.' Mamma tried to smile but her face looked puffy and her lips pale and swollen. I hugged her.

'You're a good girl, Eeva.'

I was glad I'd chosen her then. I wished Pappa would never come back, and we could forget all about him.

'Are you hungry?' Mamma asked, her face brighter. 'Shall we make waffles?'

It was an odd time to be making waffles, Saturday night, and I wondered what Pappa would say if he came back suddenly. We hadn't even had dinner yet. But I loved them, especially with whipped cream and Mamma's home-made strawberry jam. A jar was still left in the cupboard.

'Yummy,' I said. Mamma took two pinafores from their hooks and put one on me, and the other on herself. She asked me to get the waffle iron from the cupboard while she mixed the dough. The sweet smell of the cooking filled the kitchen. It was almost as delicious as the waffles themselves. We ate quickly at the table. Mamma kept an eye on the car park where Pappa had his car space. For now it was still empty. Not many cars were coming or going, perhaps only one since we'd sat down to eat. The streetlights had an orange glow to them. It looked as if it was snowing, but Mamma said it was just drizzle.

'Where's Anja?' Mamma said suddenly. 'It's already past ten o'clock. She should have been home by nine, she promised!'

'They don't close the youth club until half past,' I said.

'Really?'

'Yes, on Saturdays it's later.'

'Of course! It's Saturday,' Mamma said with relief. She looked over the car park again. 'Let's hope she gets in before Pappa.' As Mamma spoke a dark-green Volvo pulled into our view.

Twenty-three

MY ROOM looked empty again, just as it had the first night after our arrival in Rinkeby. I'd managed to keep to only three boxes. They stood side by side in the middle of the room. Mamma had told me there wasn't as much room in our new flat in Sundbyberg. I wondered if Anja and I would share a room like in Tampere. I imagined the new place would be just like Irena's flat, which was close by, Mamma said.

The bed in my room looked naked, with just the yellow foam mattress on top. Mamma had taken the sheets and blankets that morning in the first car full. Since then she'd been back and forth lots of times with Lew. I wondered what the time was now. Would Harriet be coming along the path soon? I thought about the day before when we'd said goodbye.

'I'll come and see you if you haven't gone by the time I get back from school,' she'd said when we parted on the path.

'I wish I could stay here, and in your class,' I said miserably.

'It's only three stops on the Tunnelbana. We can meet up every Saturday,' she'd said.

'Mamma told me we won't have a telephone for two weeks,' I said.

Harriet had hugged me and given me her colouring pencils, all of them.

'I don't need them,' she said when I stared first at the steel case and then her. 'You're much better at drawing than me.'

I watched her walk towards her block, her red head bent. Just before she turned the corner, she smiled and waved to me.

Now I took the pencils out of my school bag and put the case against my cheek. I heard the door go and ran into the hall. There I stopped. It was Pappa. He gave me a quick glance, and walked past me into the lounge. He sat down on the yellow sofa and started reading the paper. He looked cold and angry. I walked silently back to my room. I wondered where Anja was. She was supposed to be helping, but as usual she'd vanished as soon as she was needed. I'd been packing all the cutlery and china with Mamma. Those boxes had gone in the last load. I wondered what Pappa would say if he noticed how much stuff was missing from the kitchen. I sat still, not breathing. Then the door went again and I heard voices. It was Lew talking to Mamma. Suddenly the voices stopped and I heard Pappa speaking loudly in Finnish, 'Saatanan akka!'

I put my head in my hands.

Mamma stood at my door, 'Ready, Eeva?'

'Yes, Mamma,' I said lifting my head. My voice was quiet and shaking.

Lew came in and picked up a box. He smiled at me and glanced at Mamma. She said, 'Eeva, you take your bag and go with Lew on this trip. Irena is waiting for you at the other end. I'll tidy up here and gather up the last bits and pieces and wait for Anja. OK?'

Her face was pale. She had no make-up on. Her hair, though tied up in a ponytail, looked messy. A few, curly strands had come loose and were tucked behind her ears. Her beige jumper was baggy and looked dirty.

I didn't move and Mamma looked at me and said, 'C'mon, Eeva, you've got to go now. I'll see you in an hour or so.' She hugged me.

I got up and followed Lew out of the door. By the large archway I turned and looked at Pappa. He had his work clothes on and his legs were crossed at the ankles. His face was hidden behind the paper. I waited. He moved his hands to turn a page and saw me. He looked at me for a long time with cold eyes, as if he didn't recognise me. I stopped breathing.

Then he lifted the paper up and started reading.

I walked towards the door, put on my red coat and tied the Ilves scarf around my neck. Pappa cleared his throat and I turned around. He moved his legs, but didn't lower the paper.

'Hejdå, Pappa,' I said and ran out of the door.

Twenty-four

Tampere 2004

THE MORNING of the funeral was sunny. Janne and I had breakfast at the round table by the window. I'd estimated that it would take us twenty minutes to drive to the chapel in the Kalevankankaa cemetery. The funeral was at eleven o'clock. It was still only eight. I thought how odd that this was the first time I'd attended a funeral at the cemetery I'd spent much of my early childhood overlooking. I'd forgotten there was a chapel, and it was the obvious place for Saara's blessing. Janne put some bread and cheese on the table and poured me a cup of hot, black coffee.

'Here, Eeva, drink the coffee at least,' he said and touched my shoulder.

It hadn't been as strange as I thought it might be, sleeping in Saara's small bedroom. For Janne, the single bed was too short – his legs stuck out at the end. We laughed about it on the first night, after he'd held me gently in the other narrow bed.

'Just cry as much as you need to. It helps,' he'd said and stroked my hair.

I stopped when I could cry no more and the linen pillow-case was damp under my cheek.

'How do you know?' I asked, thinking I knew so little about this man, this gentle man, whose presence in my life was starting to make sense.

'Oh, I lost a close friend when I was younger,' he said. I heard his voice go dry at the mention of him, or was it a 'him'?

'What happened?' I said, and turned over to face him. The bed forced us to be so close to one another that I couldn't see the whole of his face, just his mouth and the top of his nose. I strained my neck to look at his eyes and nearly fell off the side. Janne tightened his grip on me and pulled me back. I put my head in the crook of his neck and listened. I felt his Adam's apple move when he spoke.

'It was a stupid accident. We were riding our bikes in Djurgården. It was the last day of May, in 1979, and the sun was high and blindingly bright.' Janne stopped speaking and swallowed. This is hard for him, I thought, and waited. 'Kristian and I had just finished school. We were both going to Uppsala to study. He was very bright, much better at school than me. If he hadn't wanted to go to university, I wouldn't have even thought of it...but he made me work hard. 'It'll be so cool, us studying together, we'll live in the same block of flats,' he said. I worked late at night, learning my books by heart because I didn't have the brains he had. Kristian didn't need to study. He was clever. Anyway, a lorry came trundling down the road, turned the corner and Kristian didn't see it. He rode straight under the wheels of the...'

Janne squeezed me harder. 'I can't cry for him anymore; I lost my tears with him,' Janne pulled me off him, still holding tight, and looked into my eyes. 'I love you, Eeva.' He said quietly and kissed my lips.

'I know so little about you,' I said and pressed myself closer to him.

'Now you know more,' Janne said. His body was warm and strong against me. We were silent for a while and then he said, 'Now it's your turn to tell me about you, about Tampere where you grew up. This is all new to me.' I got up from his bed and went to sit on the one opposite. I took the sheet and blanket and wrapped it against my naked body. I pulled my feet up and looked at Janne. He'd got up as well and came over and sat next to me. He put his arm around me and again I felt secure in his embrace.

'What you have to know about me is that my father is an alcoholic wife-beater.' I looked Janne in the eyes and saw his gentle face. His sad look made me cry. I bent my face down between my knees. Janne said, 'Shhh, it's OK, Eeva, it's OK.'

I looked at him through my tears and said, 'But you don't know the rest.'

'Then tell me,' Janne said calmly. What if he'll leave me, I thought, but knew I couldn't lie to him anymore. 'I slept with someone on the ferry.'

The silence that followed was heavy with my dread. I didn't look up, I still had my head buried inside the blanket between my knees. 'Please say something,' I prayed. Then I couldn't bear it any longer. I lifted my head up slowly and looked sideways at Janne. He had his head in his hands.

'A stranger?'

'No,' I whispered. Janne hadn't moved, but now he lifted his head and his eyes met mine. They were sad, the eyelids heavy.

'I met Yri, by chance, and…'

'Yri!'

'Yes, I don't know why, it was so strange seeing him there, I was caught unawares, and with all this, it just happened…' I sighed. I couldn't explain it. I looked over to Janne and put my hand on his knee. But, I love you, I know that now, I've changed. The last two days, seeing Pappa and Anja, and losing Saara, seeing you here. Oh, please, Janne, forgive me.' I was leaning my head against his shoulder. At first his body was tense against mine, but slowly as I talked it relaxed and he put his arm around me. Then he straightened himself up and looked at me, hard into the eyes.

'Eeva, you know I love you too; I have since the first moment I saw you on that platform at T-Centralen. But, I won't play second fiddle to some philandering Polish dentist.'

'He's a bastard and I don't love him.' I said quietly. I felt so ashamed for being such a fool. When I'd told Janne about my previous relationship, after the first time we slept together in my flat in Stockholm, he'd been sympathetic and taken me in his arms and squeezed me gently. He'd had no such dramatic stories to tell about his previous girlfriends – there'd been one serious relationship started at university, which had ended amicably when they both realised they wanted different things from their lives. The girlfriend was now working in a bank somewhere abroad, I'd forgotten where.

Janne wiped my tears with a corner of the sheet and said,

'Sometimes you are just a little foolish, Eeva. We all have our moments.' And then he pulled his lips into a straight line.

'Can you forgive me?' I whispered.

Janne was quiet for a long time. Am I asking too much of this gentle, lovely man, I wondered.

Janne took me deep inside his arms, rocking me from side to side, 'Yes, Eeva, I forgive you.' I sighed and felt I was breathing normally, without the pain that had been in my chest since I'd spoken to Pappa in my flat just days before.

'You ought to try to eat something,' Janne now said. He was sitting at the round table, facing me.

I smiled and looked out of the window. The swings in the children's play area were new and shiny. The sand had been replaced by bark chippings. It was Saturday morning, too early for people to be about or for the Konditoria to be open. It looked cold outside; I'd needed to wear a vest underneath my silk blouse. I looked at Janne. He was wearing a pair of pyjamas we'd bought him at Stockmann's. I had insisted he needed a pair. The top looked baggy on his lean body and I could see the vertical creases from the packaging. I smiled when I thought how he didn't wear anything in bed. He only wore the pants and the top to please me when we had break-fast. Then tears rose to my eyes, and I put my hand over my face.

'What is it, Eeva?' Janne said. He put his long fingers over my hand, and I managed to smile at him, a smile that turned into a grimace. 'Oh, you know, it doesn't seem right to be happy on a day like this.'

Janne looked hard at me. I saw the lines around his straight lips and I put my hand out and touched his cheek. He turned his head and kissed my hand, 'I'm sure Saara would want you to be happy.' He looked serious, 'But are you, Eeva – are you really happy?'

'Yes, I'm happy to be with you, very happy. I couldn't do this without you. I'm glad you came, Janne.' I said and leant over to kiss his lips.

At ten o'clock we were ready to leave. Janne had bought a black tie and scarf from Stockmann's, and I was wearing my black suit with the heavy Ulster and a warm grey shawl over the coat. I stood and looked at myself in the mirror in Saara's orange hall. I remembered standing there next to Saara's large body, watching her dab a small amount of red lipstick on her thin lips. How she adjusted and readjusted her artificial breast, never happy with how it looked, asking me if it showed under a flowery dress, or should she wear a jacket to hide her uneven chest? I'd bend my head this way and that, making sure I looked as if I was really considering the matter, then lied, 'It's fine. Both look exactly the same.'

Saara would smile at me and take my hand, 'Well, if your young eyes can't tell the difference, no one can.' And we'd go out to the shops or visit her friends.

I was thinking of her friends. I could only remember Marja. There were others, but I guessed they were long gone. Then I thought about the men who were going to be the pallbearers. Pappa told me Uncle Keijo was going to be one. I'd been surprised to hear Saara and Mamma's brother had been in touch, but then I guessed they both lived in Tampere, so why wouldn't they? Pappa also told me Marja's grandson,

Pauli, with whom I'd played when Saara and I visited, had also volunteered. In her letters Saara had told me about Pauli's two broken marriages. He had one child, a boy, from the first, but the mother refused him access. Pauli and I were exactly the same age. Saara and Marja liked to imagine that we'd marry when we grew up because we enjoyed playing together so much. I smiled at the embarrassing memory of those whispers. Then there was Anja's husband, Bengt, of course, who was flying over in the morning and would no doubt also help to carry Saara's coffin.

Janne drove my car and parked it underneath a row of pine trees. Some had large cones on them, and a few twigs were lying on the snowy banks beneath their trunks. The chapel was surrounded by a brick wall, and the car park was between this and the outer cemetery wall. It was built of grey granite in two tones. The bell was tolling as Janne and I sat in the car. We were the first to arrive.

Seeing Pappa's pale blue Peugeot, I said to Janne, 'Let's get out.'

Pappa carried a large wreath of white lilies. He handed me the bouquet and returned to the car to fetch another one. I read the inscription on the flowers I was holding. 'To my dearest mother, rest in peace. Your loving son, Mikko.' I swallowed hard and leant myself against Janne. He put his arm around me, holding my elbow with his hand. A cold wind blew in my face and I shivered. Pappa straightened himself up and said, 'Here, this is from you and Anja.'

I looked at the beautiful arrangement of flowers; there were blue cornflowers, white carnations, pale white, almost green roses, and lilies of the valley.

'She would have liked these,' I said.

Pappa lifted his eyes to me and wiped his nose with a gloved hand. He looked formal in his black coat and felt hat. He said nothing. I saw he was fighting tears. I read the inscription, 'To Saara, our rakas grandmother. Sleep well, Anja and Eeva.'

We'd agreed that we would read a sentence each, Anja first.

'Can you do that?' Anja had asked me on the phone. I was looking at Saara's pictures on her bookcase when I replied. 'Yes, I'll be alright.'

'It doesn't matter if you just whisper the words. People know it's difficult. It doesn't matter if you can't on the day, they can always read them at the cemetery afterwards. The most important thing is to be there,' she said.

Anja explained the format of the day to me. I hadn't been to a funeral in Finland since I was a child, and then we'd been ushered out of the church as soon as possible. That had been Mamma's other brother, Jussi. I remembered seeing Mamma in tears by the coffin. I hadn't known Uncle Jussi very well, but even so I had cried in church.

'Do you remember Uncle Jussi's funeral? It will be just the same. Afterwards the coffee and sandwiches will be here at Pappa's house.'

I thought now how much Anja must have done for the funeral. I hadn't even asked if she needed help. To read half of the inscription seemed nothing.

Pappa was standing looking at the flowers. He said, 'Eeva, Anja isn't here yet, so can you take the wreaths into the church. I'll have to go and find the pastor.'

Janne took Pappa's flowers and said, 'What do you want to do? Wait for Anja or go inside?' I could tell he was cold, his nose was red and he kept his shoulders hunched.

'What time is it?' I said.

'Half past.'

'We'll wait for a few minutes,' I said. I was watching Pappa's large shape as he walked slowly up the path to the chapel. His legs looked heavy as concrete, he could hardly lift one in front of another. Then I saw Bengt and Anja arrive in a black hire car. Bengt was a large man; his frame reminded me of Pappa, I realised, as I watched him get out of the car. His belly was large but unlike Pappa he had red cheeks and a ready smile. Today, though, even he looked sad, He'd lost more hair from the top of his head and his face was lined. Anja was wearing a black cape over a woollen suit and short black boots. She flung one end of the cape over her shoulder and walked towards us.

Bengt took my hand first and said, 'I'm so sorry, Eeva.' Without asking he took the wreath from me and patted my back, letting his left cheek touch mine in a brief embrace. Then Anja hugged me hard and whispered, 'This is the hardest part. You'll be alright, Eeva.' I smiled through my tears at her. Then another two cars pulled into the churchyard. I saw Pauli, a grown-up version of the full-lipped child with the dark, naughty eyes. He came over and took my hand, 'I'm so sorry,' he said and performed the same brief embrace Bengt had given me. Then Marja, walking with a stick, supported by Pauli, hugged me and said the same words. There were five or so other people who I didn't know but Anja seemed to. They all took my hand and said, 'I'm so sorry.' Some hugged

249

me and looked sadly into my eyes. I watched the line of black-clad people walk up to the chapel and looked at my watch. It was quarter to. I turned to Anja and said, 'Should we go in?'

'Yes,' she said, but she didn't look at me. She was scanning the road beyond the churchyard. Then a large, black Mercedes pulled in. I watched as it parked next to Bengt's hire car. A woman in a smart black coat came out first and then a man with curly blond hair stepped smartly out of the driver's side. I recognised him straight away.

'Uncle Keijo,' I said turning to Anja. Then to Janne in Swedish, 'This is my Uncle.' Anja didn't say anything. She kept her eyes on the couple, who were getting a wreath out of the book of the car. I could see the woman had a pair of expensive shoes on, not boots, and thick black-and-grey patterned tights. Then, as Uncle Keijo shut the boot and they both turned towards us, I gasped. I looked at Anja, 'It's Mamma!' I said.

I hugged Mamma but kept my eyes down. She glanced quickly at me. She'd been crying and was holding a bright white cotton handkerchief in her gloved hand.

'I'm so glad you came,' she whispered.

When she pulled away I said, 'Of course I came.'

Mamma patted my hand and then went to hug Anja. I watched them briefly whispering to each other. Mamma's hair looked very light next to Anja's new copper-coloured bob.

Standing in front of me, Uncle Keijo looked smart and fashionable in his square-rimmed glasses. He embraced me for a long time. I felt his hot breath in my ear when he said, 'This is such a sad occasion but it's good to see you here in Tampere, Eeva.'

We walked along the path and into the church with our heads bowed. Janne and I were last. The silence in the church was breath taking. Mamma went to sit in the second pew from the front. Whispering something to Anja, she gestured towards the front pew. Anja turned around and gave me a look, pointing her head towards a space next to her. Somebody coughed and the sound echoed along the stone walls of the chapel. Janne took my hand in his, and Anja leant over to me and whispered, 'Make room for Pappa at the end.' I moved along the cold, hard pew. I was afraid I'd damage the flowers on my lap. I heard a shuffle break the silence and saw people were standing up. The pastor had appeared in front of the altar. Anja stood up, rolling her eyes at me to indicate I should do the same. I turned around and saw a white coffin, carried by Pappa at the front, with Bengt on the other side, move slowly along the aisle. Tears ran down my cheeks. The six men lowered the silk-covered coffin in front of the pastor and slowly, heads bent, found their seats in the church. Bengt went past me to sit next to Anja, and Pappa lowered himself heavily next to me. He didn't look at me. I smelled aftershave on him.

The pastor was wearing a long white gown and in his hands he held a black leather-bound bible. He looked at the congregation for a long time, his eyes pale under bushy grey eyebrows. Then he started talking about the frailty of life, the sadness of death and the necessity of grieving.

'But God gave you this wonderful woman, a wife, mother

and grandmother, whom you loved and who loved you.' He looked straight into my eyes. I couldn't meet his gaze. Music from the organ filled the church. The psalm was one I recalled from School Graduation Day in the spring. After the first familiar verse I started to weep. Pappa put his hand on my knee and squeezed it. Then he removed it and took a grey-looking hankie out of his trouser pocket. After the last notes sounded, the pastor turned around and went to stand on one side, still holding his bible. His fingers were long and bony. I saw him nod to Pappa, who got up slowly. Janne saw him move and handed him the wreath.

With his head bowed, Pappa placed the lilies at the head of the coffin and without looking at the silk ribbon, mumbled his goodbye. It was inaudible. I heard sniffles behind me and wondered if it was Mamma. Pappa stood silently praying by the coffin, his hat in his hands. The thin wisps of hair had fallen over his face, covering his eyes. Then he turned back towards the pew and stood at the end, nodding to Anja. She got up and I let her pass, then followed her up to the altar. We stepped up and stood by the coffin, side by side, leaning onto each other as we had done in the hospital just a few days ago. Anja took hold of the ribbon and said in a clear, thin voice, 'To Saara, our rakas grandmother.' She nudged me, her head bent, tears running down her cheeks. I didn't have a voice. My throat was sealed up. I took hold of the ribbon and whispered, 'Sleep well.'

I sniffled and then continued, 'Anja and Eeva.'

Anja placed the flowers carefully on the floor, letting them lean against the coffin. She straightened the ribbons, neatly arranging them along the dark-green stems. She took my hand and we stood there, heads bent, tears running down our faces for what seemed to me an eternity. When Anja finally moved to leave, I looked across to the pastor. He nodded to me, closing his eyes briefly.

One by one, the congregation placed their wreaths on or around the white coffin. I scarcely heard their messages, but they were not meant for me, for any of us, I realised; they were meant for Saara. And she would hear them all. When each party turned away from the coffin, they made a brief bow to Pappa.

When Mamma went up with Uncle Keijo, I watched her closely. He supported her like Anja had me, and her words were thin and inaudible like mine had been. Once again I was startled by her blonde hair. It looked artificial against the black of her clothes. She looked foreign, too polished for the church. I wondered briefly if I looked out of place here, too.

Uncle Keijo said his message more confidently, 'May you rest in peace, dear Saara.' Mamma and Keijo also bowed to Pappa afterwards. I wondered how Mamma felt; seeing Pappa must be even more difficult for her than it was for me.

'Let us pray,' the pastor said. I was surprised how I remembered the words for the Lord's Prayer in Finnish. But they seemed more natural, stronger than in Swedish. For the first time since childhood I felt I really meant them.

The organist started playing a slow hymn, and Pappa and the other pallbearers got up and carried the coffin out. I worried about what would happen to the wreaths. Then I saw a woman dressed in black collecting the flowers and handing them back to those who had brought them to the altar.

As the coffin passed us, with the pastor close behind,

Anja got up and said, 'We go first, then others follow us to the graveside.'

The day was bitterly cold and windy. A weak sun was peering out from behind thin clouds. We followed the slow progress of the pallbearers down the church steps, then along a path leading to the grave of Saara's husband. Daffodils and even some tulips were in flower by the rows of headstones. Their colours against the patches of greying snow and brown, dead grass filled me with hope. This is a beautiful cemetery, I thought.

By the open grave, the pastor said a prayer, and threw earth over the beautiful, white, clean lid of the coffin. The scraping sound hurt my ears and I closed my eyes. I wondered what Saara looked like inside, but brushed the thought away. I shuddered, and Janne took hold of my arm. I let him support my body while we watched as the pastor, with his head bent, spoke with Pappa. Then Anja made a coughing sound. She said, 'You are all welcome to Lauttakatu 7. I'm sure most of you know where it is; if not, follow our car.' She took hold of Pappa's arm. With her other hand she pulled me next to her. The three of us stood there, arms linked, watching the white coffin rest in the deep grave.

The pastor was still standing at the head of the grave. Pappa looked up to him and said, 'Do you have a car or would you like to come with me?'

It felt odd to me that ordinary arrangements needed to be made. I looked at both Pappa and the pastor and saw the pastor say in a low voice to Pappa. 'It's very kind, but I have transport.'

Slowly people started to leave. I didn't see Mamma or

Uncle Keijo at the graveside and I wondered if they were going to come to Pappa's house.

'I think we'd better leave too, Pappa,' Anja said. Bengt was standing a little further away, talking to Janne. He had his head bent down to hear what Bengt was saying. I thought how good it was that at least they had each other, when everyone else around them was speaking Finnish. I felt great gratitude towards Janne for being here with me, not understanding a word of the service. He wouldn't understand what people were saying at the house either. It would be a long day for him and Bengt, I thought. Just then, both turned and smiled at me. I said, 'We'll see you in a minute,' to Anja and Pappa, and went over to Janne.

Twenty-five

We drove to Pappa's house in silence. Janne kept glancing at me but I was afraid I'd start crying if I even as much as looked at his sympathetic face. He parked the car on the road alongside the post box with the number 7 on it and put his hand on my knee.

'You OK?' he said. Then seeing my face, he added, 'I'm useless, what I meant was, is there anything I can do? He looked hard into my eyes, 'Eeva, please let me be there for you.'

I smiled at his miserable face. How can I have failed to notice what a wonderful man he was?

'Yes, Janne, I will,' I said and put my hand on his and squeezed it. 'Let's go in, Anja and Pappa will need our help in there.'

The dining room was packed with men and women dressed in dark, depressing clothes. The table had gone and chairs had been placed all around the walls of the room. There were even seats in the middle, in a row. The room looked like a church hall. Or an office set up for a presentation. People had white cups of coffee in their hands and were chatting in low voices. When we walked in some of them turned around. Pauli gave me a nod and Marja smiled. I smiled back, but when I saw her touch Pauli's arm and move forward I turned to face Janne behind me, 'Let's go into the kitchen to see if Anja needs any help,' I whispered.

Anja was standing facing the work surface, wearing a pinny over her dress. She lifted her eyes briefly to me when I came in but didn't say anything. Her face looked lined and drawn.

A large-framed man with blond, unruly hair was sitting at the table. I recognised him as one of the pallbearers. Though the tallest, he was also the youngest of the men carrying Saara's coffin, and I thought he must be a distant cousin. I stepped forward and put my hand out, 'I'm Eeva Litmunen.'

The legs of the chair screeched on the floor as he got up quickly. Glancing at Anja's back he said, 'Heikki Litmunen.'

I was a little taken aback by the name. Something about him was familiar. Perhaps it was his square shoulders and large body. I felt dizzy looking at him. He didn't smile but his eyes were laughing, like he was having a private joke with himself.

'Have we met?' I said.

The man looked past me at Anja. He opened his mouth and then shut it again, biting his lower lip. I turned to Anja while letting go of the man's hand.

Anja turned around and said, 'Eeva, this is your half-brother.'

I put my hand on the side of the kitchen cupboard to steady myself. Janne moved behind me and stretched his hand out to the man. Janne hadn't understood what Anja said to me. The two men shook hands and nodded to each other. Then Janne turned to me. He put his hand under my elbow and said, 'Eeva?'

I heard the concern in his voice, but couldn't talk to him. I looked past his quizzical eyes at Anja. She had her head bent over the work surface. I saw she was cutting up a sandwich cake. There were thin slices of ham rolled up on top of the cake and all around it sprigs of flat-leafed parsley. The green and the pink colours against the white covering of the loaf looked harsh and bright. Anja cut into the cake and set the slice carefully on top of several others arranged neatly on an oval silver plate. She lifted her head and said, 'Not now, Eeva.' Her eyes didn't meet mine.

I stared at her. Her cheeks were hollow, as if she was sucking in a breath. Then the man at the table shifted. He'd been half-standing, supporting himself with the tip of his delicate fingers against the round kitchen table. He sat back down and said, 'I'm sorry about your loss.'

Pappa appeared at the door and said, 'Eeva, Anja: the pastor is about to speak.' Then, seeing Heikki, he coughed and said, 'You'd better come in, too.' Pappa turned around. I took hold of Janne's hand and said in Swedish, 'We have to go in and listen to the pastor.'

People were now sitting down in the chairs. As soon as Pappa appeared at the doorway, the seats in the middle of the room were vacated. I looked around. I wanted to sit somewhere in the back, but was ushered by Anja into the middle.

I sat next to Pappa. Janne took a seat to my left. Anja walked in front of us, nodding to the pastor as she passed him and sat next to Pappa on the other side. The pastor was now the only person standing. He took a step forward and said, 'We are going to say a few words about Saara.' His eyes were dark. They looked like pools of sorrow.

The pastor spoke softly. 'Saara wanted to keep this very informal and we will honour her wishes. I'd like to start with a short prayer and afterwards each one of us can say what Saara meant to us. How we are going to remember her. Just a few words are needed, if you are able. From experience I have learned that it helps enormously to talk amongst family and friends, as we are gathered here, about our grief.' He fell silent for a few moments, linking his fingers together and lowering them in front of his black suit. The white dog collar shone brightly against the dark jacket and his grey face.

'We must rejoice in the love of God and the love that Saara gave us and we gave her.' The pastor moved his kindly eyes from one face to another. I heard sniffles from behind me and I felt the ache in my chest and face, the ache that meant the tears were coming again. I closed my eyes and lowered my head.

'Let us pray.'

I didn't hear what the pastor said, just the monotonous, soft tone of his voice. After he finished speaking there was a long silence, broken only by more sniffles and coughs. Then Pappa stood up and said, 'My mother was unlike any person I have ever known. Not only was she loving, forgiving and kind,' Pappa turned to look at me. He had a piece of paper in his hand. I returned his gaze, looking squarely into his eyes.

Pappa lowered his eyes to the piece of paper again and said, 'She was also an artist, and I am going to miss her very much.' He paused. 'I don't know how I will...' Pappa bent his head and the paper in his hand started shaking. Anja stood up and put her arm around Pappa's shoulders and pulled him down to the seat.

'We understand. God be with you, Mikko,' the pastor said and bent his head.

After a while Anja stood up and said, 'I loved Saara very much, she was a good person and a wonderful grandmother,' and sat down. Again there was a silence. I looked up to the pastor. He met my eyes and nodded imperceptibly. As in a dream, I found myself up on my feet. I wiped my eyes and said, 'I'm sorry, this is very difficult for me.'

'That's quite alright, my child,' the pastor said. 'Take your time.'

'Saara wrote to me every week,' I whispered. 'I don't know what I would have done without her letters. They meant so much to me. I'd wait and wait for the next one. Then I didn't have one for three weeks...' I looked at Pappa's bent head. 'I just wish...' Pappa looked up and said, 'It's alright Eppu, you came and she saw you before she...' I nodded to him and sat down. Janne squeezed my hand and whispered, 'I love you.'

Behind me Heikki stood up next and said in a high-pitched, shaky voice, 'I'd just like to say Saara was the best Grandmother you'd ever want to have. She was brilliant.' He sat down quickly with a heavy thump and a deep sigh. I have a stepbrother, I thought. Pappa has a son, the son he always craved. But where was the mother? Another divorce? I thought then about Mamma and Uncle Keijo, neither of them was here. I must speak with Anja, I couldn't believe she had been keeping all of this from me.

After a long pause, while people had been whispering to each other, Marja said, 'Saara was my best friend. You'll have to excuse me sitting down, my old legs aren't much good anymore.'

There were mumbles and noises of approval. I turned around and saw Marja behind me. Her eyes were wet from crying, but she was smiling when she said, 'Only two weeks ago, was it two weeks, Pauli?' Marja looked at her son sitting next to her. Pauli said, 'Well I think so. I wasn't there!' He rolled his eyes to me and smiled.

Marja laughed and said, 'Sons, they can never be trusted. Of no use whatsoever! Anyway, say it was two weeks ago when my best friend Saara and I were walking to the Konditoria, more like shuffling we were, a young woman with a baby in a pram was walking in the other direction. Well, you know Saara, she will talk to anyone. She stopped the woman and asked to see the baby in the pram. They start talking about this that, about how well the baby slept, how old it was, how the feeding went. I was getting a bit tired, standing there on the cold pavement, so I said to Saara, 'Are we going to the Konditoria or are you going to waste the whole of the day chatting to other people?' She smiled to me and took my arm and waved to the woman as if to an age-old friend. Up we walked and eventually we reached the shop. There was no queue, thank God – Oh, sorry pastor,' Marja said and rolled her eyes. 'But did we get our cakes and swiftly move on to coffee at my place? Oh no, we had to hear the whole of the personal history of the young girl behind the till. Her boy-friend, whom neither Saara nor I had ever clapped eyes on. Come to think of it, I don't suppose Saara had ever even met this girl, with red-coloured hair in pigtails and darkly polished fingernails! But, Saara had to hear the whole story. By the end of it, the girl took Saara's hand and kissed it. I could have been knocked over with a feather! When I go there alone, the girls don't even look me in the eyes, just take the money and shove the cakes in a paper bag. But people treated Saara differently. They loved her whether they knew her or not.'

Marja dug out a large linen handkerchief out of her brown handbag with a noisy clasp and blew her nose. Pauli put his arm around her shoulders. People around her patted her shoulders and muttered something to her. Again, I wished I'd come to Tampere before, long before.

Then the pastor, standing up, cleared his throat and said, 'I believe there is some food and kotikalja on offer in the kitchen.' Anja got up and said, 'Please, do help yourselves!' She went past the rows of chairs and opened a door to a room where the dining table was laden with cups, plates and food.

I remained seated. I wanted to talk to Janne about everything, but I heard a voice next to me, 'Eeva.' It was Heikki. He'd sat down on Pappa's seat. I was struck by the similarity of their build, and face. Heikki looked exactly like the man next to Mamma in the wedding picture at Saara's. I wondered briefly why I hadn't seen any pictures of Heikki on the same shelf. I tried to remember, if I had, not knowing who it was, but couldn't.

'So I finally meet you.' Heikki said.

'Yes,' I said.

'I'm working in Helsinki now and couldn't come until today.'

'Oh.'

I nodded and looked at him. Heikki leaned back in the chair and said, 'You didn't know about me, did you?'

I shook my head.

'Ah,' he said. He looked around the room. It was empty. Everyone was crowded into the bedroom next door, now converted into a dining area.

'Well, I certainly knew all about you,' he said.

I heard Janne shift in his seat next to me. I turned to him and said, 'Janne, this is my half-brother, Heikki.' Janne stared at me and then at Heikki.

'Hej igen,' Heikki said.

'You speak Swedish,' I said. I'd assumed he'd be the same as Pappa, incapable, or unwilling, to learn the language.

'I work for Ericsson,' Heikki said.

'I bet that's popular here in Nokia country,' Janne said.

'Yeah,' Heikki said and laughed a little.

After a while when nobody spoke, Janne got up. Looking down at me, he said, 'Shall I leave you two to catch up?'

I nodded and Heikki said, 'Vi ses.'

'That was a very Stockholm way to say goodbye.'

'I work there a lot,' he said.

'So is your mother here?' I said, swallowing hard.

'No, no,' Heikki said and lowered his eyes, 'she died when I was fourteen.'

'Oh, I'm sorry,' I said.

'No problem, I'm over it, it was a long time ago.' He

263

straightened himself and cleared his throat. Being a grown-up man, I thought.

'Can I ask you what happened?'

Heikki looked at me for a while and then said, 'Cancer. She died of breast cancer.'

'I'm so sorry,' I said and blew out air. I closed my eyes and felt the rush of tears. I put my hand to my mouth and let out an involuntary sound. A tissue was pushed into my hand and I wiped my eyes. I saw Heikki's blue eyes close to mine.

'I know why you haven't been in touch,' he said. 'Anja told me the whole story. And I understand. But he wasn't like that with my mother; they were happy together.' He looked at me again. 'But I can see why he wouldn't tell you about me, or about my mother. Or tell me about you two until he absolutely had to. He's afraid to lose you again. Besides, he's never been good at talking about anything, really,' Heikki took my hand in his and smiled deeply into my eyes.

'No,' I said and blew my nose, 'Sorry, I'm being such a child.'

'It's cool,' Heikki said and reminded me how much younger than me he was.

'So when did you find out about us?'

'When Anja first came to visit.'

'And when was that?'

'Right after my mother died.'

People were slowly filling the seats again and a man with grey hair wearing a pinstripe suit sat next to Heikki and started talking to him. Marja came to sit next to me. I got up to help her lower herself slowly and painfully onto the seat. After a deep sigh, she said, 'Eeva, you have grown so tall!'

I smiled at her and gave her a hug. Though she was much shorter than Saara, and a lot rounder, she felt frail in my arms.

'Saara never stopped talking about you, and your work in Stockholm. She was very proud of you!'

I smiled and nodded but couldn't speak. Then I felt Janne's hand on my shoulder. He was standing behind us carrying two plates of food.

'I brought you something,' he said and put one of the plates in my hand.

'Anja has done Saara proud with the spread,' Marja said. Heikki on the other side of me got up and stretched his hand out to show Janne to sit down.

'I'm going to get something to eat too,' he said in Swedish to Janne and walked away.

'Is this your young man?' Marja said and leaned across me to Janne.

'Yes,' I said. 'Janne, this is Marja, Saara's friend.'

'Päivää, päivää,' Marja said.

'Paiva, paiva,' Janne said and nodded enthusiastically.

I smiled at his terrible pronunciation and thought I must teach him some Finnish.

Marja nudged me and, smiling at Janne, said, 'You've taught him Finnish, haven't you?'

'Yes,' I said.

Twenty-six

I WAS sitting in the Siilinkari cafeteria when my mobile rang. It was Sunday morning and I'd left Janne in the flat reading an Aftonbladet I'd found in the local kiosk. It was the only Swedish paper they had, and it was a day old, but it was better than nothing.

'Eeva Litmunen,' I answered without looking at the caller display.

'Eeva,' Yri's low voice said, 'it's me.'

'Hej.'

'How are you?'

It's Sunday, I thought, how can he be phoning me on a weekend?

'I'm fine,' I said, then thought, 'yes, I'm fine, no thanks to you!' but said nothing.

'Where are you?' he demanded. I smiled at the pronunciation, but then thought how arrogant he was.

'Finland.'

'Eeva, what is the matter?'

'Nothing,' I said and thought I should just say goodbye and put the phone down. I was surprised how relaxed I felt, and how little I felt. The empty sensation in my belly I usually had when talking to Yri wasn't there anymore.

'Well, then, you wanted to see me. When are you back in Stockholm? I could come over tomorrow afternoon,' there was a silence in the other end, as if he was checking his diary, 'Eeva, are you there?'

'Yes.'

'Well then, would four o'clock suit you?'

It's like making an appointment for a check-up, I thought.

'Yri,' I said.

'Yes, Eeva,'

'You promised to call me the day before yesterday, or was it the day before that, I can't remember. No, I can: it was three days ago!'

'I'm sorry, I couldn't. I was tied up.'

I said nothing.

'But I'm phoning you now,' Yri said. His voice was low, enticing, sexy, 'And I want to see you again. I haven't stopped thinking about you. You're a very exciting woman, Eeva.'

I would have given anything for an admission like that three days ago, I thought, but not any more.

'I can't see you tomorrow.'

'What about Tuesday? You'll be back in Stockholm by then, yes?'

'No, Yri, I can't see you, not tomorrow, not Tuesday, not at all.'

There was a long silence.

'We had a good time, didn't we, Eeva?'

I said nothing. I thought about cutting him off, but decided against it. I wanted to end it so that he knew for certain it was finished. I didn't want to hurt Janne anymore, nor take the chance Yri might call again and make Janne suspicious. A part of me, a large part of me, was enjoying his squirming, enjoying the little hurt – even if it was only to his pride – I was causing him.

'So why phone me? Why follow the little fun we had by phoning me? I worry, so I make arrangements to see you. I make myself available and you change your mind. Just like that.' His voice was dry and I could imagine his eyes darken.

'I'm sorry, Yri, I made a mistake.'

Yri didn't answer and I thought he was plotting a different attack. Perhaps.

'I have to go now. I'm really sorry, Yri. It's finished, for good. Take care, but don't phone me. Goodbye, Yri.'

Now my hands were shaking. I didn't wait for Yri's reply but cut him off. Then I found his number and deleted it. I put the phone away inside my handbag and thought about Janne. How he would look if he knew I'd been in touch with Yri.

I looked up and saw Mamma walk into the cafeteria. I half stood up and waved to her.

'Mamma!' I got up and hugged her, 'where's Anja?'

'Oh, she's coming,' Mamma took off her coat and lay it neatly against a chair. Then she sat down and said, 'Is that a cappuccino? Is it any good?'

'Yes, it's nice,' I said and looked at my mother. I hadn't thought she'd changed at all through the years. But seeing her here in Tampere was like seeing her for the first time as an older woman, a grandmother. Why hadn't I noticed the wrinkles around her eyes? The blue eye shadow she was wearing now gathered in fine lines in her eyelids. Her hair was thinner and didn't shine the way it used to in Rinkeby. She had it cut into an efficient bob, but still a few strands of curly hair framed her face. It made her expression look softer. There was no grey, though.

'Shall I get you one or shall we wait for Anja?' I said.

Mamma lifted her eyes up to mine. She'd been looking for something in her shiny black leather handbag, where everything was neatly arranged. Then she glanced at her watch, 'My flight is at one thirty, I left my bags with Uncle Keijo and he's taking me to the airport in about an hour. Let's wait.' She put her handbag on the seat next to her and smiled at me.

'How was the reception?' she said.

'Oh, good,' I noticed Mamma wasn't wearing any lipstick, 'I met Heikki.'

'Ah.'

'You knew about him?'

'Anja told me.' Mamma was looking down at her hands.

'Were you in touch with Saara?' I asked. I'd chosen a seat in front of the windows, facing the entrance. I wanted to make sure I'd see who was coming in.

'I came to see her once, yes.' Mamma was still not looking at me.

'When?'

'Oh, a few years ago, when Anja's first was born,' Mamma said, lifting her eyes.

And I thought I was the only one writing to Saara. How guilty I'd felt all these years not telling Mamma and Anja about my correspondence! Instead there were these secrets, Anja seeing Pappa, Mamma making visits to Saara. Pappa's second marriage, Heikki...Suddenly I had a thought, 'Did you meet up with Pappa too?' I said.

'It was a long time ago,' Mamma said, taking my hand. I saw tears in her eyes. I couldn't bear to see her cry.

'I know,' I said, 'it's just that...' I looked down at my empty cup of coffee. The dark blue china cup was the same series Saara had. They were still producing the 1950s designs. Everything here had the effect of making me cry.

'What?' Mamma said, stroking my hand.

'Why didn't you tell me? About Heikki, about Anja seeing Pappa and Saara?'

'I didn't think you'd want to know.' Mamma loosened her grip on my hand.

I took my hand away and moved it to my mouth.

'Oh Eeva,' Mamma said and came to sit next to me on the sofa. She put her arm over my shoulders and squeezed hard. Her hair smelled of shampoo and hairspray.

'I don't want to cry, not again,' I said and looked around me. A man sitting two tables away gave me a quick glance, but otherwise nobody was taking any notice of us.

'Oh, don't worry, I can't bear it either,' Mamma said and took a tissue from her sleeve. Saara used to keep her handkerchief in her bra, in the folds of her artificial breast. I smiled at the memory, how old-fashioned that seemed now.

'What is it?' Mamma said, returning the smile. Her mascara was smudged. I took the tissue out of her hand and wiped some of it away.

'Just of bit of your eye make-up there,' I said.

She got up and fumbled in her handbag for a mirror, found it, wet the tissue with her tongue and wiped it off. Her eyes looked puffy, I thought as I watched her.

'What was so funny?' she said, 'my smudged mascara?'

'No, Mamma, no. I just remembered how Saara used to keep her handkerchief in her bra.'

We both laughed and Mamma went to sit opposite me again. I took a deep breath and said, 'Janne and I are staying in her flat. I thought I wouldn't be able to do it but actually it helps.'

'That's good, Eeva, I'm glad Janne is here to support you.'

I looked at her. She was surveying me over her small black-rimmed glasses, holding both my hands now. I wanted tell her about Janne and how happy I was suddenly. Just thinking about him made me smile.

Mamma looked at me, and said, 'What is it?' She patted my hand. Her touch was soft and warm.

'Oh, I think I'm falling in love with Janne!'

'At last!'

I bent my head down and said, 'I know.'

'Have you told him?' Mamma asked.

'Yes.'

'Oh,' Mamma said. She leant back in her chair and exhaled, looking at me.

'I feel like a teenager again,' I said and smiled.

'That's the best news!' she said.

We both sat quietly for a while, watching people drink their coffee.

'Oh, Eeva, this is such a mess,' Mamma said after a while.

I looked at her and said, 'What is?'

'I couldn't tell you everything. You were so young, Eeva. Forgive me.'

'Of course I'll forgive you,' I said gently, 'but what is there to forgive?

Mamma looked very serious, 'I must tell you, Eeva, it's been terrible not being able to.'

'Tell me what?'

'About Rinkeby.'

'What about Rinkeby?'

'Pappa was right you know.'

I said nothing. Again we both sat there silent in the middle of a busy café. I listened to people laughing, to the till sounds, to people walking back and forth behind Mamma. She looked pale now, her lipstick had worn off.

'But it didn't give him the right to hit, and...' I hesitated at the word, then leant over and whispered it, 'rape you!'

Mamma lifted her eyes from the tissue she'd been fiddling with. 'Eeva, I was so young, and your Pappa, well he was...but I know I did wrong and times were different then...'

'The seventies?'

'Well, you know what I mean. A man was the head of the household then. It wasn't all his fault.'

All these years Mamma and I had never mentioned Pappa, or Saara. I thought that was what Mamma wanted. Suddenly I realised what she was telling me.

'Was it Nils?'

Mamma's eyes were steadily on me when she said, 'Yes.'

'But still, Mamma, Pappa had no right...' I couldn't continue, I didn't know what to say.

'I know and that's why I left. When he did it more than

272

once, I knew he'd do it again. But I can see now he needed help. And he got it.'

'Oh,' was all I could say. I felt so tired, I wanted to lie down and sleep and wake up in my tidy flat in Stockholm. 'It's alright, Mamma,' I said, but I didn't dare to look at her. I was studying my hands. They looked dry and pale. I'd read somewhere that hands were the first part of the body to show old age. Blue veins were visible on the top. Saara's hands had never been like this. They were red and round with short fingers and plump palms. They were always doing something, either dabbing paint on a canvas or baking or washing dishes. In the hospital her grasp had felt thin and papery when I held her hand. I realised life had already been pulled away from her then.

'How do you know Pappa got help?' I asked, looking at Mamma.

'He wrote to me, and then we met up. Just the once, though. I couldn't bear to see him…'

'When?'

'A year or so after I left. But it was too late by then, you can see that can't you, Eeva?' Mamma took hold of my hands again. They were larger than mine and softer. I smiled at her and nodded.

'I think I'll go and get that cappuccino after all. Anja is late! Do you want another one?' Mamma said and got up.

'Yes, please.'

I watched Mamma's tall figure walk towards the till. She looked stylish, though I was shocked to see she was just slightly stooping. When she entered the self-service section to pick up a tray, she turned to me and smiled. Just then Anja

273

walked in and saw her too. She waved to me and joined Mamma in the queue. Their similarity once again startled me. Anja was wearing jeans and black high-heeled boots. On top she had the black poncho she wore to the funeral. She, too, looked out of place here. Her hair was the same length as Mamma's. I wondered now if she coloured it to make herself look a little different from her. I didn't know if she cared that much.

When they returned to the table I got up and hugged Anja. She came and sat next to me on the sofa.

'Are you alright?' she asked and looked first at me, then at Mamma.

'Yes, we've talked and talked and now we're alright, aren't we Eeva?' Mamma said.

I nodded.

'It was a nice funeral, so many people in church, did they all come to the house?' Mamma asked, looking brighter.

'Yes almost all, didn't they?' Anja said and smiled at me.

'Yes,' I said.

'And what did people say about Saara?' Mamma said.

'Oh, Pappa spoke, then I did, then Eeva...'

Mamma leant across the table and said, 'You spoke, Eeva?'

'Yes, I did; it was strange how easy it was and how good I felt afterwards. Like saying goodbye properly.'

'Yes,' Mamma said.

We sat silently for a long time.

'Oh, and Marja,' Anja said.

'Yes, I saw her in church, she looked frail,' Mamma said.

'I don't think she's very well, but she told this long story

274

about how Saara always talked to people and how they loved her straightaway.' Anja brought her hand to her mouth and stopped talking. Mamma looked at her watch.

'What time is your flight?' Anja asked.

'One something, I've got to go soon.'

'I'm glad you came, and so was Pappa,' Anja said.

'Oh,' Mamma said, her eyes wide.

'Yes, he told me this morning how glad he was that you came to say goodbye.'

Mamma took a deep breath in and nodded several times, looking past us out of the window. Anja glanced at me. She took my hand, squeezed it and pulled her mouth up in an effort to smile. I looked at Mamma and thought, she still loves Pappa, or at least cares for him.

'Mamma,' Anja said and Mamma turned her gaze to us, startled as if she'd been woken from a dream. Then she smiled and said, 'I've got to go now girls, it's past eleven and I need to pick up my bag from Uncle Keijo's.' She stood up and put on her coat. Then she hugged both of us and said, 'Ring me when you get home, Eeva.'

'I will, Mamma. Janne and I are taking the ferry over tonight.'

Anja and I watched Mamma walk out of the cafeteria. She waved to us from the street and then hurried across the road.

'Where does Uncle Keijo live?' I suddenly asked.

'Oh, not far, he's got a flat in one of the newly renovated blocks on Hämeenpuisto.'

Anja leant close to me and said, 'You OK?' She looked wary, her eyes steady and her mouth straight.

'Yeah,' I said and thought, she could have told me about seeing Pappa, the existence of Heikki and most importantly Saara's frailty, at any time. We talked at least once a week on the phone. But I just smiled and said, 'I'd better be going too.' Then it occurred to me that we might be on the same ferry, 'When are you going back to Uppsala?'

'We're flying later tonight.' Anja bit her lip and turned her head away from me for a moment, then looking back at me said, 'Eeva, you'll come and see Pappa again, won't you?'

I hadn't thought about that. Anja's eyes were pleading now, so I said, 'Yes, I suppose I will.'

She smiled and said, 'I'll tell him you said that. He'll be very pleased and you'll feel better too, I promise.'

Twenty-seven

IT WAS typical of Janne to cancel his flight back to Stockholm and come back with me on the ferry instead. I didn't ask him how much the flights had cost him and he didn't volunteer the information, but I knew he couldn't afford it. I decided to make it up to him by paying for the next two dinners when we went out, but then I knew he wouldn't let me do that either.

'I'll have to come back and sort out the cellar,' I said to Janne when we were standing in the kitchen washing up after our early breakfast on Monday morning.

'I'll come with you,' he said, then flashed his eyes at me and added, 'if you want me to, that is.'

I stroked his back with a wet hand and kissed his cheek, 'Of course I do.' He smelt of aftershave and his skin felt smooth against my lips.

'I've made your shirt wet,' I said and started wiping it with a red-and-white checked cloth.

Janne smiled at me and took his hands out of the sink and put them over my shoulders. Water was dripping down my back onto my blouse. I wriggled out of his grip and laughed, 'You did that on purpose.' I ran out of the room and into the little hall where Janne caught me. He took hold of my waist and pushed me through the doorway onto one of Saara's single beds. He kissed my neck and then my mouth. His wet hands were all over me.

'You're making my top all wet' I said, giggling.

'You'll just have to take it off then!' he said.

I felt his hot breath on my neck and thought how much I wanted his lips on me.

'We'll miss the ferry,' I whispered. The top buttons of his shirt had become undone and I rubbed my nose against the soft hairs of his bare chest. I could feel his hardness against my belly and wondered how much time we had.

'I'll be quick then,' he said and pulled his face back to look at me. His eyes were dark green and full of lust.

'Oh, Janne,' I gasped.

Afterwards I looked at my blouse. As well as wet it was now very creased. Then I looked down at my black bra, the only clean one I had left. I put on the trousers of my black Sand suit and then stuffed the blouse into my holdall. Then I put on the matching jacket and went to look at myself in the mirror in the hall.

'What do you think? Can I get away with this? It is a night ferry after all,' I shouted to Janne. He was washing-up in the kitchen. He came to the doorway and smiled.

'I should say! I'll have to fight the men off you.'

'Oh yeah,' I said and went back into the bedroom. I liked

the way I'd looked in the mirror. My face was glowing and my body looked slimmer and more relaxed somehow. I took a deep breath in and zipped up the holdall. It'll be nice to get back home to Stockholm.

All packed, standing in the hall, Janne said, 'What are you going to do with the key?'

I looked at the worn-out piece of metal and thought that I hadn't even considered it. I put it into the pocket of my Ulster and said, smiling, 'Keep it.'

'OK,' Janne said, 'So this is not goodbye, but "au revoir" to Saara's flat?'

'That's it.' I said and moved towards the front door. I looked back at the orange hall and thought how much I had missed this place and how much I would miss Saara in Stockholm. At least I had her letters and soon I would come back and bring some of her things to my flat. Quickly I turned around and walked out. By the lift I decided that I'd walk the stairs, taking my time to say goodbye properly this time.

'Walking down, are we?' Janne said.

I turned around and said, 'You take the lift. I'll walk.' Then I said, 'No, don't take the lift, come with me.'

Janne smiled and carrying both of our bags followed me down the stairs. It felt good to hear his heavy steps behind me.

If you enjoyed *Coffee and Vodka,* Helena's next novel, a spy story set in Helsinki during the Cold War, *The Red King of Helsinki,* is out now. *The Englishman*, a story of long-distance love, which came out in August 2012 is on sale at Amazon and good bookshops.

More information about Helena Halme can be found on www.helenahalme.com and www.amazon.com/author/helenahalme.

The Englishman

Prologue

KAISA realised she'd never felt like this before. This was love. The stuff she'd read about in books since she was a teenager; the films she'd watched. This was how Ali MacGraw felt about Ryan O'Neal in *Love Story*, and Barbra Streisand about Robert Redford in *The Way We Were*. Kaisa grinned. She'd wanted to pose the same question to the Englishman that Katie had to Hubbell, *'Do you smile ALL the time?'*

Chapter One

THE BRITISH Embassy was a grand house on a tree-lined street in the old part of Helsinki. The chandeliers were sparkling, the parquet floors polished, the antique furniture gleaming. The ambassador and his wife, who wore a long velvet skirt and a frilly white blouse, stood in the doorway to the main reception room, officially greeting all guests.

When it was Kaisa's turn, she took the invitation, with its ornate gold writing, out of her handbag, but the woman didn't even glance at it. Instead she took Kaisa's hand and smiled briefly, before she did the same to Kaisa's friend Tuuli, and then to the next person in line. Kaisa grabbed the hem of her dress to pull it down a little. When a waiter in a white waistcoat appeared out of nowhere and offered her a glass of sherry from a silver tray, Kaisa nodded to her friend and they settled into a corner of a brightly lit room and sipped the sweet drink.

A few people were scattered around the room, talking English in small groups, but the space seemed too large for all of them. One woman in a cream evening gown glanced briefly towards the Finnish girls and smiled, but most were unconcerned with the two of them standing alone in a corner, staring at their shoes, in a vain attempt not to look out of place.

Kaisa touched the hem of her black-and-white crepe dress once more. She knew it suited her well, but she couldn't help thinking she should have borrowed an evening gown.

Kaisa looked at her friend, and wondered if Tuuli was as nervous about the evening as she was. She doubted it; Tuuli was a tall, confident girl. Nothing seemed to faze her.

'You look great,' Tuuli said, as if she'd read Kaisa's mind.

'I keep thinking I should have worn a long dress.' Kaisa said.

Kaisa's friend from university looked down at her own turquoise satin blouse, which fitted tightly around her slim body. She'd tucked the blouse smartly into her navy trousers. On her feet Tuuli had a pair of light-brown loafers with low heels. Kaisa's courts made her, for once, the same height as Tuuli.

'What did the woman at the bank say, exactly?' Tuuli asked. Kaisa noticed her blue eyes had turned the exact same hue as her blouse. Her friend was very pretty. Students and staff at Hanken, the Swedish language university to which Kaisa had so remarkably gained entry a year ago, thought the two girls were sisters, but Kaisa didn't think she looked anything like Tuuli. As well as being much taller, her friend also had larger breasts, which made men turn and stare.

'Cocktail dresses...' Kaisa replied.

'Well, I don't wear dresses. Ever.' Tuuli had a way of stating her opinion so definitely that it excluded all future conversation.

'I didn't mean that. You look fantastic. It's just that she was so vague...' Kaisa was thinking back to the conversation she'd had with her boss at the bank where she worked as a summer intern. The woman was married to a Finnish naval officer whose job it was to organise a visit by the British Royal Navy to Helsinki. She had told Kaisa it was a very important occasion as this was the first visit to Finland by the English fleet since the Second World War. 'The Russians come here all the time, so this makes a nice change.' The woman had smiled and continued, 'We need some Finnish girls at the cocktail party to keep the officers company, and I bet you speak English?'

She was right; languages were easy for Kaisa. She'd lived in Stockholm as a child and spoke Swedish fluently. Kaisa had been studying English since primary school and could understand almost everything in British and American TV series, even without looking at the subtitles. She'd all but forgotten about the conversation when, weeks later, the invitation arrived. Kaisa's heart had skipped a beat. She'd never been inside an embassy, or been invited to a cocktail party. The card with its official English writing seemed too glamorous to be real. Kaisa now dug out the invite and showed it to her friend.

Her Britannic Majesty's Ambassador and Mrs Farquhar request the pleasure of the company of Miss Niemi and guest for Buffet and Dancing on Thursday 2 October 1980 at 8.15 pm.

'Whatever, this will be fun,' Tuuli said determinedly and handed the card back to Kaisa. She took hold of her arm, 'Relax!'

Kaisa looked around the room and tried to spot the lady from the bank, but she was nowhere to be seen. There were a few men whose Finnish naval uniforms she recognised. They stood by themselves, laughing and drinking beer.

'Couldn't we have beer?' Tuuli asked.

Kaisa glanced at the women in evening gowns. None of them were holding anything but sherry. 'Don't think it's very ladylike,' she said.

Tuuli said nothing.

After about an hour, when no one had said a word to Kaisa or Tuuli, and after they'd had three glasses of the sickly-tasting sherry, they decided it was time to leave. 'We don't have to say goodbye to the ambassador and his wife, do we?' Tuuli said. She'd been talking about going to the university disco.

Kaisa didn't have time to reply. A large group of men, all wearing dark Navy uniforms with flashes of gold braid, burst through the door, laughing and chatting. They went straight for the makeshift bar at the end of the large room. The space was filled with noise and Kaisa and Tuuli were pushed deeper into their corner.

Suddenly a tall, slim man in a Navy uniform stood in front of Kaisa. He had the darkest eyes she'd ever seen. He reached out his hand, 'How do you do?'

'Ouch,' Kaisa said and pulled her hand away quickly. He'd given her an electric shock. He smiled and his eyes sparkled.

'Sorry!' he said but kept staring at Kaisa. She tried to look down at the floor, or at Tuuli, who seemed unconcerned by this sudden invasion of foreign uniformed men around them. 'What's your name?'

'Kaisa Niemi.'

He cocked his ear, 'Sorry?' It took the Englishman a long time to learn to pronounce Kaisa's Finnish name. She laughed at his failed attempts to make it sound at all authentic, but he didn't give up.

Eventually, when happy with his pronunciation, he introduced himself to Kaisa and Tuuli, 'Peter Williams.' He then tapped the shoulders of two of his shipmates. One was as tall as him but with fair hair, the other a much shorter, older man. Awkwardly they all shook hands, while the dark Englishman continued to stare at Kaisa. She didn't know what to say or where to put her eyes. She smoothed down her dress. The Englishman took a swig out of a large glass of beer. Suddenly he noticed Kaisa's empty hands, 'Can I get you a drink? What will you have?'

'Sherry,' she hated the taste of it, but couldn't think of what else to ask for.

His dark eyes peered at Kaisa intensely. 'Stay here, promise? I'm going to leave this old man in charge of not letting you leave.' The shorter guy gave an embarrassed laugh and the Englishman disappeared into the now crowded room.

'So is it always this cold in Helsinki?' the short man asked. Kaisa explained that in the winter it was worse, there'd be snow, but that in summer it was really warm. He nodded, but didn't seem to be listening to her. She tried to get her friend's attention but Tuuli was in the middle of a conversation with the blonde guy.

Kaisa was oddly relieved when the dark Englishman returned. He was carrying a tray full of drinks and very nearly spilled it all when someone knocked him from behind. Everyone laughed. The Englishman's eyes met Kaisa's. 'You're still here!' he said and handed her a drink. It was as if he'd expected her to have escaped. Kaisa looked around the suddenly crowded room. Even if she'd decided to leave, it would have been difficult to fight her way to the door. The throng of people forced the Englishman to stand close to Kaisa. The rough fabric of his uniform touched her bare arm. He gazed at Kaisa's face. He asked what she did; she told him about her studies at the School of Economics. He said he was a sublieutenant on the British ship.

Kaisa found it was easy to talk to this foreign man. Even though her English was at times faltering, they seemed to understand each other straightaway. They laughed at the same jokes. Kaisa wondered if this is what it would be like to have a brother. She had an older sister but had always envied friends with male siblings. It would be nice to have a boy to confide in, someone who knew how other boys thought, what they did or didn't like in a girl. An older brother would be there to protect you while a younger brother would admire you.

286

Kaisa looked around what had been a group of them and noticed there was just the Englishman and her left in the corner of the room. She asked where her friend was. The Englishman took hold of her arm and pointed, 'Don't worry. I think she's OK.' She saw a group of Finnish naval officers. Tuuli was among them, drinking beer and laughing.

When the music started, the Englishman asked Kaisa to dance. There were only two other couples on the small parquet floor. One she recognised as the Finnish Foreign Minister and his famous model wife, now too old for photo shoots but still envied for her dress sense and beautiful skin. She wore a dark lacy top and a skirt, not an evening gown, Kaisa noticed to her relief. The woman's hair was set up into a complicated do, with a few long black curls framing her face. They bounced gently against her tanned skin as she pushed her head back and laughed at something her minister husband said.

The Englishman took hold of Kaisa's waist and she felt the heat of his touch through the thin fabric of her dress. She looked into his dark eyes and for a moment they stood motionless in the middle of the dance floor. Slowly he started to move. Kaisa felt dizzy. The room span in front of her eyes and she let her body relax in the Englishman's arms.

'You dance beautifully,' he said.

Kaisa smiled, 'So do you.'

He moved his hand lower down Kaisa's back and squeezed her bottom.

'You mustn't,' Kaisa said, not able to contain her laughter. She removed his hand and whispered, 'That's the Foreign Minister and his famous wife. They'll see!'

'Ok,' he nodded and lazily glanced at the other couples on the dance floor.

After a few steps Kaisa again felt his hand drop down towards the right cheek of her backside. She tutted and moved it back up. He must be very young, Kaisa thought. When the music stopped, the Englishman put her hand in the crook of his arm and led her away from the dance floor. He found two plush chairs by a fireplace in a smaller room. It had windows overlooking a groomed garden. As soon as they sat down, a gong rang for food.

'You must be hungry,' The Englishman said, and not waiting for a reply got up, 'I'll get you a selection.' He made Kaisa promise to stay where she was and disappeared into the queue of people. She felt awkward sitting alone, marking the time until the Englishman's return. She could feel the eyes of the ladies she'd seen earlier in the evening upon her.

Kaisa smoothed down her dress again and looked at her watch: it was ten past eleven already. She saw Tuuli in the doorway to the larger room. She was holding hands with a Finnish naval officer, smiling up at him.

Quickly Kaisa walked towards them. 'Are you going? Wait, I'll come with you.' She was relieved that she didn't have to leave alone.

Tuuli looked at the Finnish guy, then at her friend, 'Umm, I'll call you tomorrow?'

Kaisa felt stupid. 'Ah, yes, of course.' She waved her friend goodbye.

The Englishman reappeared, balancing two glasses of wine and two huge platefuls of food in his hands.

'I didn't know what you liked,' he said, grinning.

He led Kaisa back to the plush chairs. She watched him wolf down cocktail sausages, slices of ham, and potato salad as if he'd never been fed. He emptied his plate and said, 'Aren't you hungry?'

Kaisa shook her head. She wasn't sure if it was the formal surroundings or all the sherry she'd drunk, but she couldn't even think about food. All she could do was sip the wine. She leant back in her chair and the Englishman sat forward in his. He touched her knee. His touch was like a current running through her body.

'You OK?'

Kaisa felt she could sink into the dark pools of the Englishman's eyes. She shook her head, trying to shed the spell this foreigner had cast over her, 'A bit drunk, I think.'

He laughed at that. He put the empty plate away and lit a cigarette. He studied her for a moment. 'You're lovely, do you know that?'

Kaisa blushed.

They sat and talked by the fireplace. The heat of the flames burned the side of Kaisa's arm, but she didn't want to move. While they talked the Englishman gazed at her intently, as if trying to commit the whole of her being to memory. Kaisa found this both flattering and frightening. She knew she shouldn't be here with the Englishman like this.

Once or twice one of his shipmates came and exchanged a few words with him. There was an Englishwoman he seemed to know very well. He introduced her to Kaisa and laughed at something she said. Then he turned back to Kaisa, and the woman moved away. Kaisa liked the feeling of owning the Englishman, having all his attention on her. She found she could tell him her life story. He, too, talked about his family in southwest England. He had a brother and a sister, both a lot older than him, 'My birth wasn't exactly planned,' he smiled.

'Neither was mine! My parents made two mistakes, first my sister, then me,' Kaisa said and laughed. The Englishman looked surprised, as if she'd told him something bad.

'It's OK,' she said.

He took her hands in his and said, 'Can I see you again? After tonight, I mean?'

'Please don't,' she pulled away from his touch.

An older officer, with fair, thinning hair, came into the room and the Englishman got rapidly onto his feet.

'Good evening,' the man nodded to Kaisa and said something, in a low tone, to the Englishman.

'Yes, Sir,' the Englishman said.

'Who was that?' Kaisa asked.

'Listen, something's happened. I have to go back to the ship.'

Kaisa looked at her watch; it was nearly midnight.

The Englishman leant closer and held her hands. 'I must see you again.'

'It's not possible.' She lowered her gaze away from the intense glare of his eyes.

'I'm only in Helsinki for another three days,' he insisted.

Kaisa didn't say anything for a while. His hands around hers felt strong and she didn't want to pull away.

'Look, I have to go. Can I at least phone you?'

She hesitated, 'No.'

His eyes widened, 'Why not?'

'It's impossible.' Kaisa didn't know what else to say.

'Why do you say that?' The Englishman leant closer to her. She could feel his warm breath on her cheek when he whispered into her ear, 'Nothing is impossible.'

People were leaving. Another officer came to tell the Englishman he had to go. Turning close to Kaisa again he said, 'Please?'

Kaisa heard herself say, 'Do you have a pen?'

The Englishman tapped his pockets, then scanned the now empty tables. He looked everywhere, asked a waiter carrying a tray full of glasses, but no one had a pen. Kaisa dug in her handbag and found a pink lipstick. 'You can use this, I guess.'

The Englishman took a paper napkin from a table and she scrawled her number on it. Then, with the final bits of lipstick, he wrote his name and his address on HMS Newcastle on the back of Kaisa's invitation to the party.

Outside, on the steps of the embassy, all the officers from the Englishman's ship were gathered, waiting for something. The blonde guy Kaisa and Tuuli had met earlier in the evening nodded to her and, touching his cap, smiled knowingly. She wondered if he thought she and the Englishman were now an item. She could see many of the other officers give her sly glances. It was as if outside, on the steps of the embassy, she'd entered another world – the domain of their ship. As the only woman among all the men, she felt shy and stood closer to the Englishman. He took this to be a sign, and before she could stop him, he'd taken off his cap and bent down to kiss her lips. He tasted of mint and cigarettes. For a moment Kaisa kissed him back; she didn't want to pull away.

When finally the Englishman let go, everybody on the steps cheered. Kaisa was embarrassed and breathless.

'You shouldn't have done that,' she whispered.

The Englishman looked at her and smiled, 'Don't worry, they're just jealous.' He led her through the throng of people and down the steps towards a waiting taxi.

'I'll call you tomorrow,' he whispered and opened the car door.

When the taxi moved away, Kaisa saw the Englishman wave his cap. She told the driver her address and leant back in the seat. She touched her lips.

The Englishman is now out in paperback and can be found on Amazon.com and in good bookshops.

Made in the USA
Charleston, SC
26 October 2014